For many years, Mel-Aqat was thought to be a mere legend, part of the many tales drifting out of the dark continent of Xen'drik. Mentioned in various ancient texts, Mel-Aqat was thought to be the prison of primal power, long locked away from the confines of the world.

But at the height of the Last War, during an exploration of Xen'drik, the scholar Janik Martell discovered the ruins of Mel-Aqat—much to his sorrow. Pursued amongst the ruins by an old rival, the one he loved most in all the world betrayed him, leaving him a shattered man.

Years later, something is stirring again in Mel-Aqat, and the only one who may be able to stop it is the one man who swore he'd never go back—Janik Martell.

THE
WAR-TORN

THE CRIMSON TALISMAN
ADRIAN COLE

THE ORB OF XORIAT
EDWARD BOLME

IN THE CLAWS OF THE TIGER
JAMES WYATT
(JULY 2006)

BLOOD AND HONOR
GRAEME DAVIS
(SEPTEMBER 2006)

IN THE CLAWS OF THE TIGER

THE WARTORN • BOOK 3

JAMES WYATT

IN THE CLAWS OF THE TIGER
The War-Torn • Book 3

©2006 Wizards of the Coast, Inc.

Cover art by Wayne Reynolds
Map by Rob Lazzaretti
First Printing: July 2006
Library of Congress Catalog Card Number: 2005935539

9 8 7 6 5 4 3 2 1

ISBN-10: 0-7869-4015-8
ISBN-13: 978-0-7869-4015-8
620-95543740-001-EN

U.S., CANADA,
ASIA, PACIFIC, & LATIN AMERICA
Wizards of the Coast, Inc.
P.O. Box 707
Renton, WA 98057-0707
+1-800-324-6496

EUROPEAN HEADQUARTERS
Hasbro UK Ltd
Caswell Way
Newport, Gwent NP9 0YH
GREAT BRITAIN
Please keep this address for your records.

Visit our web site at www.wizards.com

**This book is lovingly dedicated to
Amy and Carter:**

*"The touch of her hands always seemed to soothe
away the aches and bruises and hurts of the day
even more than her spells of healing did. Her love
for him had always felt like tangible proof of the
Sovereigns and their divine love."*

*Special thanks to David Silbey and Chris Perkins,
who reviewed the manuscript in various stages. I
am grateful to my editor, Mark Sehestedt, for his
confidence in me throughout the process.*

*A note of thanks to Blizzard Entertainment for the
incentive to write every day. ("If I write 700 words
a day, then I can play WORLD OF WARCRAFT.")
Thanks to Rieta, whose advancement to 60th level
was delayed until after the novel was finished.*

*More thanks to Keith Baker and Bill Slavicsek,
for EBERRON and the chance to help create it. And
to the folks who play D&D there with me—David
Noonan, Andy Collins, Gwendolyn F.M. Kestrel,
Stephen Schubert, and Cameron Curtis.*

*This book was written almost entirely at the
Panther Lake Starbucks in Kent, Washington.
Thanks to Sharon and Tom and their staff for a
steady diet of for-here venti mocha Valencias, as
well as a relatively low-rent desk.*

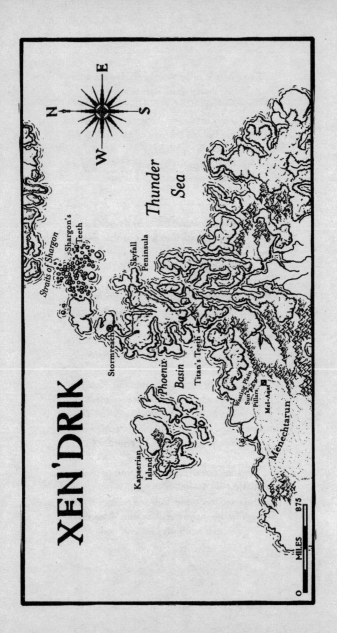

TABLE OF CONTENTS

Airborne Attack

CHAPTER 1

Janik Martell?"

Not looking at the black-haired man beside him, Janik stared at the Blackcap Mountains far below the airship. He had watched the man since the voyage began, having pegged him as one of the Royal Eyes of Aundair. He gave a slight nod even as his left hand moved to the hilt of his short sword at his belt.

"I'd like to ask you a few questions." The man's voice was low and heavy. "In the name of Queen Aurala of Aundair."

Janik pushed a wayward strand of tawny hair over his right ear and lifted his eyes toward the horizon, where the mountains sank down into hills and flowed into the plains and vineyards of Aundair. "We're not across the border yet."

"And it's my job to make sure you don't get across the border if I don't like your answers."

Janik looked at the other spy, studying him. He was shorter than Janik by a hand's breadth, and his hair was cut short. He wore a midnight blue coat open in front, revealing light armor—and the hilt of his sword—underneath. The two eyed each other for a moment, then Janik turned back to look down at the mountains again. "So ask," he said.

"What's your destination?"

"Fairhaven."

"How long are you staying there?"

"As short a time as possible."

"What's your business there?" As the man asked the question, Janik felt the pressure in his mind that meant someone wanted access. No way, he thought, and mentally slammed a door in the intruder's face while looking around to see who had cast the spell. A wiry man lurked in the shadows across the deck, holding a scroll. Janik spotted an open pouch bulging with scrolls at the man's belt and guessed that he was an artificer. Janik scowled and gripped the hilt of his sword.

The other man shrugged, raising both palms as if to ward off an angry outburst. "Just a spell to check the truth of your words, Martell. Understandable in our line of work."

"I don't like sneaking spellcasters." Janik jerked his head toward the artificer, who was rummaging in his pouch for another scroll. The Aundairian agent looked lazily over his shoulder, then turned back to Janik.

"I don't suppose there's any way we're going to convince you to submit to this spell? Prove you have nothing to hide?"

"Not a chance."

"All right. Haunderk—" The man made a sign to the artificer, and the wiry man slunk off toward the rear of the ship. "So what is your business in Fairhaven?"

"It's personal."

"Well, I hope you won't take it personally if I have you put off the ship."

Janik held his adversary's steady gaze. No, the man wasn't

bluffing. After a long moment, he gave a grim smile and held out his hand. "You never told me your name."

The Aundairian hesitated for a moment, then smiled and shook Janik's hand. "Kelas ir'Darran."

"All right, Kelas ir'Darran." Janik released his hand. "I'm visiting your fine capital to find my old friend Mathas Allister, who worked with me during the war. No doubt you have him under constant surveillance. I hope to enlist his aid for another mission."

"Another expedition to Xen'drik, in Breland's service?"

"Maybe Xen'drik, but not for Breland. We've been invited to Thrane, to an audience with the Keeper of the Flame herself." Janik smiled to himself as he watched Kelas stiffen. Aundair and Breland had been enemies during the Last War, but had also been allies at times. Nothing but bad feelings ran between Aundair and Thrane. "Look, Kelas," he said. The Aundairian turned away from Janik to look at the fields of his homeland drawing closer beneath the airship. "I'm going to Aundair to collect my friend and leave. Honestly, I don't know what the Keeper wants with us. But if it's the least bit political, I'm out. I'm not interested in that kind of work for Breland, let alone Thrane."

"You don't know what she wants?"

"No idea. But she summoned me, so I can only assume it has something to do with my expertise, which is Xen'drik, not subterfuge against Aundair."

"And why would Janik Martell emerge from three years of quiet teaching in Sharn to answer a summons from the Keeper of the Flame? I thought you followed the Sovereign Host."

"I used to. And I certainly have no interest in the faith of the Silver Flame. This isn't about religion. It's—well, like I said before, it's personal." A sudden flash of anxiety hit Janik as he thought again about Dania's letter. He fought it down, but his voice was choked as he said, "Another old friend asked me to come."

Perhaps aware of Janik's discomfort, Kelas stared out over the bulwarks without saying anything. Janik turned away as well and stared blindly at the ring of elemental fire that surrounded the airship, keeping her airborne and propelling her through the skies. As they stood in silence, the mountains dwindled to foothills and Aundair stretched out in autumnal splendor beneath them. Janik lowered his gaze to the mosaic of red, yellow, orange, and brown leaves radiant in the evening light far below, enjoying a different experience of autumn than he had in Sharn—where the change of seasons just meant more rain.

"Well, Janik Martell," Kelas said at last, "welcome to Aundair." He clasped Janik's hand again and smiled. "I hope your stay in Fairhaven is pleasant—and short." He turned and walked aft, leaving Janik alone with his thoughts.

Janik pulled Dania's letter from the breast pocket of his coat and tapped it idly against the bulwarks. He hadn't seen Dania or Mathas since leaving them at an airship dock in Sharn three years ago. They had just returned from their famous expedition to Xen'drik. On a mission for King Boranel of Breland, Janik had led his friends to ancient Mel-Aqat, a temple-city known from numerous ancient inscriptions. That mission had cemented Janik's reputation as a scholar and explorer, and it had shattered his life.

He had spent the last three years hiding—hiding from Mathas and Dania, hiding from the memory of that expedition and its disastrous outcome. The memory of Maija, his wife, betraying him.

He had thrown himself into his work—his teaching at Morgrave University, his translation of the stone tablets he had brought back from Mel-Aqat. Working, constantly moving, he had succeeded in suppressing those memories, at least during daylight. But the letter had brought them all back, and as he looked at the page in his hand once more, after reading it over and over for three days, it still made his chest tighten.

Janik lifted his gaze to the horizon, watching a hippogriff soaring in the distance. He stuffed Dania's letter into his coat pocket and tried to force his thoughts back to where they had been before Kelas interrupted—planning his search for Mathas. He rattled off a mental list of places the old elf favored: fine restaurants, booksellers, perhaps a wizard's college or even a university. Mathas could teach Xen'drik history as well as Janik could, if he ever desired to do so. But soon he felt the same clenching anxiety that hit him every time he tried that line of thought. Searching for Mathas was one thing. Finding him was something else entirely.

"Sovereigns! What's he doing?"

The cry jolted Janik out of his reflections. A woman had shouted, part of a well-dressed couple who had kept to themselves on the trip so far. Janik guessed they were newlyweds, celebrating their recent marriage with an airship journey. The young bride was pointing into the sky above the port side while her husband craned his neck curiously.

A hippogriff swooped low over the airship, and Janik saw what had drawn the woman's attention. A man was on the hippogriff's back, not strapped into a saddle and harness, but *standing*. Just as Janik realized what was happening, the man jumped.

Janik pulled his short blade from its sheath and leaped

toward the wheelhouse, where the windwright pilot steered the ship. The jumper landed hard on its roof—hard enough to drive the airship's stern downward. Janik stumbled as he ran across the rocking deck toward the wheelhouse, but he kept his feet. He watched the man drop from the roof to the stairway leading up from the deck, and saw one of the House Lyrandar guards, stationed there to protect the pilot from just such an event as this, crumple under the man's blade. Janik reached the bottom of the steps as the man disappeared into the wheelhouse.

He sprang up the stairs by twos, just in time to see the other Lyrandar guard fall, his neck slashed by a broad arc from the killer's sword. The windwright stood clutching the helm, his knuckles white and his eyes wide with terror. The attacker turned, and Janik got his first look at the man's face—except he was not a man. A featureless mask of metal formed his face, and beneath a black cloak, his body was similarly composed of metal, wood, stone, and strange sinewy cords. His bastard sword was the gleaming silver-black of adamantine, with gold tracings etched into the blade. He gave Janik the merest of glances, then turned his attention to the windwright. "Martell," he said as he stalked toward the terrified pilot, "they told me you'd be the first one here."

Janik did not waste time responding. He leaped over the first guard's body toward the warforged, hoping to push him away from the pilot and into the bulkhead. He ducked under the swinging adamantine sword and slammed hard into the killer's chest, but his opponent didn't even miss a step. Janik tottered backward and slashed at the thing's elbow, aiming for sinews between hard plates. The warforged jerked his arm to the left and Janik's blade clattered against the hard plating on the forearm. The bastard sword went up and slashed down on the windwright's skull, sending a spray of blood into the air as the pilot collapsed.

The airship lurched as the elemental bound into a fiery ring surrounding the ship felt the hands holding its reins fall slack. The warforged stumbled. Janik pressed the momentary advantage, slashing at his opponent's neck. The adamantine sword batted Janik's smaller blade away.

"You wield your blade with skill, Martell," the warforged said, his voice strangely human coming from such an inhuman frame, "but there is no strength behind your blows."

"You're giving me fencing lessons?" Janik decided to buy time by letting the warforged have his conversation. "How do you know my name?"

"I know all about you, Martell." The killer's voice was mocking as he launched a fierce offensive with his whirling blade. "Your life and loves, your strengths, and especially your weaknesses." Janik dodged and parried the relentless assault, his breath coming faster with the exertion. "Captain Kavarat told me." The voice of the warforged betrayed no hint of fatigue.

Krael Kavarat, Janik thought. I should have guessed.

When Maija had left him, she had delivered the Ramethene Sword right into the hands of Krael Kavarat, an officer of the Emerald Claw who had been Janik's rival and enemy for a decade.

First a letter from Dania, now an assassin sent by Krael.

"It seems my past is determined to catch up with me," he said. Striking the adamantine blade as hard as he could to knock it wide, he slashed from his right, trying to drive the warforged toward the stairway. Momentarily surprised by Janik's renewed barrage, his foe stepped closer to the stairs, turning his back to the wheelhouse's only entrance.

Just where I want you, Janik thought with grim satisfaction. Now we wait.

He fell into a defensive stance, intent on keeping the adamantine sword away from him.

"So Krael sent you to kill me," he said. Continuing the conversation was the best way to keep the killer distracted, he figured, though speaking had become a real effort.

"That's right. Crashing the airship was my idea, though." There was a trace of a smile in the voice of the warforged, though his face was expressionless.

Crashing the airship?

Since the initial lurch at the death of the windwright, Janik had not paid attention to the ship's movement, but he suddenly noticed that the deck was slanted toward the prow.

Better finish this up quickly, he thought, though he had little hope of success.

Janik's patience was rewarded as another man appeared in the wheelhouse doorway, almost directly behind the warforged. It was Kelas, the Aundairian spy, bastard sword in hand. His eyes flicked from Janik to his opponent, to the dead guards and the pilot, and quickly back to the warforged. Swiftly and silently, he stalked up behind the warforged and brought his sword down in a deadly arc. At the last instant, the killer twisted and the sword cut into his shoulder instead of cleaving his skull. Roaring in surprise and pain, the warforged spun around to retaliate—and Janik took the opportunity to hack with his short blade at his opponent's shoulder. This time, it was a solid blow. The warforged nearly dropped his sword, but quickly shifted it to his left hand.

"About time you got here, Kelas," Janik said, smiling at the Aundairian.

Kelas nodded, his eyes wide and fixed on their opponent,

the warforged had turned sideways, and Janik could see that he was trying to keep both humans in view while sizing up his opportunities for escape.

"Whose idea was it to get yourself trapped in a small room with two opponents?" Janik said. "Probably Krael's. He's never been too concerned about the lives of his minions—especially those who fail."

The warforged had lost interest in idle conversation. But Janik's words apparently reminded him of his purpose, and he renewed his assault on Janik, swinging his sword left-handed with undiminished strength, trying not to expose his back to Kelas. Again Janik focused on defense until Kelas could distract the warforged. Just as Kelas maneuvered behind their opponent, the warforged took a halfhearted swing at Janik and then rushed for the door. Kelas's sword glanced off the back plates of the warforged, then their foe was out the door. Janik saw him knock the Aundairian artificer off the steps as he bolted down. Hurrying to the door himself, Janik watched the warforged run to the bulwarks and throw himself over the side.

For an instant, Janik prepared to rush to the bulwarks himself, to see what happened to the assassin. But a commotion on the deck wrenched his attention to a more immediate concern. Passengers clung to each other, sought shelter belowdecks, or knelt down and prayed for deliverance. The ring of fire that normally burned steadily leaped and crackled as if trying to break free of the magical bonds that held it in place around the ship. From the deck where the warforged had knocked him flat, the artificer cried out, "The airship's going to crash!"

CHAPTER 2

Janik spun around and hurtled up the stairs to the wheelhouse, pushing past Kelas in the doorway. Standing over the fallen windwright pilot, he examined the helm of the airship. "I wonder how you use this thing," he said to himself.

"No pressure, Janik," Kelas called from the doorway, "but if you're going to figure it out, you'd better do it soon."

Hearing the fear in the Aundairian's voice, Janik gripped the wheel. He felt pressure at the edges of his mind again, similar to the artificer's divination only a short time ago. Janik's instinct was to snap his mind shut as he had before, but he forced himself to receive this contact. It was a wordless voice of rage and rebellion, and Janik recognized it as the elemental bound in a fiery ring around the airship.

"It wants to be free," he muttered.

No, damn you. Up! He used the strange telepathic connection to command the elemental. *Up!*

Janik felt as if he had caught a dragon turtle on a fishing line. Pain stabbed through his head. He felt the elemental trying to throw the mental yoke from its mind. He sensed, though he could not see, the wild leaps of the fiery ring and thrashing tongues of flame coursing along the veins of magical tracery that covered the body of the ship. The deck of the ship bucked wildly—but she remained airborne.

Janik's fists clenched the wheel. He pulled on it as if it were a horse's reins, willing the elemental to obey him. He squeezed his eyes shut and the ship disappeared from around him—the bucking deck, the screaming passengers, the dead pilot. He felt as if he stood alone in the middle of a giant ring of wildly burning fire. As he pulled on the wheel with his hands and pulled on the fiery ring with his mind, it seemed to grow smaller, tamer.

"Up!" he shouted, and the ship moved up.

Surprised, Janik opened his eyes. Immediately, the ship jerked hard to port as the elemental felt his hold weaken. *No! Obey me!* With his renewed focus, the ship moved smoothly once more.

"Take her higher, Janik," Kelas said, still standing in the door of the wheelhouse. "We're still awfully close to the ground." He paused. "But that was well done, I must say."

Janik allowed a smile to flicker across his face before exerting his will on the elemental once more. This time, it responded immediately and smoothly to his telepathic command, gently lifting the airship higher while keeping the deck level. He was vaguely aware of cheers and a quiet babble of relief from the passengers on deck, but the more he stretched his attention beyond the little wheelhouse, the more he felt his control over the elemental slip.

"Now what?" he said to Kelas. "I can't keep this up forever."

"I'll get word to House Lyrandar," the Aundairian replied. "Maybe they can get another pilot up here."

"Another pilot? How are they going to do that?"

"Call in a favor from the teleporters of House Orien, maybe? They're dragonmarked. They'll figure it out." Kelas jumped down the steps to the deck, leaving Janik alone in the wheelhouse.

❋ ❋ ❋ ❋ ❋ ❋ ❋

Janik had no idea how much time passed while he goaded the elemental forward. He was only dimly aware of Kelas returning and offering a course correction to point them toward Fairhaven again. Through a haze of exhaustion, he watched moonlight creep into the sky and brighten the deck. Before long, a man appeared in the wheelhouse—a half-elf whose Lyrandar dragonmark covered much of his muscular chest, only partly covered by the loose, open shirt he wore. The windwright stepped up and gripped the wheel, thanking Janik formally. It was the last thing Janik remembered until he woke in his cabin the next afternoon.

"Fairhaven!" A steward's voice outside his cabin door penetrated the depths of his exhaustion, and Janik sat up in bed. Looking out the window, he could see the square towers and carefully planned streets of the Aundairian capital below. He jumped up and threw the clothes that were scattered around the cabin into his backpack, then slung it over one shoulder. He felt his pocket to make sure Dania's letter was still there, then hurried out of the cabin with a backward glance to make sure he hadn't forgotten anything.

In his years of travel, Janik had never become accustomed to crowds—standing amid a sea of people waiting to disembark, feeling somehow like a sheep being herded for shearing. Even though he was tall enough to see over the heads of many people, he still felt swallowed up in crowds, as though he might drown in their relentless tides. So he breathed a relieved sigh when he finally made his way off the airship, through the busy mooring tower, and down to the relatively quiet, wide streets of Fairhaven.

Now what? he thought. He stood in the red brick plaza outside the mooring tower and tried to collect his jumbled thoughts. He had spent much of the four-day journey from Sharn planning what to do at this moment, but the assassin's attack and his stint as airship pilot had driven his careful plans from his mind.

First things first, he thought. I've got to put this bag down somewhere, and I might not find Mathas today.

He looked around to get his bearings. In contrast to Sharn, with its mile-high towers reaching up to claw at the slate clouds above, Fairhaven spread serenely beneath a clear blue sky. Only the great alabaster palace at the city's center, to Janik's right, towered more than several stories. Neat clusters of white-plastered houses lined wide, clean streets. In this part of town, the houses and shops all sported carved lintels and elegantly arched windows. He was surprised by all the green—orderly rows of trees displaying gold and red leaves divided the major roadways, and lush ground covers hinted at beds of colorful flowers in the spring. He spotted the blink dog emblem of House Ghallanda on a large building near the plaza. Shifting his pack on his shoulder, he started walking.

Janik settled himself in a luxurious room in the Ghallanda Inn then wandered into the city. He set out to master Fairhaven, as though he were on another Xen'drik expedition, learning its streets and shops, paying particular attention to fine restaurants and booksellers. He spent the whole of his second day wandering the University of Wynarn, amazed at its size and grandeur compared to Morgrave University, where he taught between expeditions. Everywhere he walked, he kept thinking he saw people he knew—not just Mathas, but Dania, Krael, and—setting his pulse pounding—Maija. But none of his exploring turned up what he sought.

● ● ● ◉ ● ● ●

The morning of the third day, Janik sat on his bed, one boot on and the other in his hands, planning the day's search. He was startled out of his reverie by a sharp knock on the door. "Who's there?" he called, stuffing his foot into his boot and looking around for his sword.

"Kelas ir'Darran."

"Kelas?" Janik found his sword, drew it, and walked to the door. "What are you doing here?" Holding the sword in his left hand, he hid it behind the door as he swung it open, forcing a smile to greet the Aundairian.

Kelas's smile looked genuine enough. "I've got some information that might help you, Janik," he said.

"Information?"

Kelas held out a scrawled note. "Mathas Allister will be pleased to dine with you at the Dragonhawk Towers for luncheon today. That's the address," he added, as Janik took the parchment.

Janik shot Kelas a quizzical look. "You found him for me? Why?"

"Too slow!" Kelas laughed. "You should have left for Thrane by now. Instead, you've spent two days learning every back alley of Fairhaven and apparently not asking a soul where you might find your friend." Kelas's face grew serious. "You saved my life and the lives of a lot of other people on that airship, Janik Martell. So I'm willing to believe that you weren't lying to me about your business here. But that doesn't change the fact that you're a Brelish spy, and certain people would like you to complete your business and be on your way."

Janik studied the address Kelas had given him, momentarily speechless.

"Besides," Kelas continued, "it wasn't hard to find him. As you said, we've got him under surveillance." Smiling, he turned and started walking down the hall. "Enjoy your lunch!" he said over his shoulder.

"Thanks," Janik called after him, still staring at the note in his hand.

Dragonhawk Towers, Janik thought. He remembered the restaurant—he had walked past it several times in the previous days. It looked like the kind of place Mathas would frequent: finely carved columns at the door, warm firelight spilling out the windows, high-class clientele, probably very expensive.

I never went in. Why? Janik closed the door and sat down on the bed.

Because I thought I might find him, he admitted.

Again he found himself rehearsing the meeting in his mind. Always he saw the old elf's face wearing a mixture of horror and reproach, not at all the kindly expression Mathas had worn most of the time Janik had known him. His breath started coming faster and he stood up, pacing around the room as he tried for the hundredth time to think of something he could say—something that would make the horror of Maija's betrayal and the shame of his ill-advised romance with Dania go away. The spacious room felt much too small. Grabbing his coat, he strode out the door and down to the street.

Walking always helped to clear his mind. Years of long overland treks had taught him to subsume his mind into the pace of his long legs, to think of nothing but the rhythm of his own steps. Some part of his mind was always alert for danger—it had to be, in the wilds of Xen'drik—but he was able to turn off the part that planned and remembered and worried. So he walked, winding through the now-familiar streets of Fairhaven. Almost without conscious intent, he found himself standing in front of the Dragonhawk Towers at luncheon time.

"All right, Janik," he muttered, finding to his relief that the long walk had stilled his mind. "Mathas is your friend, or was once. Trust him."

He pulled on the door and went inside.

He cast a quick glance around the crowded restaurant and spotted Mathas, sitting at a table by a window, staring out at the autumn leaves. The elf's hair was grayer and cut shorter than the last time Janik had seen him—but they had just returned from a long expedition when Janik had seen him last. In civilization, Mathas always kept his appearance up.

A genuine smile spread slowly across Janik's face as he crossed the room. Mathas saw him and got slowly to his feet, deep wrinkles surrounding his mouth and eyes as he returned Janik's smile.

When he reached Mathas's table, the old elf threw his arms around him. Janik returned the embrace, then settled himself into the chair across from Mathas.

"I can't begin to tell you how pleased I was to receive your invitation," Mathas said.

"It's great to see you, old friend," Janik replied, his throat tight. "I—"

"I was particularly amused," Mathas interrupted, "by its bearer. I was not aware that Kelas ir'Darran was a mutual acquaintance."

Janik laughed, suddenly at ease. "I only met him on the

airship here. After he threatened to throw me overboard, I started to like him."

"For three years he's kept an eye on me," Mathas said, lifting a cup of tea to his thin lips. He took a sip, then said, "He's starting to feel like an old friend." He smiled. "But that might be because I was starting to forget what the company of old friends feels like." His voice was utterly without blame or anger, and Janik returned his smile.

"I had as well, Mathas, and I'm sorry for that."

"Kelas indicated that I am soon to leave the country. I must admit to some curiosity regarding our destination." Mathas sipped his tea.

"Did he now?" Janik laughed.

"Well, not in so many words. I pieced it together."

"Held his hands just so while glancing toward the horizon?" Janik had often joked that Mathas could read volumes from the slightest gesture.

"Something like that. So where are you taking me?"

Janik took a deep breath and let it out slowly. "I got a letter from Dania."

Mathas arched an eyebrow. "Really? What did she have to say?"

"Not very much, actually, but she urged me to come to Thrane."

"Thrane? Hmm. Last I heard, she was in Karrnath."

"What have you heard, Mathas? I've been so completely out of touch—it was all I could do to find you here."

Mathas leaned back in his chair and stared at the ceiling. "Precious little, I'm afraid, and it's been some time. I saw Dania before we both left Sharn. She told me she'd written to a friend of her father's in Karrnath, and he'd agreed to give her some work—mercenary work, I believe. I came here shortly after that, so if she ever wrote me a letter, I never received it."

"When was that?" Janik asked.

"Just after the war ended. We had been back less than a year."

A waiter approached, and Janik realized he hadn't looked at the menu. He glanced at it quickly while Mathas ordered, decided on a Cyran duck dish, then fiddled with his fork as he asked, "So, did she talk about me?"

"What do you think, Janik?"

"I think you two probably discussed me to death, but that might just be my inflated sense of self-importance."

Mathas smiled. "Of course we did—as we have done many, many times over the years. As usual, we came to no conclusions."

"I hurt her pretty badly, didn't I?"

"Yes, you did."

Janik turned sideways in his chair, scanning the crowded room. Mathas turned his gaze out the window for a moment, then looked back at Janik. "What did she say in her letter?"

Janik sighed. "Nothing about . . . what happened. It was actually the third letter I received. The first two were from the Cathedral. It's really the Keeper of the Flame who has invited me to Thrane."

Mathas leaned forward. "The Keeper of the Flame? What does she want with you?"

"Unclear. I pretty much ignored the first two letters. I didn't feel like taking up any holy quests. Of course, Kelas assumes the Keeper wants to send us on a mission against Aundair." Janik smiled.

"And Dania wrote to reinforce the Keeper's invitation?"

"Exactly. Here, I've got the letter." Janik pulled the folded page from his coat pocket and handed it across the table. He quoted the words he had read a hundred times. "Dear Janik, I'm writing to add my voice to the invitation you've already received. I urge you to come to Thrane and hear what the Keeper of the Flame has to say. And so on."

Mathas read the last few lines of the brief letter, then handed it back to Janik.

"So she has allied herself with the Church of the Silver Flame?" Mathas asked. "Interesting."

"Yes, that's one of the things that puzzles me."

"Well," Mathas said, looking at the ceiling. "Now that I think about it, I believe that the friend of her father's in Karrnath was affiliated with the Church. Perhaps she has simply risen through the ranks to some military position with the Church?"

"Possibly. Anyway, as you can see, the letter says nothing important—nothing about our past together, nothing about Xen'drik or Maija . . ."

"Or me," Mathas interrupted.

"Nothing about you."

"So why have you come to take me to Thrane?"

"If the Keeper wants to send me on some expedition, then I need you." Janik sighed and studied his wine glass. "And I can't face Dania without you."

Mathas smiled kindly. "What are you afraid of, Janik?"

Janik sipped his wine, thinking, while the waiter set their food in front of them. After the waiter left, he said, "I'm afraid—" His voice was shaking, and he took a deep breath to steady it. "I'm afraid of the past, Mathas. I'm afraid that seeing her will make missing Maija hurt that much more." He looked down at his plate.

"Three years have not dulled its bite?"

"Not in the least. I've been keeping myself busy—always

on the move. It keeps my thoughts from running away with me. But I dream about her all the time, and I keep thinking maybe she's going to just show up and apologize and make things the way they used to be. I even talk to her sometimes, as if she were still with me."

"Then you have no clearer idea of what happened?"

"What happened? You saw as well as I did—she took the Ramethene Sword from me and gave it to Krael."

"No, I mean what happened in her heart. Did you see any sign of a change in her, some dissatisfaction or anger that might cause her to leave us that way?"

"Did we have a big fight in the ruins—is that what you're asking?" Janik's voice rose. "Did I drive her away? You think maybe she caught me in bed with Dania?"

"That's not what I mean, Janik. Nobody thinks what Maija did is your fault, and I know perfectly well what happened with Dania. All I'm saying is that you were obviously closer to her than Dania or I was. I like to think I'm a pretty good judge of people—even you humans—after all these years, and I was completely surprised by what she did. If you have any insight that could help me understand her behavior, I would certainly like to hear it. That's all."

"I'm sorry, Mathas." Janik shook his head. "I was as surprised as you were. I still lie awake some nights trying to understand it, and I just can't."

Mathas cut a bite of venison and chewed it slowly, then set his fork down. "So when do we leave for Thrane?"

CHAPTER 3

In contrast to the ride from Sharn, Janik enjoyed the journey from Fairhaven to Flamekeep. *Agate Star* was an airship built for luxury, easily twice the size of the ship Janik had sailed on from Sharn. Her main deck boasted a grand pavilion containing a luxurious dining room, a lounge, and even a small library, though Janik found nothing on its shelves to catch his interest. The deck had room for chairs, and the cabins below were spacious and comfortable.

Janik and Mathas had boarded in the late morning and expected to arrive in Flamekeep shortly after dawn the next day. The old friends enjoyed a fine luncheon together. As always, Janik let the elf choose wine for him, and did not regret the decision—Mathas had extensive knowledge of wines and exquisite taste. Their conversation ranged widely over their shared past without ever straying too close to Maija or dwelling on Dania. Janik was eager to hear of Mathas's activities over the past three years, and found with some surprise that he had plenty of tales to share as well.

Janik spent the afternoon on the deck while Mathas

retreated to his cabin to study. He watched the plains and rolling hills of Aundair far below, idly wondering at what point they became Thrane. No natural feature marked the border, which he supposed might be the reason it had been so hotly contested during the war. He saw two different places—easily a three-day journey apart—where the land still had not recovered from some pitched battle fought there in the last years of the war. He supposed one or the other might lie on the border set in the Thronehold Accords. He wondered how long it took for the earth to heal a scar like that.

As the autumn sun drew near the horizon behind the ship, bathing the deck in golden light and long shadows, Janik changed into formal clothes and joined Mathas in the dining room. In place of the sunlight and chatter of luncheon time, the dining room was now dancing with candles and alive with the soft music of a small orchestra. Janik found Mathas at a small table near the window, just as he had in Aundair the day before.

"I find myself drawn to windows these days," Mathas said as Janik took his seat. "I don't know what it is—I can find endless amusement in just staring out, no matter what's on the other side."

Janik peered out the window himself. The fiery glare of the airship's elemental ring all but drowned out the Ring of Siberys in the deep blue sky, the golden belt of dragonshards that circled the world. He looked at Mathas and grinned. "You must be getting old."

"Nonsense," Mathas said. He sipped his wine. "I was old when you were born. In fact," he continued, "I believe the last time I was in Thrane was before you were born. King Thalin was such a strange man, so . . . devout. His presence made those around him feel uneasy, as though they might be called upon to praise the Silver Flame at a moment's notice. I expect the Keeper of the Flame will be much the same."

"Is it true she's a child, this Jaela Daran? Eight years old?"

"I believe she must be eleven by now, but yes, a child," Mathas said. "Ruling part of Galifar like a queen, Sovereigns help us."

"There must be a regent or something—someone who does the work of government on her behalf?"

"I believe so—a council of clergy of some sort. It's absurd to imagine an eleven-year-old in charge of affairs of state."

"Quite. Do you think we'll be dealing with this council, then? Or someone else?"

"I have no idea," Mathas said, then he gave a laugh. "Maybe Dania."

"Sovereigns help us," Janik replied, rolling his eyes dramatically.

When a waitress approached the table, the two fell silent, not wanting to offend the young woman, who proudly displayed the emblem of the Silver Flame around her neck. She took their order and withdrew, and Janik took the opportunity to change the subject.

"I neglected to mention—Dania is not the only old friend who has suddenly inserted herself back into my life."

Mathas raised his eyebrows. "Who else?"

"I received a . . . communication from Krael Kavarat on my way to Aundair. The messenger nearly crashed the airship."

"An Emerald Claw assassin?" Mathas looked shocked.

"A warforged assassin. I don't know about Emerald Claw. But he admitted Krael sent him. To kill me."

"That's bizarre. Why now?"

"Exactly. I haven't heard a word from or about Krael since he walked off with Maija and the Ramethene Sword.

And why should I? I've been no threat to him these last three years—he's had plenty of opportunity to send assassins after me in Sharn. But no, he sends his latest killer after me now, after Dania has invited me to Thrane."

"Clearly he knows something about our mission. Probably more than we do at this point."

"My thought exactly," Janik said. "It gives me a bad feeling. Whatever the Keeper, or Dania, or whoever has in mind, it's clear that Krael will be involved."

"On the bright side, maybe we'll have the opportunity to kill him this time." Mathas smiled grimly.

"That would be good," Janik said. "That would be really good."

❋ ❋ ❋ ⊛ ❋ ❋ ❋

After dinner, Janik and Mathas retired to their cabins. As he often did, Janik dreamed of Maija—her head on his shoulder, her brown hair tickling his nose, her skin pressed against his. When the steward called "Flamekeep!" outside his door in the morning, he awoke confused, unable to figure out where he was or where Maija had gone. He called her name twice before he came back to the present, and the familiar dull ache settled around his heart again. He threw on the clothes he had set out the night before, hoisted his pack, gave the room a quick glance, and stepped out.

Janik looked up and down the crowded hall, but saw no sign of Mathas. He walked to the elf's cabin and pounded on the door. "Mathas! Are you awake?"

"I'm an elf, you idiot. I don't sleep." Even so, the voice inside sounded groggy, and Janik heard some frantic sounds of motion. A few moments later, Mathas stumbled out, looking uncharacteristically disheveled. Wordlessly, the two made their way through the crowd to the mooring tower.

Flamekeep was far different from Fairhaven. While the capital of Aundair was spread out in ordered streets, Flamekeep sprawled over a small island and the nearby mainland shore. At its heart was the great Cathedral of the Silver Flame, standing like a beacon above the rest of the city, clearly visible from the mooring tower. Even the shops and houses in the city had a soaring architecture that suggested Thrane's devotion to the Church, lending an elegant beauty to the relative jumble of the city's streets.

Janik was so focused on making his way through the crowds in the mooring tower that he didn't notice the knights converging on him until Mathas nudged him. They were heavily armored—"easily outrun," in Janik's mind—and wore the insignia of the Church of the Silver Flame beautifully engraved on their breastplates. They carried longswords at their belts and bows slung on their backs. The only visible threat in their approach was the way they moved from opposite sides to approach Janik from the right and left, narrowing his chances of escape.

Fair enough, he thought, but I won't bolt just yet.

"Janik Martell," one of the knights said, stepping forward and standing formally at attention. The other knight adopted a similar pose, and Janik stopped with Mathas just behind him. "Welcome to Thrane."

"Thank you," Janik said. "Was that a real welcome or a 'you're under arrest' welcome?"

The second knight, a blond woman at least ten years younger than Janik, smiled at that, but her male companion frowned. "We are Knights of Thrane," he said, "and we do not speak to deceive. You are an honored guest of the Cathedral, and you are most welcome." He gave a small bow, which his still-smiling companion echoed, and Janik nodded slightly in return.

"Thank you, Knights of Thrane," he said with a glance back at Mathas. "I apologize for appearing to question your honesty—it's just that I was not aware the Cathedral knew of our arrival on this particular airship."

"The knowledge and wisdom of the Keeper of the Flame admit no limitations," the smiling woman said.

"Indeed," the male knight replied. "If you will accompany us, we will take you to your quarters in the Cathedral."

"Thank you."

As the knights began to walk toward the stairs, Janik and Mathas fell into step behind them. "My friend also requires lodging," Janik said. "Are there accommodations prepared at the Cathedral for him as well?"

"Our apologies, master," the male knight said, looking at Mathas for the first time. "We were not informed of your coming. However," he turned to Janik, "I'm sure you'll find that your lodging at the Cathedral includes adequate room for your companion."

"I do not sleep on benches," Mathas said with only a slight smile.

"There will be no need for you to do so," the knight replied.

"The Cathedral's hospitality admits no limitations," Mathas said under his breath.

Janik chuckled as the knights led the way down the mooring tower's stairs to the street. There, a large and ornate coach waited for them, hitched to two white horses that looked prepared for a parade. The driver jumped down from his perch and opened the door when he saw them approach, holding the door as Mathas and then Janik climbed in and settled themselves on the comfortably padded seats. The female knight stood at the door. "It's just a short ride to the Cathedral," she said. "We'll be on the back." She closed the door quietly, then Janik heard the knights' armor clanking as they climbed onto the back of the coach. Hooves clomped on cobblestones as the carriage began to bounce and roll.

"That's strange," Janik said, looking across the carriage at Mathas. "How would they know I was coming on this airship but not know that you were coming? At first, I thought Kelas had notified them of our departure from Aundair, but wouldn't he have told them about you?"

"It's more likely they have agents watching the mooring tower in Fairhaven," Mathas said. "Or House Lyrandar sends passenger lists ahead of the airships. Why would Kelas tell them we were coming, anyway? He has no love for Thrane."

"You're right. I'm probably reading too much into this. They have access to the passenger lists. Looking over the list, they'd have no idea we were traveling together. A live agent in Fairhaven would have seen that." Janik rested his head on the cushioned seat back behind him. "Politics make my head swim. I'd rather head back into the Xen'drik jungle."

Mathas smiled. "If only we could ride in cushioned coaches through the jungle."

"That would be a sight!" Janik laughed.

Mathas closed his eyes while Janik gazed out the window. The coach made its way down the long coastal road to one of the bridges that connected the island-city to the mainland. A low wall ran the length of the bridge, carved with reliefs depicting the religious history of Thrane. Once across the bridge, the coach wound up a steep hill toward the Cathedral.

Janik's heart started beating faster, and he felt somehow as if he were about to step into some new, unexplored ruin in Xen'drik. Another adventure, he thought.

Still, I'd rather be walking into a crypt or ruin than this, he mused. That kind of adventure I know how to handle.

The carriage came to a halt. Mathas shifted in his seat and Janik looked anxiously out both windows. They heard the Knights of Thrane step off the back of the carriage, then the female knight opened the carriage door.

"Welcome to the Cathedral of the Silver Flame," she said formally. Then she smiled again, looking Janik in the eye. "And no, you're still not under arrest."

Behind her, Janik could see the male knight's disapproving frown. He returned the woman's smile as she helped him step down from the carriage. Mathas followed him out, and the male knight stepped toward the front doors of the Cathedral. The two friends paused, staring up at the soaring bulwarks and reaching towers of the Cathedral.

"Quite impressive," Mathas said to the smiling knight beside him. "It lifts the spirit, does it not?"

"It does stir the blood," she replied. "Come. I'll show you to your accommodations. You will be staying in the old palace." She gestured toward a magnificent edifice to the left of the Cathedral.

The male knight gestured toward the Cathedral and spoke to Janik. "And I will take you directly to your audience," he said. "The Keeper of the Flame awaits."

The knight began walking and Janik followed.

"Well, good luck, Janik," Mathas said, but the words barely registered in Janik's rushing thoughts.

"All right," he said to the knight. "Let's get this over with, then." Only when the ornate silver doors of the Cathedral closed behind him did he look back.

The knight led Janik up a set of stairs into one of the towers that flanked the Cathedral's spacious narthex. They went up only a single flight, though Janik could see many more landings above them, and through a door to a sumptuous sitting room. Dominating the far wall, a tapestry gleaming with silver thread depicted the paladin Tira Miron joining with the Silver Flame to prevent the escape of a mighty demon from Khyber. A fire raged in a hearth below the tapestry. Half a dozen cushioned chairs were arrayed facing the fireplace, and the knight swept his arm across the room.

"Please make yourself comfortable. I shall return in a moment." The knight went out a narrow door in the left wall, and Janik started to pace.

His mind was not on the Keeper of the Silver Flame or on the content of his impending meeting. Rather, a series of images of Dania filled his mind, threatening to consume him with guilt. He recalled the way she used to look at him when he'd done something particularly well, whether it was maneuvering to catch a troll in a gout of flame or successfully leading the expedition to Mel-Aqat. For years he had denied that Dania had any romantic feelings for him. He had loved Maija with all his heart, and treated Dania as another great friend, just like Mathas. When he had taken comfort in her arms after Mel-Aqat and then abandoned her in Sharn, he had not just betrayed the love she had harbored for him all those years—he had betrayed their friendship as well. What kind of reception could he expect from her? Why had she contacted him at all?

The narrow door opened again, and Janik wheeled to face it. The knight stood beside the open door, inviting Janik in with a gesture. With a deep breath to steel his nerves, Janik stepped past the knight and entered a well-appointed audience chamber. The vaulted ceiling rose as high as a cottage roof, framing a colorful mural, another depiction of Tira Miron. The walls were hung with simple banners carrying various symbols Janik didn't recognize. The left wall was pierced with four high windows through which daylight streamed, making the room warm and bright. The floor was black marble laced with veins of silver.

She's not here, Janik thought with relief. As the knot of anxiety in his chest started to unwind, he surveyed the room and its occupants.

A large dais rose on the far wall. At its center, a sculpted wooden chair dwarfed the young girl perched in it—yet somehow Jaela Daran, the Keeper of the Flame, managed to avoid looking like a child. She sat erect, her soldier-straight back not touching the ornate wood behind her. Her hands rested lightly on the chair's arms, occasionally moving to rub the smooth wood, almost like a lover's casual caress. Her eyes took in Janik with intelligent curiosity, noting the short sword at his belt, his metal-studded leather armor, the traveling dirt on his boots. She wore a simple white robe tied with a cord of pure silver. A plain silver circlet was her only badge of office.

Janik sized her up quickly, then gave a start as a hulking shape on the floor next to the throne opened two small silver eyes and raised a monstrous head to peer at him. How had he not noticed it first? He supposed he had taken it for a large dog, but its four curved horns marked it as something other than canine. It looked at him for a moment, then settled its head back down on its two front claws, apparently returning to its nap.

Janik forced his attention to the half-dozen attendants standing beside and behind the Keeper. Their heads shaven and their bodies draped in shapeless robes, they gave Janik the impression of being ageless and sexless creatures, almost inhuman. He noticed one or two of them inclining their heads slightly to whisper in a neighbor's ear. One was bending down to whisper to the Keeper herself.

So here we have the hands that hold the reins, he thought, and he began watching the attendants closely, trying to determine who really ruled Thrane.

"Janik Martell." The knight announced him, then backed out the door, bowing. He closed it behind Janik.

"Welcome, Janik Martell," the Keeper of the Flame said. Her high voice was a girl's, but was strong and clear. "The Silver Flame has summoned you."

Janik ducked his head in a minimal bow. "I'm honored," he said, more than a hint of sarcasm in his tone. *You* summoned me, he thought, and I wouldn't have come at all except for Dania. "How can I be of service to you?"

One of the attendants spoke. "You are aware of our Church's mission?"

"You mean fighting evil, casting out demons, that sort of thing?" Janik couldn't quite suppress his smirk. Back home in Sharn, the Church of the Silver Flame didn't so much fight evil as curl up in bed with it. He studied the attendant who had spoken more carefully—the second from the left. He thought he detected the hint of a sneer on that one's face.

"We are called," another attendant said, more than a hint of disgust in her voice, "to wage war upon the evil spirits that prey upon mortals, and sometimes to do battle in the flesh with evil when it takes bodily form."

"Hasn't our world seen enough war?" Janik retorted.

"Enough is when the war is won," the same attendant replied.

"No wonder Aundair is still looking warily across its borders."

"We are not speaking of a war that can be fought with armies across borders." This was a third attendant, the one directly to the Keeper's left. She cast an imperious glance at the one who had been arguing with Janik, and Janik decided to watch this one more carefully.

Now here's some authority, he thought.

"I am well acquainted with wars fought on a smaller scale," he said. "I assume that this summons has something to do with my service for Breland during the Last War."

"Thrane has no need of spies."

Right, Janik thought, thinking of a few Thrane spies he had encountered during the war. "Then why have you called me here?"

The attendant on the Keeper's left looked over her shoulder at the one on the end of the line, who stepped down off the dais and took a few steps toward Janik before speaking. These attendants had no visible weapons, but Janik moved his left hand to rest on the hilt of his sword as he adjusted his stance to face the approaching attendant.

"Your fame is considerable, Janik Martell," this one said. "In particular, your discovery of the ruins of Mel-Aqat has drawn our attention."

Janik could not hear the name of that place without Maija's face forcing its way into his thoughts—the delight she had taken in Janik's success, and then the utter contempt she had worn as she handed the Ramethene Sword to Krael. His eyes flicked over all the attendants again, his thoughts a jumble of questions.

"Yeah, I discovered Mel-Aqat. Found it, fought over it, came back alive. I'm not eager to go back there, if that's what this is about."

"It will be worth your while to return there." The Keeper of the Flame spoke this time, her first words since she issued her welcome. Her eyes rested on Janik but they seemed out of focus, almost glazed over. Her hand had ceased its restless wandering over the arm of her chair.

Here we go—now for the bribes, Janik thought. Somehow, it was a comfort to know that the Church of the Silver Flame was just like any other government or organization. It's always about money, even when you dress it up in vestments.

"Don't waste your breath," he snorted. "There's not enough money in the world."

The girl seemed not to hear him, and Janik suddenly noticed that all the attendants had shifted their attention to the Keeper, looks of surprise and—was that reverence?—on their faces. Even the beast at the foot of the throne was staring at her.

"What you have lost lies still in those ruins, still within your grasp." Her eyes regained their focus and fixed on his, riveting his attention. "The Silver Flame calls you there."

He held her gaze for a moment, drawn in by her mysterious tone. Then he looked away, shaking his head.

I have to admit, this girl is good, Janik thought. Whoever holds her strings picked a perfect puppet—she says her lines with feeling.

He met the Keeper's gaze again. "No," he said. "I'd sooner die than return to Mel-Aqat."

He spun on his heel and stormed out of the chamber.

* * * ◉ * * *

The same knight still waited for Janik, and escorted him to his quarters in the palace. He slammed the door to his suite right in the knight's face, then stalked to a divan and threw himself down.

Mathas sat on a chair facing Janik, a heavy book opened on his lap. The elf's eyebrows rose high on his forehead, but he waited patiently for Janik to speak. It was a long wait.

At last, Janik vented some of his churning anger with a heavy sigh. "I'm sorry to have wasted your time, old friend," he said, shaking his head in frustration.

"I hardly consider time spent in your company after all these years a waste," Mathas replied gently. "What happened?"

"They want me to go back to Mel-Aqat."

"Why?"

"We didn't get that far. They promised to make it worth my while, but I told them to forget it and I walked out. I'm not going back there. There's no way." He leaned back on the cushions, folding his arms behind his head and staring up at the ceiling.

Mathas nodded slowly, his eyes focused somewhere over Janik's shoulder. "And Dania?"

"She wasn't there."

"Ah." They sat in silence for many moments.

"Well," Mathas said finally, gesturing at two doors behind him. "There are beds in those rooms. I think I'm going to see how comfortable they are, and determine whether the Cathedral's hospitality truly knows no bounds."

"Sleep well, Mathas." Janik didn't shift his gaze from the ceiling.

"I don't sleep." The elf seemed older than Janik remembered as he rose slowly to his feet and shuffled into the other room.

What am I doing here? Janik fumed, not sure why he was so angry. *I came because I wanted to see Dania. So the Keeper of the Flame tries to buy my services—why not? It's a job, right? But no, not Mel-Aqat. Nothing could get me back* there. Not even Dania.

He pulled Dania's letter out of his coat again, carefully unfolding it for the hundredth time. "I urge you to come to Thrane and hear what the Keeper of the Flame has to say."

"All right, Dania," he muttered, "I came to Thrane. I heard the Keeper's little speech. Where are you?"

His eyes closed. His thoughts still raging through his mind, he fell into a fitful sleep.

He wasn't sure how long he had slept when a gentle knock at the door roused him. From where he sat, he could see light pouring in the windows of the empty bedroom. Janik stumbled groggily to the door and threw it open. The smiling blond knight stood there. Beside her, a man in a servant's uniform steered a cart laden with food. Janik stepped aside as the servant wheeled the cart into the room.

"I hope you find your rooms acceptable," the knight said. Janik grunted and managed a half smile. "We invite you to enjoy the hospitality of the Cathedral as long as you wish. My name is Tierese, and your comfort is in my charge."

"Thank you." Janik was confused. He had dreamt of Maija again, and Tierese's smiling face reminded him of her.

"If you would be gracious enough to return to the Cathedral in the morning, your presence would be appreciated."

Ah, the Cathedral, he thought. Dream and reality became more distinct in Janik's mind. "All right," he said, "I'll hear the Keeper one more time."

"I am pleased to hear it." Tierese's smile was unwavering, and Janik began to distrust it. "After breakfast tomorrow, I will escort you to your audience." She gave a small bow, which Janik returned.

"Thank you," Janik said again, feeling stupid and still quite groggy. Tierese turned and left, and the servant hustled after her, leaving a fine lunch spread on the table in the suite's outer room. Janik closed and bolted the door, then stumbled into the vacant bedroom. He threw himself down on the bed and fell at once into a much deeper sleep, leaving the food untouched.

CHAPTER 4

Janik awoke with a much clearer head and made his way to the main room of the suite. Mathas had returned to his chair and his weighty tome, which was draped over his lap. An empty plate lay on a side table beside the elf, and plenty of food remained spread on the larger table.

Mathas looked up and smiled as Janik emerged. "A day on an airship is like two on the ground," he said. "Traveling always exhausts me."

Janik laughed. "It wasn't that long ago you spent a year traveling to Mel-Aqat and back." He sat on the edge of the chair facing his friend and started loading a plate for himself.

"And a year in the wilderness is like ten in the city. No wonder I feel so old."

"No wonder." Janik bit into a ripe plum, then dabbed his chin with a white napkin. "I've been summoned back to the Cathedral tomorrow."

"Of course you have. They served us lunch."

Janik smiled. "Rather than turning us out on the street?

You're right. Apparently whoever is behind this isn't going to give up that easily."

"And who is behind this? Did you get any sense of that?"

"It's hard to say." Janik took another bite of his plum and continued with his mouth full. "The Keeper had six attendants who did most of the talking." He swallowed. "Four of them spoke, and none said more than a sentence or two. I couldn't tell whether one of them was pulling the strings." He stared thoughtfully at the wall and took another bite of his plum.

"Well," Mathas said, "while you were there, I learned a little more about the government of Thrane. The girl has mostly abdicated control of the government to a Council of Cardinals, and she concerns herself primarily with the spiritual well-being of the people."

"Interesting," Janik said. "I don't think I was dealing with Cardinals."

"No, I'm sure you would know if you had been."

"But if they're the ones really running the country, why wasn't I talking to them?"

"Perhaps this isn't the kind of job you thought it was." Mathas watched Janik consider this for a moment. "Did the Keeper speak at all?"

"She spoke first, just welcoming me here. Then when she spoke again, all the attendants looked surprised, like she had strayed from the script." He poured himself a glass of wine. "Probably played trump too early."

"Trump?"

"Oh, she was good. She pulled almost a prophetic vision thing—had me going for a moment."

Mathas leaned forward with interest. "What did she say?"

"Something like, 'What you have lost is still in those

ruins.' And then, 'The Silver Flame calls you there.' Trying to make it sound like this job's divinely ordained, and hoping to make it personal."

"What have you lost, Janik?"

"Oh, don't you start now! I work for money, not out of some quest for personal fulfillment. I don't care what this one pays. I'm not going back there."

"It seems to me you've lost a great deal, then." Mathas's voice was quiet, in contrast to Janik's outburst.

"Yes, I have." Janik stood. "I've lost the woman I loved and one of my best friends. I've lost any belief I used to have that the universe was a just and fair place ruled by a Host that cares about such things. I've lost my passion for my work, my thirst to learn more about the ancient civilizations of Xen'drik. I've lost everything that matters to me. But I've been to Mel-Aqat and I know what's there, and I'm not going to find those things there." He stormed to the door, grabbing his coat from a nearby chair.

"Where are you going?" Mathas asked.

"I need to walk, clear my head," Janik said. He threw the door open. The knight Tierese was there, a respectful distance away. He called to her. "Am I allowed to go into the city and look around?"

"Of course," the knight replied. "If you would like, I can arrange a carriage for you."

Janik stepped out of the room, then looked back at Mathas. "I'm sorry I lost my temper, Mathas," he said, then pulled the door closed behind him and addressed Tierese. "Thank you. That won't be necessary." He swept past the knight and stalked down the hall toward the stairs.

"An escort?" Tierese said to his back. "Flamekeep is quite safe, but to be sure . . ."

"No." He sped down the steps, out of the palace, and into the city beyond.

❋ ❋ ❋ ❋ ❋ ❋ ❋

Janik walked for over an hour, but saw very little of the city. He drifted along the jumbled streets, oblivious to the autumn chill, too lost in his thoughts to notice the architecture, the statuary, the murals, and especially the people.

Not noticing the people of Flamekeep, he also didn't notice the distinct lack of people when he turned down a narrow street. He was only vaguely aware of the buildings standing more closely together, forming a narrow canyon that blocked the sun, shrouded in shadow. Something about the sound of footsteps behind him, though, triggered his combat reflexes, and he snapped out of his reverie and spun around, his short sword springing to his hand.

It was a warforged holding a gold-traced adamantine sword—no, it was *the* warforged, the same one that had attacked Janik on the airship to Aundair. It had tried to creep up behind Janik quietly, and looked surprised as Janik spun to meet his approach. As Janik settled into a combat stance, though, he heard someone running up behind him as well, and he knew he was in for a tough fight.

"You again," he muttered. He stepped sideways, trying to bring both opponents into his line of sight. The warforged stood warily, almost close enough to strike, and Janik risked a quick glance around him.

His other assailant was a woman, apparently human, wearing a hood that covered her face. Her armor shone beneath a black cloak, and she carried a heavy bastard sword. In her left hand, she held a battered shield that contrasted sharply with her well-kept armor and sword.

As the woman reached him, the warforged closed the distance and both assailants moved to attack at once. Janik decided that being flanked by them was not a place he wanted to be, and he dove toward the feet of the warforged. The adamantine sword swung over his head as he rolled on the ground and sprang up behind the warforged and out of reach, spinning to face his attackers.

"What is this about?" he said, already starting to breathe hard from the exertion. "If Krael's trying to make sure I don't go back to Mel-Aqat, he needn't worry—it'll take more than the Keeper's gold to send me back there."

"What makes you think Krael sent me this time, Martell?" the warforged said. Again Janik could hear the mocking smile in his voice behind the utterly emotionless face. "Maybe I'm just angry about a fall from an airship."

The woman gave the warforged a sidelong glance, and Janik thought for a moment that he recognized her eyes.

"You jumped!" Janik blurted out as both assailants rushed him again. His sword blocked the adamantine weapon as the warforged swung it toward his head. The powerful blade bit into Janik's sword and stuck for a moment. As the warforged struggled to pull his weapon free, Janik twisted his own sword, trying to pull the hilt out of his opponent's grasp. At the same time, he kicked in a high arc to knock the woman's sword arm away as she swung in under his defenses.

How am I going to get out of this? he thought, trying to remember the lay of the streets around him, mentally searching for possible escape routes.

The warforged yanked his sword free and stumbled backward a step. The woman edged around Janik's left flank.

"You're right, Martell," the warforged said. "Krael sent us."

"Evidently he no longer trusts you to get the job done alone," Janik said. "Of course, he'd never face me with less than a dozen soldiers between us."

"Maybe I just wanted to come along to watch you die," the woman said. Janik could see the smile in her eyes and suddenly realized where he had seen them before.

"Ah, Tierese," he said, backing away so she couldn't maneuver behind him. "I knew there was a reason I hated your smile."

"Damn you to the Outer Darkness, Janik Martell," Tierese said. She glanced at the warforged. "He really has to die now, Sever. If he escapes . . ."

The warforged roared and charged, his blade slashing down to cut into Janik. At the same time, Tierese rushed him from the other side. Janik spotted his only chance to escape. He stepped toward Tierese and ducked under her swing as she tried to compensate for his new position. He crouched and reached for her legs. She slammed into him hard, but he used her momentum to propel her over his shoulder and into the warforged. Both of his opponents sprawled on the cobblestones, and Janik took off running as fast as he could, the same way he had come.

He did not look back. He heard their shouts of fury behind him and heard them scrambling to their feet, then running after him. Janik knew their heavy armor would slow them. With his head start, he would be safe as long as he kept running. In moments, the jangling of armor faded behind him and he knew he had lost them, but he didn't slow his pace. He spotted the Cathedral rising high above the rest of the city, making it easy to find.

He finally slowed to a walk as he approached the door of the palace. He worried that Tierese's participation in this assault spelled danger at the palace, but the knights at the gate let him pass without a word. He made his way back to the suite he shared with Mathas, where no knight stood watch. Still breathing hard from his exertion, he flung open the door and stormed in.

Mathas sat on the divan with his book, leaning back with one arm stretched across the tops of the cushions.

"What kind of twisted nest of vipers has Dania drawn us into?" Janik growled, shrugging out of his coat and tossing it on a chair—atop another coat. He paused for an instant, then spun around to see a half-elf woman leaning against the wall behind him. She pushed a strand of red hair off her face and folded her arms.

"Dania!" Janik blurted.

"Hello, Janik," she replied. "What nest of vipers are you talking about?"

"Krael Kavarat." Janik spat the name. "He sent an assassin after me on the airship to Aundair—clearly he knew what your Keeper wanted from me before I did. And I just met the assassin again, in the company of one of your Knights of Thrane. Which would explain Krael's source of information."

Mathas and Dania were speechless.

"What is going on here, Dania? And what are you doing here?" Janik looked her up and down. "You're dressed like a Knight of Thrane—right down to the Silver Flame around your neck! I suppose Tierese is a friend of yours, smiling to your face while feeding news to Krael?"

"I should have known you'd come in here throwing blame around at everybody but yourself, Janik Martell," Dania said. "This isn't some conspiracy to make your life miserable."

"No, just a conspiracy to get me killed, courtesy of Krael Kavarat."

"Well, Krael's done his level best to kill me, too, while you've been hiding at Morgrave University. Welcome back to the front lines! It's about time you came out of your rabbit hole and started fighting again!"

"Rabbit hole? Hey, the war's over, Dania. Are you having trouble accepting that? Is that why you've put on the armor of a Knight of Thrane? So you can keep fighting the war?"

"I'm not a Knight of Thrane, Janik. I'm a paladin of the Silver Flame."

"A paladin?" Janik's eyebrows shot up in surprise. "So that's it. Now you've got what the Last War could never give you—right and wrong. You think you're on the side of good and virtue now, is that it? And because you've chosen sides, I need to come out of a comfortable retirement and fight evil with you? So how do you explain an Emerald Claw spy in the Cathedral? How can you fight evil when you can't see it in front of your face?"

"This isn't about the Last War, Janik—you're right, it's over. And there's greater evil in the world than Emerald Claw spies. But you wouldn't understand that, would you? As far as you can tell, evil is what hurts you, and good is what you like. Get your head out of the sand! It's bigger than you! And—" She broke off suddenly and turned to face Mathas, inhaling slowly.

"Why don't you sit down and join us, Janik?" Mathas said. Dania let out her breath and sank into the seat facing Mathas, her hand at her throat, touching the Silver Flame pendant that hung there. Janik turned his back on them both, crossing the room to a small table and pouring himself a glass of water from a pitcher. Uneasy silence settled over the room.

"So there's a traitor among the Knights of Thrane," Dania said, addressing Mathas since Janik refused to turn around. "That explains a great deal, more than just your airship assassin. Tierese is her name?" Janik grunted. "I don't know her, but I'll make sure she is dealt with."

"And how does the Church of the Silver Flame 'deal' with spies and traitors in its midst, Dania?" Janik spoke to the wall. "The same way Breland does? Or the Order of the Emerald Claw? Can I look forward to seeing her smiling face hanging from a gibbet?"

"Would that make you happy, Janik?" Dania's voice stayed calm. "Would that reaffirm your conviction that the whole world is callous and uncaring? Would that take the edge off your anger, or justify it, give you an excuse to go on being angry?" Janik took a long drink of water, still refusing to turn around. "You've got no right to be angry at me, Janik. None at all. Turn around and hear this."

Janik drained his cup and turned around, not looking at Dania.

"You hurt me, Janik," she said. "About as badly as it's possible to be hurt. I was stupid to let you into my heart when I knew you didn't love me, but that's not my fault. It's yours." Janik looked ready to respond, but she cut him off. "Listen. It doesn't matter. It's in the past. What matters now is finding a way to fix what we did in Mel-Aqat. More than my heart or your pride is at stake here, Janik. Let's put it aside."

Janik opened his mouth several times, but no words came out.

"As Dania was telling me when you arrived," Mathas said, "apparently our last visit to Mel-Aqat caused more harm than dropping the Ramethene Sword into Krael's hands."

"What harm?" Janik said.

"As far as we have determined," Dania said, "there was an evil spirit imprisoned in the ruins of Mel-Aqat. Without knowing it, we released it. That's why you're here, Janik, as you would know if you had listened to the Keeper of the Flame. We need to go back and find some way to imprison it again or destroy it."

"An evil spirit," Janik said. "What kind of evil spirit?"

"We don't know. Actually, we were hoping you might. You know more about Mel-Aqat than anyone in the world. We thought you might have some insight—"

Janik cut her off. "We? You mean you and the Keeper of the Flame? You and a little girl have decided that I should risk my neck to go back to the place where my life fell apart? Oh, but that doesn't matter, it's in the past."

Dania rose to her feet. "What?" Her calm slipped away. "I cannot believe that you would take the forgiveness I offered you and twist it like that. What happened to you, Janik?"

"You know perfectly well what happened to me. You were there."

"Janik, Maija hurt all of us. We were all her friends, we were all wounded by what she did. But we haven't filled our hearts with bile and anger, Janik. You need to—"

"Don't tell me what I need to do." Janik interrupted her again. "You've filled your heart with Silver Flame hypocrisy. Don't try to push it on me."

For a moment, a hint of holy anger flared in Dania's eyes—an almost visible fire of wrath. "Do not presume to judge what is in my heart, Janik! Has Maija poisoned you against everything? She was a cleric, so everything divine is hypocrisy—is that it?"

"No. It has more to do with what I've seen of your Church—especially in Sharn." Janik was almost smiling. "It didn't take Maija to convince me that the Silver Flame clerics in Sharn were hypocrites. And practically the first words out of your precious Keeper's mouth yesterday were bribes."

"Bribes? Perhaps you heard her wrong, Janik."

" 'It will be worth your while to return there,' she said. I said I didn't want to go, and she said she'd make it worth my while."

"She wasn't talking about money." Dania's wrath had settled down to simple anger.

"Sure she wasn't." Janik scoffed.

Dania threw up her hands. "Forget it, Janik. Just forget it. It's like arguing with a dragon. Just come to see her again tomorrow. If she doesn't convince you then, fine. Go back to Sharn and your teaching and your comfortable retirement from dangerous adventures. Twiddle away your days until Krael's fangs finally close on your throat. I don't care." She stalked to the door and opened it, then turned back. "Just come tomorrow. Mathas, it was wonderful to see you again." She smiled warmly at the elf, cast one final glare in Janik's direction, and stormed out, closing the door firmly behind her.

Janik threw himself down in the chair Dania had vacated, holding his head in his hands. Mathas hadn't moved from his seat, and he slowly stroked his chin as he gazed at his friend. Silence settled over the room for several moments.

"Well," Mathas said at last, "wasn't it nice of her to stop by? It was so pleasant to have the three of us together again."

"Oh, shut up," Janik said, still staring at the floor.

"She always was a hotheaded girl."

"Sea of Fire, yes!" Janik sat back, draping his arms over the sides of his chair. "And now she's got holy fire to back it up!" He returned Mathas's smile.

"She has a wisdom beyond her years, too."

"Shut up again, Mathas." Janik's smile didn't waver.

"Hmm." Mathas stared over Janik's shoulder at the door.
"Yeah, 'hmm.' Plenty of 'hmm.' " Janik rubbed his forehead.
They sat in silence for a long time.

* * * * * * *

Servants delivered a fine dinner to their room, which
Janik and Mathas ate together without much conversation.
Mathas settled into bed early for his elven rest, despite his
long meditation in the morning. Janik sat awake for hours,
not bothering to light a lamp when the sun faded from the
sky, going over his conversation with Dania in his mind over
and over again.

Countless times he had imagined seeing her again and
planned what he might say to her, but the encounter never
played out in his mind the way it had earlier that day. He had
planned to apologize and he'd never gotten the chance. He
had started to, but she interrupted him to say it didn't matter.
Of course, he had started the conversation off on a bitter
note, flushed with anger after being attacked in the city.

The last thing he'd expected was to find that Dania had
become a paladin of the Silver Flame. That, more than
anything, had thrown him off. Dania had never been a
religious person. She had been a soldier—initially, a willing participant in the Last War, not because she believed in
Breland's cause or King Boranel's claim to the throne of the
shattered empire, but because the war got her away from the
expectations placed on the daughter of a noble family. The
war had made her hard—at least on the outside, though Janik
had always suspected that the horrors of the battlefield had
scarred her soul more deeply than she ever revealed.

Now that he thought about it, maybe her new place as a
paladin wasn't that surprising after all. He had always sensed

that her greatest difficulty with the war was that she didn't see any right or wrong in it. She didn't believe in Boranel's cause, and if Breland wasn't fighting for what was right, then it followed that the other nations weren't in the wrong. That, in her mind, made the whole war meaningless, a futile exercise of human arrogance and stupidity. And that made the whole thing feel wrong, including her participation in it.

So perhaps it made sense that with the war over and her adventuring career with Janik cut short, she had found a way to fight for something she thought was right. Better the Church of the Silver Flame than the Order of the Emerald Claw, Janik supposed—though on the other hand, perhaps it was better to be evil without pretense than to cover a corrupt heart with a veneer of holiness.

And now she was trying to draw Janik into her holy crusade. Why? If she had found meaning and purpose in her life without him, why drag him back into it? She knew he had no love for the Silver Flame, not after growing up in Sharn. But certainly what she had said was true: no one knew more about Mel-Aqat than Janik Martell. Maybe she genuinely needed his help.

So what about this evil spirit? Janik turned his thoughts to his years of research into the history of Mel-Aqat. He himself had argued that a passing mention in the *Serpentes Fragments* to a "place of imprisonment" referred to Mel-Aqat, and that one of the great princes of the ancient demons was imprisoned deep beneath the ruins. But if they had released something like that when they were in Mel-Aqat, Janik was sure he would have noticed—and the world would have felt the impact by now.

Thinking this through felt like entering ruins that had lain abandoned for years. Janik had been writing, publishing articles about Mel-Aqat, but he realized now that he'd been coasting, letting the momentum of his discovery carry him through article after article, that all of them really argued little of substance. He had not thought this deeply in years, and he was a little surprised at how good it felt.

I need my books, he thought. I don't remember half of what matters.

With that thought, he got up from his chair and stumbled in to bed.

❧ ❧ ❧ ❧ ❧ ❧ ❧

It was not Tierese but the other knight from the previous day who came after breakfast to escort Janik to the Cathedral.

"Janik," Mathas called as Janik started out the door behind the knight.

"Yes?"

"Hear her out."

"I'll try."

"Thank you."

Janik followed the knight out of the palace and into the Cathedral. They walked to the same sitting room, but the knight did not ask Janik to wait. He walked to the door leading to the audience chamber and held it open for Janik to walk through.

No attendants flanked the throne this time. The Keeper of the Flame sat on her ornate chair, and Dania stood in front of her, to Janik's right. Both smiled as Janik entered.

"Welcome, Janik Martell," Jaela Daran said again. "Thank you for returning."

"I am grateful for your hospitality," Janik said with a bow. He caught Dania's gaze as he straightened, and held it for a long moment before Dania looked back to the Keeper of the Flame.

The girl spoke again. "Dania tells me that you uncovered a spy among the Knights of Thrane who serve our Cathedral. I am grateful for this information, and deeply sorry for the trouble she caused you. This woman, Tierese, has fled Thrane, but we will continue in our efforts to bring her to justice."

"Thank you," Janik said.

"We think she's heading for Sharn, Janik," Dania said. "Which suggests that Krael is there."

Janik started to respond, but the Keeper cut him off. "Dania tells me that you are still reluctant to return to Mel-Aqat, Janik."

"Reluctant is putting it rather mildly," Janik said.

"Janik, listen," Dania said. "Maybe you don't care about this evil spirit we released, or fixing the harm we've done. I find that hard to believe. But think about what we left there."

"Half those ancient passages still lie unexplored," Jaela said, "untouched by any human hand. You found the Ramethene Sword in the ruins, and it might have changed the course of the Last War. What else might still be in there?"

"It would be unusual to discover more than one artifact of power at a single site," Janik said. "And we explored more than half the ruins. At least, I think we did. No telling how much is left, really."

"Should we leave it to Krael to find out?" Dania said. "Will you let him pillage the ruins? He's got the Ramethene Sword already, thanks to Maija. What if there are other relics there? Do you want more artifacts in his hands?"

"And what makes you think he's going there?" Janik was starting to feel the solid ground shift beneath his feet.

"If he's in Sharn, you know what that means," Dania said.

"He's heading to Xen'drik. He's going back there."

"Which is why he has sent assassins after you," Jaela said. "He wants you out of the way so his path is clear."

Janik looked at the Keeper of the Flame, surprised at the poise and authority this child brought to her position. He had to admit that she was impressive, and he no longer suspected her of delivering lines that had been scripted for her.

"We don't know whether Krael's interest has anything to do with the spirit we released there," Dania said. "Maybe the two events are completely unrelated, though I doubt it. But that makes two good reasons for us to return to Mel-Aqat."

Something stirred in Janik's heart. It had started with the merest trickle the night before, a sense that he wanted to plunge deeper into his research, think harder about the issues his visit to Mel-Aqat had raised. Now that trickle was building to a flood. For three years, the name of Mel-Aqat had conjured a single thought, like a dagger in his mind. Now other images were reawakening. He recalled the sight of the ruins looming before them for the first time as they crossed the desert. He felt the thrill of moving through the ancient halls, shining his lantern on inscriptions that verified all his theories and speculations. He remembered fighting shoulder to shoulder with Dania, keeping a pack of insectlike waste-dwellers away from Mathas and Maija. I've missed this, he thought. Maybe I could go back . . .

"For *us* to return?" he asked Dania. "You would come?"

Dania smiled. "Of course I'll come, Janik. You think I'd miss it?"

Janik knew exactly what she meant. Another image forced itself into his mind: Krael's superior smirk as Maija handed him the sword.

"All right," he said. "I'll go."

The three companions boarded an airship the next morning, destined for Sharn. Janik spent the bulk of the first day pacing the deck, casting a wary eye at the skies all around the ship. He slept fitfully, Krael's warforged assassin featuring prominently in his dreams and usually living up to his name—Sever, Tierese had called him.

He rose early the next day and resumed his pacing. Dania approached as he stood at the stern, following his gaze out at a speck in the distant sky.

"It's a dragonhawk," she said.

"Too far east," Janik replied.

"I don't know anything about their range," Dania said, "but I know a dragonhawk when I see one."

"You're just saying that because you know it'll never come close enough for us to be sure."

"It *is* close enough for me to be sure." Dania smiled. "The fact that your inferior human eyes can't make it out doesn't make it false."

Janik grinned. They had shared this argument many times, playing endless variations on essentially the same lines of dialogue. "So if it's a dragonhawk, and it's flying over southern Thrane, does that mean someone's riding it?"

"No," Dania replied. "No one is on its back."

"I hope your superior half-elf eyes are right." He turned around and leaned back on the railing. "It's good to see you again."

"It is good," she replied, still watching the circling dragonhawk. "And good not to be arguing."

"Dania," Janik said seriously, "I never apologized."

"No, you never did."

"I am sorry for everything."

She gave him a sideways glance. "I already told you it's all forgiven." She smiled, then looked outward. "Look, it's diving!"

Janik saw the distant speck plummet earthward, pulling up an instant before colliding with the ground. He imagined he could see the beating of powerful wings as it climbed back into the sky, but it was like seeing the twinkling of a star.

"It caught a sheep," Dania said. "That will be one unhappy farmer."

"You're making this up."

She turned to him and smiled. "Hey, Mathas is down there having breakfast. Let's join him. We can talk about what we need to do in Sharn."

"I guess I could eat breakfast."

They walked together across the deck and went below to the elegant dining room. Mathas, as usual, sat gazing out a window on the starboard side. Janik pulled a chair from a nearby table while Dania sat across from the old elf.

"It's the most remarkable thing," Mathas said. "I just watched a dragonhawk grab a sheep. It's unusual to see them this far east."

Dania burst out laughing, and Janik scowled at them both.

"I don't know how you did it," Janik said, "but somehow you two planned that."

Dania laughed harder, but Mathas was utterly bewildered. Janik glared at them as he accepted a menu from a waiter.

"I thought we could start planning our time in Sharn," Dania said after she and Janik ordered their food.

"Good idea," Mathas said, picking at his plate of fruit. "Janik, our passage to Xen'drik is all set?"

"Yes," Janik said. "I stopped at the Sivis enclave and spoke with Captain Nashan before we left Flamekeep. It's a good thing I did, and probably the first time of many that

I will express my gratitude for the Church's generous letter of credit. We'll arrive in the city in the evening on Zol, then we'll have only Wir and Zor to prepare before we leave on Far."

"Only two days!" Dania said. "There's a lot to do in a short time."

"Yes. Of course, we'll have as much time as we need to really stock up for the journey once we hit Stormreach."

"Will we have trouble with the letter of credit there?" Mathas asked.

"We shouldn't." Janik answered. "House Kundarak still has a bank there, I think. I'll check on that. I'll also have to talk with the sahuagin to get us safe passage through Shargon's Teeth."

"Right," Mathas said. "Is your contact—what's his name?—still around?"

"Shubdoolkra," Janik said, punctuating the sahuagin name with a weird popping sound around the D. "I don't know. I'm completely out of touch. A lot can change in three years."

"Speaking of change," Dania said, "I hate to bring this up, but there are fewer of us than last time. Should we think about finding a fourth?"

"I've been thinking about it," Janik said.

"For all her faults," Mathas said, "Maija proved very useful in certain areas. Healing, for example."

"That's true," Dania said. "The Silver Flame has granted me some ability to heal wounds, but I would be happier with a cleric along."

"Do you have contacts in the Church of the Silver Flame who might fill that role, Dania?" Mathas asked. "You were working with a cleric in Karrnath, were you not?"

"I'm not eager to work with Kophran ir'Davik again," Dania said. "Pompous ass," she muttered, and Mathas laughed.

The waiter returned, set plates of food in front of them, then bustled off to another table.

"My thought," Janik said, "is that it might prove fruitful to find someone who can cover a couple of weaknesses. I don't want to go in there with more than four people—with too many, we'll be stumbling through the ruins like a thunder-herder in Sharn. But in addition to healing, remember that we had trouble in Mel-Aqat with traps, as well as unsafe walls, ceilings, and floors."

"Yes," Mathas mused, "it would be fine with me if I did not get separated from the group by a collapsed wall this time." Dania and Janik both laughed.

"We found you eventually, Mathas," Dania said.

"Eventually." Mathas scowled briefly.

"But that's exactly the sort of thing I want to avoid," Janik said. "My own skills only go so far, as Mathas will attest. So I was thinking about trying to recruit an artificer to join us."

Mathas nodded, but Dania looked slightly skeptical. "That could be an ideal solution," the old elf said. "An artificer would support all of our abilities—make us all better."

"Maybe," Dania said. "But three days to find someone we can trust makes me nervous."

"It makes me nervous as well," Janik admitted. "But believe me, I'm not going to accept anyone I don't trust."

"Well, we'll see how that goes," Dania said. "Let's ask around while we're making preparations and see who we can find."

"Sounds good," Janik replied. "You two will need a place to stay. You're welcome to stay at my apartment, but . . ."

Mathas interrupted. "Thank you for your hospitality, but I will stay in Skyway as I always do. I prefer to stay as far above all those towers as I possibly can."

"And I will find lodging with the Church," Dania said. "I've seen your apartment."

"I hired someone to clean the place weekly. I have every expectation that she's been in twice while I've been away. I had no opportunity to dirty it up in between, so it must be sparkling right now."

"That's fine, Janik," Dania said, "but all the same, I'll stay with the Church."

"Mathas, will you purchase our food for the trip to Stormreach?" Janik asked. "Nothing too extravagant, but I'd like to eat well enough on the ship to keep our strength up."

"Certainly," Mathas said.

"Dania, I'd like you to take care of securing letters of marque so we can loot Mel-Aqat with impunity."

"I'm happy to do that, Janik," Dania said thoughtfully. "But maybe it would be better if you did. You discovered Mel-Aqat, and I'd think the Antiquities Bureau would like to see your name on the application."

"Feel free to throw my name around all you like," Janik said. "But I know quite well that the old fools at the Antiquities Bureau like even more to see a pretty face holding the application."

Dania raised her eyebrows. "I'll take care of it."

"Once you've got the letter in hand," Janik said, "I'd like you to go to the Wayfinder Foundation and find out if they've sent anyone to Mel-Aqat since we got back. I'll double-check at Morgrave, but I think I would have heard if the university sent a team. I like to think the Wayfinders would have told me as well, but I want to be sure."

"Checking to see if any new information has come out of there?" Dania asked.

"I'm pretty sure the answer will be no. I'm still working my way through inscriptions I copied there three years ago, and publishing bits and pieces as I get them translated. But there are some scholars who would like to add their voices to the ongoing conversation about Mel-Aqat and don't want to wait for me to publish my findings. I'd also like to be warned if we're likely to run into other explorers while we're there."

"Got it."

"I think the rest can wait until we're in Stormreach," Janik said. "We'll need more food there—though if you find something good you don't think we'll be able to get in Stormreach, Mathas, go ahead and buy that. We'll need tents, boats . . . oh, you should get new boots in Sharn and break them in on the ship. You still have your packs?"

"Of course," Dania said, and Mathas nodded.

"I have no intention of sleeping in a tent," the old elf added, "as you are well aware."

"Just as I have no intention of walking into the wilds of Xen'drik without a tent on my back," Janik replied, "whether I ever use it or not. Some day, somehow, your magic might fail. And my tent will be there, ready to serve."

They all laughed and settled into an easy banter as they finished their breakfast and walked up onto the deck. As they emerged, Janik gave a careful look at the sky, but soon forgot his worry.

Two days later, the mile-high towers of Sharn came into view. Dania joined the crowd of people at the bow peering over each other's shoulders to watch the city approach, but Mathas and Janik hung back, sitting on the ladder leading to the aft deck.

"Are you excited to see Sharn again, Mathas?" Janik asked.

"My favorite view of the City of Towers has always been from the quiet solitude of the Seventh Wind in Skyway," the elf responded.

"Out the inn window, eh?"

"Exactly. I suppose this fascination with windows is not altogether new." Mathas stroked his chin. "And you? It's old and familiar to you now, is it?"

"I've been gone only two weeks," Janik responded. "It seems a lot longer. Much has changed." He ran his fingers through his hair. "I left this place alone and wracked with worry about seeing you two again. Now I've brought you both back and we're heading off on another expedition—just like the old days. And yet so different."

"It's not the same without Maija," Mathas said quietly.

"Not at all."

From their seats on the ladder, the pair could see the spires of Sharn silhouetted against the vibrant reds and oranges of the sky as the sun began to sink behind the horizon. Janik watched Dania hold a small child up to get a better view above the crowd.

"Janik," Mathas said, "Dania didn't get a chance to tell you—she saw Maija."

"What?" Janik nearly stood up in surprise, but he eased himself back down onto the ladder.

"Yes, in Karrnath. With Krael. It was not an amicable meeting."

"I can imagine not! What was she doing there? What did she say?"

"Dania did not report every word of their conversation, but she said that Krael was seeking an ancient tablet and Maija was working with him. She seemed to think that Maija was utterly lost to evil."

Janik scoffed. "She really is a paladin, then. All the world's in black and white. If only it were so easy to tell good from evil, friend from foe."

"If only it were."

The towers of Sharn were all around them now, and the pair rose to their feet.

"We'll be mooring soon," Mathas said. "We should collect our belongings."

"Let Dania know, will you?" Janik replied, heading down the ladder to his cabin.

CHAPTER 5

It's good to be home, Janik thought as a skycoach shuttled him among the towering buildings of the city toward his apartment near Morgrave University. Even if only for a few days.

Janik had his own mental list of tasks to accomplish during their two days in Sharn, and he hadn't shared every item on the list with Mathas and Dania. Foremost among them was digging through some historical texts and perhaps talking to a few colleagues to see if he could determine what the Church of the Silver Flame might want from Mel-Aqat. He was the acknowledged expert on that site, but his knowledge of the teachings and history of the Church of the Silver Flame was lacking, and he wanted to know what interest the Church might have in those ruins. Searching for a way to re-imprison some vaguely-defined evil spirit, he felt sure, was a cover for a more concrete goal.

Recruiting a fourth member for their group was higher on his list of priorities than he had let on to the others. He could tell that Dania would rather have a cleric on the expedition—preferably a cleric of the Silver Flame. He fully expected her to return with a cleric sent by the Church. The last thing he wanted was to be forced to bring some Silver Flame crusader along because he didn't have a stronger candidate to offer.

As he jumped off the skycoach onto a balcony near his apartment, he made a mental list of the most important books and scrolls that mentioned Mel-Aqat, planning his research. In contrast to his exhaustion upon arriving in Fairhaven and Flamekeep, he found himself energized and excited to be back in Sharn. He paused a moment on the balcony, looking at the towers stretching as far as he could see. Above him, it was nearly impossible to distinguish the lights of high windows in Morgrave University from any stars that might have been in the sky. He breathed deeply, savoring the air and its myriad odors, glad to be back in familiar surroundings.

Turning the key in his apartment door, he suddenly remembered that Adolvo Darriens had been an outspoken follower of the Silver Flame. His commentary on the ancient elven text known as the *Darriens Codex*, named in his honor, might shed some light on the Church's interest in Mel-Aqat. He pushed his door open, and the key fell from his hand and clattered on the bare stone floor.

The place was a shambles. The outer room—his study and sitting room—was littered with books that had been torn from the shelves and tossed carelessly aside. His two cushioned chairs were overturned and a glass case in which he stored his private collection of antiquities had been smashed. At a glance, Janik judged that only one or two items were missing, though several others were damaged. Through the open doors in the hallway, he could see that the kitchen and his bedroom had been similarly ransacked.

"Damn you, Krael," he swore under his breath. He drew his sword, stepped into the outer room, and pushed the door closed behind him. He made his way on silent feet around the small apartment, making sure that no agent of Krael's remained. When he was satisfied that the place was empty, he sheathed his sword, barred the door, retrieved his dropped key, and started putting books back on their shelves.

An hour later, Janik righted one of the overturned chairs and collapsed into it, feeling the weight of his exhaustion settling on him. With one hand on his forehead, he looked up at the bare spaces on his shelves.

"The *Darriens Codex*," he said, pointing at the empty shelf. "Edgeler. The *Scorpion Hymns*. Gautier. Zhavaan. And the *Serpentes Fragments*. Well done, Kavarat. You got everything important. Well damn done."

He sat there staring at the empty places until sleep seized him.

Sometime during the night, Janik must have shuffled from the chair to his bed. He woke up lying on top of the covers, still wearing his clothes, blinking as the dawn light poured through the uncurtained window. He got up, washed, and changed his clothes. With a last rueful glance at the empty spaces on his bookshelves, he made his way out the door.

He walked a long route he had walked hundreds of times before, from his apartment to the university and its teeming Commons, his favorite place to eat breakfast. He noticed for the first time how many dark alleys opened along his path, how many places an attacker could hide. Every time he saw a warforged, his hand reached almost involuntarily for his sword, though he recognized none of them as Krael's assassin.

This is ridiculous, he thought. I'm jumping at shadows. Fifteen years of all kinds of adventure, digging through ruins, spying for Breland, hiking across Xen'drik, and I've never been like this.

He rested his left hand on the hilt of his short sword and strode more deliberately along the streets and bridges of the City of Towers, forcing himself not to peer around every corner.

Janik reached the Commons and bought a piece of fried dough sprinkled with cinnamon and sugar. Food in hand, he looked around at the students and faculty clustered at tables throughout the plaza, hoping to spot a colleague he could talk to about Mel-Aqat. Seeing no familiar faces, he made his way to his office, eating as he went.

He paused outside his office door, licking the last sugar crystals from his fingers. He fully expected to find his office ransacked, even though nothing there was as precious or important as the books that had been stolen from his home. He turned the key in the lock, dropped his right hand to his sword hilt, and pushed the door open with his left.

Nothing seemed out of place, to Janik's surprise. Everything was as he had left it two weeks earlier. Which meant that either Krael's agents hadn't managed to gain access to his office since it was in a public area, or they had known that what they really needed was in his apartment. Maybe it had been a lucky guess—they tried his apartment first and found everything they were looking for. It was hard to imagine that anyone working for Krael knew that much about his books.

Except Maija. That thought stung like a Xen'drik scorpion. Dania had seen Maija and Krael together in Karrnath. Was Maija still working with Krael, telling him where to find Janik's books? Was she Krael's lover now?

He pushed those thoughts aside. He dropped his pack on the desk, pulled a journal and writing set out of it, and left the office again, locking the door behind him. The university library couldn't afford a copy of the *Serpentes Fragments,* but it did have copies of all Janik's published papers, including the article in which he first spelled out everything the *Fragments* said about Mel-Aqat. As he walked to the library, he formulated a plan. All thoughts of Krael and his warforged assassin fled from his mind.

❋ ❋ ❋ ❋ ❋ ❋ ❋

Janik did not emerge from the library until it was time to meet Dania and Mathas for dinner. He hurried to the edge of campus to catch a skycoach that would take him to Mathas's favorite restaurant, the Azure Gateway, in the floating district of Skyway. Once aboard the rowboatlike craft, he pulled out his notebook and looked over his writings.

The *Serpentes Fragments* was a loose, disjointed collection of short verses and fragmentary prose from Xen'drik. The exact provenance of the texts was the subject of much scholarly debate. Janik had made what many scholars considered convincing arguments that some of the lore contained in the *Fragments* dated to roughly the time of the quori invasion and the fall of the giant kingdoms of Xen'drik, some forty thousand years ago. Other fragments were much later, and the first attempt to bring any semblance of order to the fragments seemed to have been about three thousand years ago, when a tiny city or temple-state of drow undertook the task of collecting and editing the jumbled pieces of a tradition they inherited.

The most ancient fragments were the ones that concerned Janik, for they spoke of a Place of Imprisonment that lay at the feet of the Pillars of the Sky. They described it as being surrounded by lush jungle—"trees that bear fruit and vines that climb, all manner of creeping thing and everything that grows," in the quaint words of the first modern translation. One of the important realizations that had finally led Janik to the site of Mel-Aqat was that this jungle was gone, replaced by the great golden desert Menechtarun.

The Place of Imprisonment described in the earliest fragments was vastly different from the crumbling ruins Janik and his friends had found when they finally reached Mel-Aqat. Only the great ziggurat at the heart of the ruins remained relatively intact, and Janik had not located an entry to the structure on his last visit. Gone were the great columned halls, the towering statues of tiger-headed men and women, the sprawling relief carvings of dragons making war on demons.

In reviewing his own writings about the *Serpentes Fragments,* Janik had been drawn to two things: the description of the ziggurat and the mention of the carvings. In some places, the ziggurat itself was described as the Place of Imprisonment, while in other passages, the term clearly applied to the whole site. Zhavaan's hypothesis, expounded in one of the books Krael had stolen, theorized that the more specific references were more ancient and thus more accurate. That theory would confirm that Janik's earlier expedition could not have released whatever was imprisoned there—he never got close enough to the ziggurat to release any ancient binding.

Janik, however, suspected that the more general description of the site actually predated the construction of the ziggurat—that the ziggurat was built much later in Mel-Aqat's history as a way to mark the Place of Imprisonment. That was the argument Janik had propounded in one of his published papers. Even in that case, it was likely that the ziggurat was the location of the actual binding. Janik was quite sure he had not released whatever was imprisoned at Mel-Aqat.

But what was imprisoned there? The *Fragments* related a myth introduced by the phrase, "As recorded in stone at the Place of Imprisonment." It went on to describe a great war between dragons and demons—a common theme in the mythology of Xen'drik's ancient civilizations. This war was supposed to have ushered in the golden age of the giants. Before the birth of the giant civilizations, the legends said, demons ruled the world, which was a place of fire and unbridled torment. The great dragons, united in a coalition if not in a single species (the legends disagreed), waged a great war on the demons that lasted over a million years. In the end, angelic spirits who had allied themselves with the dragons—the winged rainbow serpents called couatls—had bound the demons inside the earth, sacrificing themselves to form the spiritual prisons that held them fast. From the ashes of this epic war, the giant civilizations were born.

A war that lasted a million years, Janik found himself thinking as the skycoach neared the floating towers of Skyway. And from its devastation a great new civilization was born. What will be born from the ashes of the Last War? he wondered. Such a pretty myth—that new birth might come from so much ruin.

The myth of the couatls' sacrifice was undeniably important in the history of Xen'drik—and even the recent history of Khorvaire. Serpent cults appeared among the native races of Xen'drik with surprising frequency through the ages, right down to the present day. Giant cults, ancient elf cults, even modern drow cults revered the winged serpents, just as there were other cults that worshiped the imprisoned demons. Many of the texts in the *Serpentes Fragments*—perhaps most of them—could be traced to cults such as these, giving the collection its name.

Of greatest immediate interest to Janik, was a theory that identified the Church of the Silver Flame as a modern version of a Xen'drik serpent cult, transplanted to Khorvaire. He wondered what connections might exist between the Church that now ruled Thrane and the primeval cults that revered the couatls and used Mel-Aqat as a place of worship. Might the Keeper of the Flame be sending him—and Dania—to Mel-Aqat in hopes of finding some artifact that would establish the connection between the Church and the ancient ruins? Did the Church hope to establish its antiquity, give itself an added degree of respectability by proving its ancient ties? Or was it seeking to prevent Krael and the Order of the Emerald Claw from learning the same thing?

Janik returned his notebook to his backpack and before long was walking the peaceful streets of Skyway toward the Azure Gateway. The floating city district boasted three prominent restaurants with panoramic views of the city, extensive menus of fine cuisine, and exorbitant prices. Mathas preferred the Azure Gateway for its food and its friendly half-elf headwaiter, a wizard with whom Mathas had struck up a casual friendship in years past. Janik preferred it because it was generally less crowded than the others.

When Janik entered the restaurant, Mathas was talking with the headwaiter in the foyer, apparently catching up after his two-year absence from the city. Dania stood nearby, politely attentive without participating in the conversation. She smiled at Janik as he walked in, then Mathas and the headwaiter turned to welcome him.

"Ah!" the headwaiter said. "Janik Martell, welcome! But where is the lovely Maija?"

I guess Mathas didn't tell him very much, Janik thought.

Mathas and Dania looked at him uncomfortably, unsure how he would react.

"She will not be joining us this evening, Ravvan," Janik said quickly.

"Very good, master," the half-elf replied graciously. "Your party is complete, then? I will show you to a table."

Having spent the day poring over manuscripts in ancient elven tongues, Janik suddenly saw Mathas and the two half-elves walking before him in a strange new light. He thought about their ancestors, living in Xen'drik and slaving under the giants. Were Dania's elf ancestors part of a serpent cult? Was there some predisposition in her blood that had led her to worship the Silver Flame? Dania and Mathas were as familiar to him as the short sword at his side, but for just a moment, they seemed as alien as the distant elves of Aerenal or the cyclopean ruins of Xen'drik.

Those thoughts dissipated quickly once the trio was seated. Janik told his friends about the burglary at his apartment, drawing shocked and angry exclamations from both of them.

"You think Krael was behind it?" Mathas asked.

"Of course he was," Janik said. "And I think it was probably Krael himself for a change, not some lackey doing his dirty work. He knew exactly which books to take."

"So he's definitely planning his own expedition to Mel-Aqat," Dania said.

"No doubt. And interfering with our plans in every way he can."

"It's not a great blow to our expedition, is it?" Mathas asked, peering a little too keenly at Janik.

"No," Janik replied quickly. "We had enough historical background to make the trip last time, and we still have everything we need. I had hoped to refresh my memory on some details, but it's no great loss. Quite a loss to me personally," he added ruefully. "Those books are very rare and cost a lot of money."

"You'll get them back sooner or later," Dania assured him. "If I have anything to say about it, Krael will not survive his trip to Xen'drik."

Janik smiled warmly at her enthusiasm. "So, how are our preparations coming? Do we have a letter of marque?"

"We do," Dania said with a smile, "and you were absolutely right about the nice gentlemen at the Antiquities Bureau."

"I hope they didn't give you too much of a hard time."

"Oh, no. They were patronizing as anything," she rolled her eyes, "giving me a load of, 'Xen'drik is a dangerous place, are you sure you're up to it?' But your name and my dress"—she indicated the moderately low neckline of the midnight blue dress she was wearing—"got the documents approved in no time."

"I'm glad it wasn't too arduous," Janik said, trying hard not to look at Dania's collarbone, suddenly overwhelmed by a memory of the feel of her skin. Mathas was half-covering a grin with one hand. "And the Wayfinders?"

"Ah." Dania's smile faded. "Unfortunate news from the Wayfinder Foundation. They did, in fact, send an expedition to Mel-Aqat, hoping to supplement the flow of information that, they felt, was not coming fast enough out of Morgrave University."

"In other words, I'm not publishing fast enough to please them."

"No one could publish fast enough to please them," Dania said. "I must say, I was a little surprised to learn how popular Mel-Aqat still is."

"It was a very major find—a large explosion in my little world of scholarship," Janik said.

"Anyway," Dania said, "the expedition left Stormreach nine months ago. No word has come back. The team is feared lost."

"Sovereigns," Mathas swore under his breath.

"Well," Janik said after a moment, "perhaps we'll find them." His voice was flat, holding little trace of optimism. "Or at least learn of their fate."

It was never pleasant to be reminded of the risks they faced every time they ventured into the wilds of Xen'drik. Janik and his friends had cheated death more times than they could count, always escaping the Keeper's fangs through wits, skill, or sheer blind luck. Apparently the Wayfinders had not shared their luck. Looking at Mathas and Dania, Janik could tell they were both thinking similar thoughts.

He lifted his wine glass and forced a grim smile onto his face. "Here's to dodging the fangs of the Keeper one more time."

Mathas and Dania touched their glasses to his. "To survival," Mathas said. Dania briefly closed her eyes but said nothing.

"Speaking of survival, Mathas," Janik said, "did you get a good start on our food stores for the trip?"

"I got more than a good start," the elf replied. "I think I'm done. And I found an artificer I want you to meet."

"Did you?" Janik was surprised.

"Someone we can trust?" Dania asked, looking skeptical.

"I believe so," Mathas replied. "His name is Auftane Khunnam."

"A dwarf?" Janik asked.

"Yes, though he was born and raised in Stormreach," Mathas said. "He has traveled extensively—he impressed me with the breadth of his knowledge."

Janik marveled at the elf's report. Anyone who could impress Mathas with his knowledge must be impressive, indeed.

"How did you find him?" Dania asked.

"I was talking to Pradam, that outfitter in Cliffside, as I bought some of our supplies. I told him we were heading to Xen'drik, and he told me that he'd heard of a dwarf who was looking to earn passage to Stormreach, and might be available for work there as well."

"I wouldn't think an artificer would have any trouble making money in Sharn," Janik said, his suspicions aroused.

"When I talked to Auftane, it turned out that Pradam hadn't gotten it quite right," Mathas said. "Money isn't the issue for him. He was just planning to return to Stormreach and wanted some company on the trip, and perhaps some work once he got to Xen'drik."

"You say he's well traveled," Dania said. "Who has he been adventuring with?"

"Various people, and that's perhaps the one thing that makes me a little uncertain about him. I don't know if he just hasn't found companions who share the extent of his wanderlust, or if there's some reason he doesn't journey with one group consistently." Mathas stroked his chin for a moment. "My sense is that he enjoys the experience of traveling with different people as much as he enjoys visiting different places."

"So he might not stay with us long," Janik said.

"Is that bad?" Dania asked. "As long as he finishes the trip to Mel-Aqat, does it matter if we never see him again?"

"I suppose not," Mathas replied. "It's just . . ."

"A change from how we've always done things," Janik finished for him. "And again, maybe that's not such a bad thing.

Well, I'm willing to meet him, Mathas. Did you arrange a time?"

"Luncheon tomorrow."

"All right. At luncheon tomorrow, we'll meet this Auftane Khunnam. And we'll see if he can be ready to leave the next morning."

* * * * *

Janik had one more task in mind before going to bed that night—a task best left until darkness. He and Dania walked Mathas to the Seventh Wind, a simple but elegant inn at the southern edge of Skyway, then rode in a skycoach together back to the city below. Dania got off the skycoach at a small shrine of the Silver Flame in the Hope's Peak district on the city's upper west side. Janik wished her a good night, then continued to the waterfront.

Making his way to the southern end of the waterfront, Janik stepped into a floating boat town—hundreds of rafts, keelboats, and other vessels lashed together and moored to the shore to form one of Sharn's seediest districts. He followed the sounds of raucous laughter and drunken singing across the decks of a half-dozen boats. Moments later, a tavern came into view, the faded painting of a dagger on a black background the only indication of the establishment's name—Knife in the Dark. Nobody called it that—people in the Ship's Towers district just called it "the tavern," and few people outside of Ship's Towers had any reason to call it anything. Janik pushed the door open and the noise inside suddenly roared in his ears.

He squeezed through the press of boisterous patrons to get to the bar, if only because Thurva, the owner, was prone to get angry at people who came to her tavern to do business and didn't buy drinks to keep *her* in business. He bought a tankard of ale, tasted it on the off chance the fare had improved in the last three years, and spat it out on the wooden floor.

He leaned his back against the bar and looked around the crowded room. For a moment he was afraid the trip had been wasted, but then a big orc stood up from a table in the corner and stormed toward the door. Janik spotted Shubdoolkra at the orc's table. Finding a sahuagin in a room full of humans was rarely difficult, but the orc had blocked Janik's view. Relieved, Janik ducked and squeezed across the room and sat down across from Shubdoolkra.

"Ah, Janjan," the sahuagin croaked, mangling Janik's name as he always did. "Good to see you once." His accent was thick and his Common terrible. His eyes bulged as he spoke.

Janik answered in fluent Sahuagin, though he had trouble with some of the clicks and pops of the language. "Seeing you again is like returning to the dark water," he said formally. He found himself thinking idly that it was almost true, in exactly the opposite way that the sahuagin meant it—talking to Shubdoolkra was a bit like drowning.

"With meat on one shoulder and gold on the other," Shubdoolkra responded in kind, and Janik couldn't help thinking that he was meat in the sahuagin's eyes. "Are you sailing through Shargon's Teeth?"

"I am, and once more I offer tribute to Baron Kushe—" Shubdoolkra's eyes bulged wider and he spat, cutting Janik off.

"Do not speak that name!" the sahuagin yelled, causing many nearby patrons to wheel around and stare, expecting a fight. Janik doubted any of them could understand their conversation, but Shubdoolkra's angry voice sounded horrific. If that weren't bad enough, the sahuagin's ear fins stuck out in anger, and the spines on his back pulsed up and down. "The one of whom you speak is dying the thousand deaths in the jaws of the Devourer! Curse his name and curse any who speak it!"

Janik was taken aback. If Kushek'ka was dead, would that change the usual bargain? The old baron had ruled his village peacefully, negotiating with sailors from Sharn for safe passage through Shargon's Teeth to Xen'drik. A new baron might take a different attitude toward human sailors, or drive a harder bargain. The violence with which Shubdoolkra had responded to his name suggested that he and his policies were not in favor under the new baron, whoever he was. All the same, Shubdoolkra was here, which suggested that he was still making deals.

"Curse my ignorance and stupidity," Janik said carefully, hating the formalities of the language but apparently calming the sahuagin. "Who is the baron of your people?"

"Baron Yadkoppo governs us with wisdom and strength, as long as it pleases the Devourer that he may do so," the sahuagin responded.

"May his reign bring meat to the village," Janik said with some relief. Shubdoolkra had said, "with wisdom and strength," which meant another relatively peaceful reign, as opposed to "in strength and slaughter," which would bode ill for his mission. "I offer tribute, then, to Baron Yadkoppo through his loyal servant Shubdoolkra, and ask the baron's favor upon my journey."

"What tribute do you bring, Janjan?" The sahuagin's bulging eyes glittered, and Janik watched his long, webbed fingers stretch greedily.

Better go high, Janik thought. "For the baron's pleasure, I offer five thousand coins of gold. For his people, I offer one hundred steel tridents and one thousand bolts tipped with steel. For his loyal servant Shubdoolkra, I offer an additional five hundred coins of gold. I hope that my tribute is acceptable to Baron Yadkoppo." Janik held his breath and kept his eyes away from Shubdoolkra's, watching the sahuagin's scaled and webbed fingers scratching idly on the table.

"Your tribute is acceptable to Baron Yadkoppo," the sahuagin said, and Janik let his breath out slowly. "When will your ship leave Sharn, Janjan?"

"We sail with Captain Nashan on *Hope's Endeavor,* departing from Sharn on the morning of the third day from this one."

"Baron Yadkoppo promises that *Hope's Endeavor* shall not come to harm on its passage through Shargon's Teeth, in gratitude for the tribute you have promised. If promises be broken, the Devourer will judge."

"My thanks, Shubdoolkra." Janik stood, nodded a bow to the sahuagin, and left the tavern as quickly as he could manage, glad to be out of the crowd. He walked the noisy streets of Cliffside until he could find a skycoach to take him home, and collapsed gratefully in bed.

* * * * * * *

He awoke about four hours later, much less gratefully, to someone pounding on the door to his apartment. He shuffled to the door, trying to wrap a blanket around himself with one hand while rubbing his eyes with the other.

"Janik, open up!" Mathas's voice came through the door.

"I'm coming," Janik croaked as he fumbled with the locks.

"We've got a problem," Mathas said as soon as the door was open. "Captain Nashan sailed for Xen'drik three days ago."

CHAPTER 6

Krael," Janik said, the name like a curse on his lips.

"Almost certainly," Mathas replied, walking into the sitting room. He took a seat on the chair that Janik had righted two nights before, arching an eyebrow at the one that was still overturned. Janik closed the door, bolted it, and turned to Mathas, lifting the chair off the floor and setting it upright so he could sit down.

"This is ridiculous," Janik said. "He sends an assassin after me—twice!—breaks into my apartment and steals my books, and then steals the ship we've commissioned to take us to Xen'drik! What's next?"

"If I had to guess, I'd say that next is getting to Mel-Aqat before we do, and getting his filthy hands on whatever it is we're looking for."

"That cannot happen," Janik said. "I'll give my soul to the Keeper before I let Krael beat me at anything again."

"Careful what promises you make, Janik. But you're right, we've got to stop him."

"Are we almost ready to go?"

"I think we're close. I brought our food stores to the docks to stow them aboard his ship and found out that Nashan left. Dania has our documents. I bought new boots, and I think she did as well. I think we could leave today."

"Then let's see what our letter of credit from the Church of Silver Flame can buy in this town, shall we?"

Mathas grinned. "I'll contact House Lyrandar immediately." He stood up and faced the door, then turned back. "We're supposed to meet with that artificer, the dwarf."

Janik groaned. "There's not enough time to figure out who he is and whether we can trust him."

"I agree."

"Can you get a message to him? Let him know we're leaving earlier than expected and we can't meet him?"

"I will try."

"Do you think I'm being too cautious?"

"No, of course not," Mathas said quickly. He paused. "But then, we both knew Maija for years."

"So we did," Janik muttered. "Maybe the three of us will be enough." He opened the locks on the door for Mathas. "Sea of Fire, I'm not even sure I trust you any more."

Mathas smiled. "I'm glad to know the feeling is mutual." He stepped out the door. "I'll let you know what I hear from Lyrandar. Where can I find you?"

"My office. Thank you, Mathas."

"Watch your back, Janik. Krael knows he hasn't won yet."

"Thanks for the reminder," Janik called as he pushed the door closed and bolted it tight.

❂ ❂ ❂ ❂ ❂ ❂ ❂

Janik grabbed a pastry at the commons and spent the morning in his office, pulling journals off his shelves. He hoped to find the article he had read linking the Church of the Silver Flame to the serpent cults, but he could not remember where he had seen it. Frustrated, he sat on the edge of his desk, staring up at the rows of musty tomes and academic writings on the shelves above him. A knock at his door stirred him from his contemplation.

"Come in, Mathas," he called out, knowing that Dania wouldn't knock.

"Ah, excuse me," came an unfamiliar voice, low and gruff. Janik stood up quickly, his left hand dropping to the hilt of his sword, and turned to face the open doorway. His visitor was a dwarf, but he seemed tall for a dwarf—only a hand's length shorter than Mathas, in fact, though he probably weighed nearly twice as much as the slender elf. He wore his black hair moderately long, brushing the tops of his shoulders. His beard was neatly trimmed and his moustache waxed to two sharp points. At his belt was a mace with a head as big as his own head, and he wore a polished breastplate.

"Oh!" Janik blurted. "I apologize. I was expecting someone . . ."

"Your elf friend, Mathas, yes," the dwarf said. "I am Auftane Khunnam. I met him yesterday." He extended his hand as he stepped closer to Janik.

Janik shook his hand. "It's nice to meet you. I'm sorry to say there's been a change of plans . . ."

"I heard. Found a note from Mathas at the inn. That's why I've come to see you. I don't let work slip away so easily."

"I'm sorry, I—"

"Look, I understand," Auftane interrupted. "You don't know me, or anything about me. You wanted to check me out a little bit, get a sense of whether I was trustworthy. You find yourself having to leave town earlier than planned, so you think you don't have time to do that. I'm thinking you've been burned before. Am I right?"

Janik blinked. He wasn't sure he had ever heard a dwarf talk that much and that quickly. Auftane didn't give him time to respond.

"Think of it this way. You were going to meet me for lunch today, then hop on a ship first thing tomorrow, then spend a month getting to know me better before we landed at Stormreach. I can leave today—I'm ready to get on a ship right now. You'll still have a month to get to know me on the boat. You don't need to make any decision until we make Stormreach. Does the half a day we've lost really matter?"

Janik found himself liking this Auftane Khunnam already, and he chastised himself for it.

"So you're mainly interested in getting to Stormreach?" he asked.

"Well, no, I'm mainly interested in doing something new," Auftane replied. "I've been traveling Khorvaire for ten years now. I'd like to go back to Stormreach, and it's easier to do that as part of a group than alone. You can't just buy a ticket like on the lightning rail, you know? But I hear you're going pretty far into Xen'drik, and that's something I've never done before. I think I'd like to give it a try."

"Are you in a particular hurry to leave Sharn?" Janik asked.

"You mean am I trying to leave town before my horrible crimes come to light? No." Auftane laughed. "No, I'm not running away from anything or anyone, and there's nobody waiting for me in Stormreach I'm in a hurry to see, either."

"What did Mathas tell you about what we're doing in Xen'drik?"

"Very little, really. I know a little bit about your work—archeology is a bit of a hobby of mine, I guess. You can't grow up in Stormreach and not pick up some interest in the history of the place. I read a couple stories in the *Inquisitive* about the big discovery you made a few years back. Anyway, Mathas told me you were planning another expedition south into Xen'drik—he said beyond the peninsula, but that's all. But I know enough to know a trip beyond the peninsula is a pretty big deal. I assume this is no dragonshard prospecting expedition."

"That's right," Janik said. "We're going back to Mel-Aqat—that was my big discovery. And I think you can come along, at least as far as Stormreach."

"Thank you," Auftane said, his face breaking into a big smile that carved deep wrinkles around his eyes. "I'll make sure you won't regret bringing me along."

"Now I'm sure you're not being too cautious," Mathas said from the doorway. Auftane spun around to look at the elf, surprised, and Janik laughed aloud at the wry smile on Mathas's face.

"Auftane made a pretty convincing case," Janik said.

"And I'm not going to question your judgment," Mathas replied. "Glad to have you coming with us, Auftane."

"Thank you."

"So when are we leaving?" Janik asked. "What did House Lyrandar say to our letter of credit?"

"House Lyrandar was suitably impressed," Mathas said with a laugh. "They can't spare an elemental-powered galleon on such short notice, and I'm not convinced that our letter of credit would have extended that far anyway. But I've commissioned a small, fast ship with a Lyrandar windwright to take us to Stormreach, leaving this afternoon—as soon as we're ready. We should get to Stormreach at least a week before Krael."

"Excellent! Mathas, that's the best news I've heard this week."

"Who's Krael?" Auftane asked.

"An old rival," Janik said, "a captain in the Order of the Emerald Claw. We've had a number of run-ins with him over the years, and the last two weeks he's been rearing his ugly head again."

"We should be clear about this, Janik," Mathas interjected. "Auftane, I don't know how much you know about the Order of the Emerald Claw, but Krael has sent assassins after Janik. He's a serious threat, and by associating with us, you're making an enemy of a powerful and dangerous man."

"I appreciate your candor," Auftane said. "But you're not going to scare me off now."

"Anyway," Janik said, "Krael is the reason our travel plans are in disarray. We had made arrangements for a ship to carry us to Stormreach tomorrow, but Krael apparently bought the ship out from under us and left three days ago. He's likely to try to get to Mel-Aqat before we do."

"Why?" Auftane asked. "What's in Mel-Aqat that we're all so anxious to get?"

"We can discuss that on the ship," Janik said. "We should find Dania and get ready to leave. Mathas, can you get the supplies loaded on the ship?"

"Already done," the elf replied. "As soon as I left House Lyrandar, I made all the arrangements."

"Perfect. Then all that remains is getting Dania. Can we find her? She still doesn't know about our change of plans."

"I hardly expect that she's out carousing in the city,"

Mathas said. "I'll find her and meet you at the ship. It's in Grayflood, dock nineteen."

"Dania is our fourth, then?" Auftane asked.

"Yes," Janik said. "She's a paladin of the Silver Flame now, but she's always been good with a sword."

"Now? Her paladin's calling is a recent occurrence?"

"She has walked the paladin's path for approximately a year," Mathas said.

"I look forward to meeting her. I've often wondered what that sense of calling is like."

"Well, you'll have plenty of opportunity to ply her with questions on the ship," Janik said. "Let's get moving."

* * * ◉ * * *

"Sea of Fire!" Janik swore. His companions turned to look at him, surprised by his sudden outburst.

The four of them were gathered at dock nineteen in Grayflood, their gear already loaded onto *Lyrandar Dayspring*. The ship's crew was climbing the rigging and scouring the deck, making ready to sail. Janik slapped his hands to his head.

"Shubdoolkra," he said. Auftane looked puzzled at the strange name, but Mathas and Dania raised their eyebrows.

Mathas immediately apprehended the problem. "The sahuagin guaranteed safe passage to Nashan's ship, not this one," he said.

"Exactly," Janik said.

"Doesn't House Lyrandar have a standing agreement for passage through Shargon's Teeth?" Dania asked.

"The sahuagin don't make standing agreements," Janik said. "They get a lot more tribute by making deals one ship at a time."

"Can you find Shubdoolkra and renegotiate before we leave?" Mathas asked.

"I doubt it. He doesn't like daylight—I'm pretty sure he comes to shore only at night."

Dania looked worried. "Should we delay our departure until tomorrow?"

Janik glanced around at the busy crew and the ship's captain, shouting orders from the poop deck. "I don't think we can do that at this point," he said. "I think our best bet is to leave word for Shubdoolkra at the tavern, tell him about our change of plans, and hope for the best. Besides, we fought our way through the sahuagin once, remember?"

"Ugh, I remember," said Dania, one hand moving to her belly. "I'd still have scars to show if it weren't for Maija's healing."

"You'd be dead if it weren't for Maija's healing," Mathas said. "That trident went in deep. And stomach wounds kill—they just do it slowly."

"And painfully," Dania added. She turned to Auftane. "That reminds me, Auftane. Do you have some means to heal wounds?"

Auftane smiled and produced three wands from a pouch at his belt, holding them up for Dania's inspection. "This one will take care of minor cuts and scrapes. This one is good for more serious injuries. And this one will bring you back from death's door." He stuffed the wands back in the pouch. "With a little time and a lot of money, I could make a scroll that would bring you back from the Realm of the Dead. But let's hope there's no call for that!"

Janik scowled as he hurried up the dock to the street to find a messenger.

"Where's he going?" came a voice from the deck above

them. The captain, Avaen d'Lyrandar, was leaning over the bulwark and watching Janik as he disappeared into the crowds. "I thought we were leaving!"

"A momentary delay," Dania called to him. "We'll come aboard now, if you're ready for us."

"We're ready! Come aboard!"

Mathas and Auftane followed Dania up the gangplank. At the top, the captain offered them each a hand to steady them onto the gently rocking deck, though he held Dania's hand somewhat longer than necessary.

"Thank you, Captain," Auftane said with a small bow when he was firmly planted on the deck. "We appreciate your gracious hospitality."

"As well as your willingness to make sail on such short notice," Mathas added.

"House Lyrandar exists to serve the people of Khorvaire," Avaen said with a bow. "Allow me to show you your quarters."

Avaen led them aft and down a few stairs to a pair of cabins below the poop deck.

"Master Allister assured me that two cabins would be sufficient for the four of you," the captain said with some hesitation.

"Mathas and I are quite used to sharing rooms," Dania said. She peered in both cabins, then walked into the one on the starboard side.

"She thinks because I'm eight times her age that I pose little threat," the elf said, winking at the captain before following Dania into the cabin.

"I suppose that leaves me and Janik to get better acquainted over here," Auftane said.

"I will make the final preparations, and we can weigh

anchor as soon as Master Martell returns," Avaen said. He left them to settle in.

Auftane dropped his pack in the port cabin, then stood in the doorway of the opposite room. Mathas sat on the edge of his bunk as Dania paced the small cabin, anxious to get under way.

"So whose boots am I here to fill?" Auftane asked. "There was a cleric with you before?"

"That's right," Mathas said. "Maija Olarin."

"She's dead?"

"Not exactly," Dania answered. "She betrayed us to an old enemy."

"Krael? The one who took the ship we were supposed to sail on?"

"Precisely," Mathas said.

"And Maija was Janik's wife? Or lover?"

"Yes," Mathas replied. "He's still quite bitter about the experience."

"That's understandable. How long has it been?"

"Three years," Dania said. "He and Mathas haven't seen Maija or Krael since."

"But you have?"

"I saw them both in Karrnath last year." Dania scowled. "At the time I didn't know what they were up to, but I know that Maija had a stink of evil on her that went far beyond normal human corruption."

"What does that suggest, Dania?" Mathas asked.

"Probably that she has given herself over to one of the Dark Six."

Shouts from the crew indicated that the ship was about to sail, and Auftane turned in the doorway to see Janik thumping down the steps.

"Are we ready to leave?" Auftane called.

"The captain just gave the order to weigh anchor," Janik said, smiling. "I hope we haven't forgotten anything else, because it's too late now."

"Dania and Mathas have claimed the starboard cabin. I guess that leaves us next door."

"That's fine." Janik dropped his pack in the cabin. "I'm going up on deck while we sail out."

"Good plan," Mathas said. "I always like the view of Sharn as we leave it."

"Not quite as dramatic from the sea as it is from an airship, though," Janik said.

The four of them filed up the steps to the poop deck, trying to stay out of the crew's way. Already the docks were slipping away behind them. Their vantage point offered an unusual view of the city—they could see glowing lines of magical energy lifting cargo and carrying passengers up the cliff side to the bases of Sharn's towers. The towers themselves stretched high above them on one side, while a stark cliff face rose on the other. The sun glittered on the river around them.

"And goodbye again, City of Towers," Janik said.

"Goodbye, Khorvaire," Dania whispered.

❧ ❧ ❧ ❧ ❧ ❧ ❧

As the sun was setting that evening, *Lyrandar Dayspring* cleared the mouth of the Dagger River and entered the open sea. The red sky turned the sea to wine in the west, which the sailors seemed to take as a good omen for the journey. When darkness settled in, the captain left the helm in the hands of his mate. Without the magic of the captain's dragonmark, the ship's pace slowed, moving at perhaps half her earlier speed. Leaving the wheelhouse, Avaen invited Janik and his companions to join him in his dining room to celebrate their first day of sailing. At the captain's request, Janik told stories of their past adventures.

"I remember our first trip to Xen'drik. We were looking back at Sharn the way we did this morning, and coming out of the mouth of the Dagger like we just did. I stood up on the prow, peering forward as if Xen'drik might come into view at any moment." He remembered holding Maija, the feel of her, the way she laughed at him, turning in his arms and looking back, bringing her face close to his. The memory clenched in his chest.

"I was at the stern sending my lunch back into the sea," Dania said. "That was my first time at sea. I did all right on the river, but when we came into the straits, the straits won." They all laughed.

Janik was caught up in the memory of the jumbled whirl-wind of emotions he had felt that time. "I was so excited to finally see the things I'd been studying for so many years. I was a dedicated young scholar, but I'd never been out of Sharn before—I'd hardly even seen the sky in my twenty-one years. At the same time, I was terrified. The king's agents had painted a pretty frightening picture of what we could look forward to. I half expected the Emerald Claw to jump us as soon as we disembarked in Stormreach, if the sahuagin didn't get us first."

"The king sent you?" Auftane asked. "What was your mission?"

"I was a new recruit into the king's service," Janik said. "The war was raging, of course—this was fifteen years ago. And King Boranel got the idea that there were things in Xen'drik that would help the war effort. I think Cannith put the idea in his head, honestly. But other spies had brought word that agents of Karrnath were exploring Xen'drik, though really they were Emerald Claw agents."

"There's a difference?" the captain asked.

"There is now," Janik said. "The Emerald Claw was founded as an extension of Karrnath's espionage agency, but King Kaius later outlawed them. They're basically their own little government now. Nobody's quite sure who they answer to, though it's generally assumed it's someone high up in Karrnath. Anyway, the presence of the Emerald Claw was enough to get the king's brother, Lord Kor, out to the universities recruiting for the Citadel. They were hoping to find people with knowledge about Xen'drik and experience digging through the ruins."

"But they got you instead," Mathas said.

"Exactly. And I'm pretty sure King Boranel has regretted it ever since."

"So how did the rest of you get involved?" Auftane asked.

Janik looked at Mathas and Dania. "Maija," he said.

"Maija and I grew up together," Dania said. "We weren't in the same social circles, but we met when we were girls and somehow kept up a friendship after that."

"And I met her when I was studying religion, briefly, at the Pavilion of the Host," Mathas said. "She was an acolyte there for a time."

"She and Janik were pretty much inseparable," Dania added, "so she was the force that drew us all together."

"Right," Janik said. "When Lord Kor asked me to assemble an expedition to Xen'drik, I went to Maija, and she got me Mathas and Dania."

"I still don't know how you got me pulled off the front

lines," Dania said. She was staring at the middle of the table, difficult memories starting to crowd into her mind.

"You can thank Lord Kor for that," Janik said, "and Maija. She told me she wanted you, I told Kor you were essential, and he got you for us."

"You were fighting in the war?" Captain Avaen asked Dania.

"I enlisted as soon as I was old enough, which was as good a way as any to get out of my father's house."

The captain looked surprised. "Yours is a noble family, is it not?"

"Oh yes, the line of ir'Vran goes back to the first nobles of Breland. And my father could easily have kept me from combat duty, if I hadn't volunteered for it." Dania was still staring at the polished wood of the tabletop, not looking at the captain.

"So Lord Kor put the four of us on a ship to Xen'drik," Janik said, trying to steer the conversation away from Dania's painful memories of the war. "And we trudged through the jungle to a tiny ruin full of baboons, remember?"

"Rabid baboons," Mathas said, chuckling.

"Corrupted baboons," Dania said. "That was no disease— there was an evil in that place that made them that way."

"And that big one nearly ripped my arms off," Janik said. He turned to Auftane and the captain. "It was holding me right up to its face, my feet dangling above the ground, and tugging on me like a rag doll, screeching like a banshee. Then all of a sudden it got this quizzical look on its big baboon face and started to look behind it, and then it just fell over dead. Dania had neatly cut right through its spine."

"And did you find what you were looking for?" the captain asked.

"No, but neither did Krael, who was in charge of the Emerald Claw expedition. Eventually we came back to Breland with some good information about the Emerald Claw's intentions there, and that convinced the king that we were worth what he was paying us."

"And what were they doing?" Auftane said.

"Mathas, you can explain it better than I can," Janik demurred.

"They were building some kind of magical device around a manifest zone they had discovered," the elf began.

"A manifest zone?" the captain asked.

"A place where the boundaries between the planes are thin. In that particular location, the plane of Shavarath, called the Battleground, was somehow close at hand. They were building a device in the hope of bringing some of that plane's warring inhabitants into our plane to fight on their behalf."

"It could have been quite devastating," Dania added, "if they had been successful. Imagine an army of demons marching at Karrnath's command."

"Or a swarm of blades flying through the air, unhindered by any defense their opponents could muster," Mathas said.

"So we snuck in and destroyed their precious device," Janik said.

"I'm surprised Breland didn't want it for itself," the captain said. "Even the best of nations, when at war, can lose sight of the proper perspective on such things—the devastation it could cause."

"Well," Janik hesitated, then admitted, "we actually had orders to secure it for Breland, if possible."

"That turned out not to be possible," Dania added with a grin.

"In fact," Mathas added, "it's not quite fair to say we destroyed it, is it?"

"No, it was that army of archons that destroyed it," Janik said. "But we helped get it sucked into the Battleground."

"Right," Mathas said. "Through our efforts, the boundary between our world and Shavarath disappeared entirely—just for a moment, and in that particular place. The device the Emerald Claw was building passed through the boundary—"

"Taking us with it," Dania interjected.

"Taking us with it, yes, and it was quickly destroyed by a raiding force of celestial beings."

Captain Avaen looked somewhat skeptical. "But you escaped," he said.

"We did," Janik said. "And Krael did, worse luck. But the Emerald Claw mastermind behind the whole project—what was his name?"

"General Malestra," Mathas said.

"Right, Malestra emphatically did not escape." Janik smirked.

"Nor did most of his lackeys," Dania said grimly.

"How did you get back to this plane?" Auftane asked, his eyes wide with wonder.

"The planar boundary was ruptured when the device passed through," Mathas explained. "It started to repair itself almost immediately, but we were able to jump through it again, in the opposite direction, before it closed entirely."

"And Krael?"

"He and a couple of his men made it through ahead of us," Janik said. "He stuck around on this side of the portal just long enough to swear vengeance on us, and then ran off."

"And ever since then, it's always the same with Krael," Dania said. "He tries to sabotage our work, and we get in his way as much as possible without lowering ourselves to his kind of dirty tricks."

"Hmm," Janik grunted. "I'm starting to wonder if maybe we should break into his apartment to steal his books."

"Count me out," said Dania.

"I suppose that wouldn't fit well in your new lifestyle, would it?" Janik said, the merest trace of mockery in his voice.

Dania's temper flared. "No, and it wouldn't fit your old way of doing things, either," she said, her voice rising only slightly. "You used to have some ethics."

Mathas and the captain looked anywhere but at the other people at the table, while Auftane watched Janik and Dania with morbid fascination.

"Well, look where it got me," Janik responded hotly. "You can only turn away from evil for so long before it stabs you in the back."

"That's why you've got to confront it, face to face," Dania said.

"Like we did with Maija?"

"Janik, that caught us all off guard," Dania said. "We never knew she held such evil in her heart."

"Which proves my point. If we couldn't see the evil in Maija—if *I* couldn't see it—then how can we see it anywhere else in order to confront it? Maybe it's better to strike first, ethics be damned."

"So you'd betray me, or Mathas, or Auftane here, rather than risk one of us turning on you? Is that what you're saying?"

"No! Churning chaos, Dania, you're twisting my words. I meant that maybe we shouldn't think Krael's tactics are beneath us. They seem to be working all right for him."

"Wait until you see Krael, Janik. I think you'll agree that his tactics, as you say, aren't working well."

"What do you mean?"

"Maija turned on him, too," Dania said, her voice suddenly quiet. "I don't know if Mathas told you, but I saw them both when I was in Karrnath."

"Together?"

"Yes, they were still working together," Dania said. "They were both working with a shifter vampire, looking for the Tablet of Shummarak."

"The Tablet of Shummarak? Sea of Fire," Janik muttered.

"Janik," Dania said. "Krael is a vampire."

"A va—" Janik's mouth hung open for a moment. Mathas and Avaen returned their full attention to the conversation, and Auftane's eyes grew still wider.

Janik gasped. "Is Maija—?"

"As far as I know, she's still alive. At least she was when I saw her. We destroyed the shifter vampire, and then Krael and Maija disappeared. We couldn't find them again. But Janik, I don't have much hope that she can ever be redeemed. She had such a strong aura of evil around her."

"Was it an aura she didn't have at Mel-Aqat?"

"I don't know. It wasn't until I was in Karrnath that I started noticing things like that. Since seeing that, I've learned to focus it more—it was part of my training as a paladin. But at the time, it was just a powerful sense, almost like I could smell it on her."

"So her smell told you she was beyond redemption?" Janik's voice rose again. "Her smell told you I should give up hope?" He leaned across the table. "I'm not going to forget about her, damn it—I'm not going to give up on her, no matter what your nose or your special paladin sense tells you!"

Mathas's calm voice interrupted him. "Janik," the elf said.

"What?"

"What's the Tablet of Shummarak?"

"And that!" Janik said, pointing a finger at Dania. "When were you planning on telling me about that? If I'd known about that while we were still in Sharn, I could have looked into it, but now—" He broke off.

"Janik, I—" Dania began.

"Ah, never mind." Janik stood, scraping his chair away from the table. "I need to look at my notebooks. I'll be in my cabin."

❋ ❋ ❋ ❋ ❋ ❋ ❋

Janik sat on his bunk, notebooks piled around him. Each lay open, some holding scraps of parchment or quills or ribbons to mark pages he had referred to. He was still angry with Dania, and he told himself he was justified in feeling that way. But even if he had known about the Tablet of Shummarak earlier, he would only have grieved the theft of the *Darriens Codex* that much more keenly. Darriens had quoted snippets of the Tablet's text in his commentary on the elven writings, but the Tablet had been lost for centuries and no copies of the complete text were known to exist. Because of Darriens's work and his connection to the Church of the Silver Flame, the Tablet was best known within the Church, and carried religious significance for the order. In fact, the Church's use of the Tablet was one of the key points in the argument he had read connecting the Church to the ancient Serpent Cults of Xen'drik.

Janik remembered that the Tablet made reference to the couatls that had imprisoned the great demons within the earth. But he couldn't remember whether any connection had been established between the Tablet and the Place of Imprisonment mentioned in the *Serpentes Codex*, which he believed was Mel-Aqat. His notebooks were no help.

Perhaps it was sheer coincidence that Krael and Maija had been seeking the Tablet, but Janik doubted it. It seemed far more likely that Krael suspected a connection to Mel-Aqat, or perhaps had established one. Maybe he had found the Tablet. Maybe that's why he was going to Mel-Aqat. And maybe that was why he was so desperate to get Janik out of the way.

Hours had passed since Janik had left the dinner table, and the ship was silent except for soft creakings as it coursed through the open sea. Auftane had not come to bed, but Janik supposed he was sleeping on deck—it was a clear, warm night.

The quiet of the night was shattered by the artificer's cry.

"Attack! We're under attack!"

CHAPTER 7

Janik grabbed his sheathed sword from the floor as he leaped to his feet. He pulled the sword free and rushed to the cabin door, kicked it open, and sprang up the stairs to the deck. Auftane held his huge mace in one hand and a scroll in the other, dodging the tridents of three sahuagin as he tried to read the scroll. Janik ran to the artificer and plunged his sword into the back of one of the sea devils, which crumpled to the deck with a gurgling yelp.

Janik's arrival gave Auftane the opportunity he needed to cast the spell on his scroll. A ring of whirling silver blades appeared around him, cutting into the flesh of both sahuagin. They cried out but did not fall. Janik glanced around the deck.

Auftane had raised an effective alarm. The three sahuagin that had surrounded him must have been the first to reach the deck, though plenty more were crawling over the bulwarks now. Sailors appeared on deck in clusters, rushing to cut at the fishlike creatures as they tried to climb aboard. Near the bow, Captain Avaen and his first mate stood back to back, surrounded by a group of five sahuagin. Dania was charging up the steps from her cabin, and Mathas touched her to imbue a spell just before she jumped up to the deck.

The two sahuagin near Auftane backed away from the whirling blades and sought another target, and Janik proved to be the closest. They maneuvered around the ring of blades and came at Janik from opposite sides, their tridents lowered. Janik ducked their onslaught, then somersaulted past one of them and shoved it hard toward its ally. It met the leveled trident of the other sahuagin and slumped to the deck.

Janik had hoped the two sahuagin would impale each other, and he cursed his poor aim. But Auftane quickly stepped up to the remaining sea devil, and it died in the ring of whirling blades before he could even swing his mace. Janik raised his sword in a quick salute to the artificer, then ran toward the bow to help the beleaguered captain.

Two sea devils threatened Janik as he ran. He drove his sword into the chest of one, then heaved its corpse toward the other. As the sahuagin stumbled, Janik ran on, noting with a backward glance that Dania had moved to engage it. The attackers surged over the sides of the ship in an apparently unending stream, and though he and his friends had little trouble cutting them down, the sailors were not faring as well. Janik jumped over the bodies of two fallen sailors on his way to the bow, and he saw that more were falling under the sahuagin assault.

By the time Janik reached them, the captain and his mate had felled two of the creatures surrounding them, but three more arrived just as Janik did. Despite the newcomers, Janik's arrival tilted the balance dramatically. The sahuagin fell quickly when their attention was divided between the sailors inside their ring of tridents and Janik's darting blade outside it. Moving swiftly around the ragged circle of sea devils, Janik guided his sword to vital spots, never needing more than one blow to finish an opponent. He killed four and reached the fifth just as the first mate's cutlass hacked through its neck.

"Thank you, Janik!" the captain called. The first mate, a pretty woman with almond-shaped eyes, gave him a grim smile before running to help a group of sailors nearby.

Janik surveyed the deck again, looking for where his help was most needed. Auftane had fallen back to the cabins, where he and his ring of blades were providing an effective shield for Mathas, who propelled fiery rays and bolts of acid at nearby foes. Dania was on the starboard side amid a thicket of sailors and sea devils, her sword rising and falling in a deadly rhythm. An aura surrounded her that Janik had never seen before, almost a shimmer of radiance—but Janik supposed that was the spell Mathas had cast on her, some kind of protective ward. Avaen was making his way toward Dania and the sailors, while the first mate had joined another trio of sailors on the port side, who looked a little overwhelmed.

Janik hurried to help the sailors, trapping one sea devil between his own blade and the first mate's, quickly bringing it down. His arrival—and the quick deaths of three more sahuagin at the end of his blade—shook the sea devils' morale and they started edging toward the bulwarks. Out of nowhere, a sahuagin hurtled across the deck from the starboard side, crashing into Janik. The sharp points of his trident only grazed Janik's shoulder, but its body slammed hard into him, forcing him against the bulwark rail.

Janik hung there for what felt like many heartbeats. The sahuagin was wedged on top of him, its weight pushing him toward the open air and the churning sea below. It got one foot onto the rail and used the leverage to push him up higher. Over its shoulder, Janik saw the first mate's blade come down onto its back, and it threw its head backward in pain. In the same instant, the rail beneath him splintered and he plummeted into the water, holding fast to the lifeless body of the sea devil.

The cold water swallowed him.

Well, Janik thought, this is a problem.

Lyrandar Dayspring was still moving, quickly sliding past him and disappearing in the dark. Blood was flowing freely from his shoulder, though it wasn't a deep wound—and blood in the water where there were already sea devils could mean only one thing: sharks. Two things stood in his favor—his short sword was still in his hand, and the attack had come so quickly that he hadn't had time to put his boots on.

He couldn't think of any others.

Janik tore off his shirt, which had threatened to drag him down. Free of its clutches, he fought his way to the surface and filled his lungs with air, spitting out the water that had filled his throat. Away from the lanterns on the ship's deck, the sea was darker, but the Ring of Siberys stretched its arc high across the sky to paint the night in soft golden light. He saw the ship as a silhouette against the glowing sky, her torches like dancing stars as she slowed and turned her port side to him. He knew they probably wouldn't come back to him—they couldn't risk running the ship over him. As soon as they cleared the sahuagin from the deck, he was sure they'd send a launch back to look for him.

That might be too late. A half-dozen yards away, Janik saw the unmistakable shape of a shark's fin cutting through the water toward him. Bracing himself against the sting of salt water in his eyes, he took a deep breath and plunged his head underwater, quickly looking around him. So far, it looked like only one shark had arrived, and not a very big one at that.

It was upon him. At the last moment, Janik threw his body backward in the water, anticipating that the shark would aim for his wounded shoulder. The shark glided over him. Janik drove his sword upward, but without leverage in the water, he could only manage a glancing blow on the shark's belly. It was enough to draw blood—and enough to drive the shark into a frenzy.

It circled back toward him quickly, its mouth open wide. Choosing his mark, Janik thrust his sword into the roof of its mouth. It was a good blow—Janik was pretty sure he hit the brain. Unfortunately, that didn't stop the shark from closing its mouth around his forearm and raking his flesh with rows of teeth. It didn't have the strength to hold on—or to bite through the bone—and Janik wrested his arm and his sword free. The blood—his and the shark's—was blackening the water, and it was only a matter of time before more sharks came, probably accompanied by their sea devil masters.

Janik clumsily slid his sword into his belt and started to swim. He doubted he could reach the ship, but perhaps he could meet the launch before the sharks got him.

After several hard strokes, Janik looked behind him and saw the water churning with sharks in the place where he had killed the first one. Feeding on the dead, he supposed. He swam harder toward the hulking shadow of *Dayspring*, still far away. The salt water stung in the wounds on his shoulder and arm, and he knew he was leaving a trail in the water that the sharks could follow to food. But he could do nothing about that.

A dark shape suddenly stood out from the darkness of the surrounding water—a boat! A long rowboat, one of the ship's lifeboats, was creeping through the water in his direction, though at its current heading, it would pass him far to his left.

"Over here!" he called out, waving his arms over his head. With his right hand out of the water, he realized for the first time just how much blood he was losing. The boat changed its course slightly and sped up, heading directly toward him. He could see two oars working as fast as the sailors could row.

But not fast enough. One of the sharks disentangled itself from the churning frenzy. Janik could see its dorsal fin barely breaking the water behind him. He pulled out his sword, but his hand was stiff around the hilt and he was having a hard time focusing his eyes. He turned his back to the oncoming boat and drew a shaky breath before lowering himself under the water to meet the onrushing predator.

This shark was considerably larger than the one he'd killed before. He recognized it as a devil shark, named for the enlarged scales on its forehead and the leading edges of its fins, which gave it a sinister, almost fiendish appearance—and, appropriately, the creatures were often found in the company of the sahuagin. Janik fumbled with the sword in his hand, then shifted it to his left. The shark swam past Janik on the right. Janik turned to keep it in sight, and noticed that the rowboat had almost reached him. He felt a surge of hope even as his lungs cried out for air. He kicked himself to the surface, gasping.

"Janik!" Dania's voice was close, but the shark was closer. It had completed a circle around him and turned inward. He felt it slam into him, but felt no tearing of teeth—either it had already eaten its fill, or it was softening him up. An instant later, a coil of rope splashed into the water beside him. He grabbed it with his right hand, keeping a firm grip on his sword as he tried to wrap the rope firmly around his right arm.

As soon as she was sure he had the rope, Dania pulled it back into the boat, dragging Janik through the water like a fish on a line. Or like a baited hook, Janik thought grimly. As he started to move, the shark recognized the danger of losing its prey, and it lunged at him with its mouth wide open.

Carefully watching the shark's approach, Janik planted a kick on its snout just as it was about to close its teeth on his legs. It veered sharply away, but immediately started circling back for another pass. Then Janik's body slammed into the side of the boat. As Dania started hauling him up the side, he blacked out.

❀ ❀ ❀ ❀ ❀ ❀ ❀

A soothing warmth washed over Janik's left shoulder, his arms, and his legs. In those places, he felt stinging pain, or the memory of it, fading under the advancing warmth. The darkness cleared from his eyes and he realized he was lying flat on his back in the bottom of the rowboat, with Dania bending over him. Silver light glowed around her hands as she rested them on his shoulders. Two sailors, their muscled arms pumping steadily, were already rowing toward *Lyrandar Dayspring*.

"Thanks," Janik said as his head cleared. "I was getting a little concerned."

"That shark almost got you," Dania said with a slight smile. "But after not speaking to you for three years, I'm not ready to give you to the Devourer."

"I didn't think you believed in the Devourer any more."

Dania scowled. "Oh, don't be an idiot, Janik," she said. "I just saved your life. Don't you think you could refrain from provoking me—at least until we get back to the ship? I can still throw you back in, you know."

"I'm sorry, Dania," Janik said. He sat up weakly. "I am grateful, believe me." Dania's scowl melted and she smiled at him.

The boat rolled hard, and Janik and Dania were thrown to the port side. The sailor at starboard fumbled with his oar but held his position, while the man at port scrambled desperately to keep from tumbling overboard. Janik could feel something banging against the hull. He reached for his sword but it was not at his belt. Dania was on her feet, longsword in her hand and shield at the ready. The boat righted itself and they were thrown to starboard. Janik found his sword sliding across the bottom of the boat and grabbed it. Dania lost her footing and nearly fell into the water, but Janik caught hold of her with his left hand and pulled her down with him. The sailors kept their seats, but they looked around wildly, panic in their eyes.

"Something's trying to capsize us," Janik said. "We'll do better to keep low in the boat."

"We'll do best if we stop the thing before it dumps us overboard," Dania shot back, scrambling toward the port side, where they could hear the banging.

The boat rolled again and Janik slid to port. Dania leaped to the side of the boat in one big step, and at that instant a huge sea devil appeared over the side of the launch. Two muscular arms reached toward Dania, the webbed hands tipped with sharp claws easily capable of tearing through armor and flesh. Two more arms clutched the side of the boat, lifting the sahuagin up over the gunwale. It swung a foot into the boat and pulled its entire bulk over the side, throwing itself at Dania.

Dania and her attacker fell backward hard, landing against the opposite side of the boat. Janik barely managed to dodge out of their way, stabbing at the sea devil as it barreled past him with Dania caught in its four arms. He managed only a glancing blow against the thing's tough scales. He was relieved to find that he had recovered the strength in his grip, thanks to Dania's healing touch.

Dania was having trouble bringing her longsword to bear against the creature as it raked at her with all six limbs—its feet bore vicious claws as well. Janik moved in to distract it, looking for weak spots in its scaly hide, finally planting his blade where one of its lower arms met the thick torso. Janik drove his blade between the creature's ribs. It howled in rage and pain and dropped Dania from its grasp, wheeling to face Janik.

"Prepare to meet the teeth of Shargon," the creature spat in its own language.

"I have seen the Devourer's teeth before," Janik replied in the same tongue, "and always they have closed on empty water." This was another of the ritualized exchanges that characterized sahuagin conversation, but Janik reflected on the truth of the boast even as he aimed his blade for another blow.

The sea devil was clearly surprised to hear the proper response from a human mouth, and it dropped its guard just for an instant. That instant was all Janik needed to plunge his blade into the creature's eye. At the same moment, Dania's sword came down hard on the sahuagin's skull, and as Janik pulled his sword free, he felt it scrape against Dania's blade. He shuddered as a wave of disgust washed over him, and he frowned at the sea devil as it fell toward him. He tried to step out of its path, but lost his footing in the wildly rocking boat and landed hard on his seat. The sahuagin's gory head landed in his lap with a wet splat.

"Dania, will you get this thing off me?" he said sickly.

"You never would have made it on the front lines, my friend," Dania said as she sheathed her sword and bent down to grab one of the sea devil's legs.

"Yes, we've established that many times over the past fifteen years," Janik replied. "Ugh, look at this. It spilled its brains all over me."

Dania smiled as she heaved the sahuagin overboard. "Why don't you take a dip and rinse off?" The water churned with sharks swarming in to feed on the bloody corpse.

Janik gingerly got to his feet and noted with some satisfaction that the sailors at the oars wore looks of disgust like his own. *Lyrandar Dayspring* now loomed nearby, and he saw sailors on the deck above, lowering ropes to hoist the launch back aboard.

"Dania," he said softly as the men on the launch tied the boat to the ropes dropped from above.

"What?"

"I'm sorry for the things I said at dinner. I was needlessly harsh."

"I let my temper get the better of me as well," Dania said.

"Just like old times, eh?" Janik said with a smile.

"No, Janik, and it never will be." Dania looked up at the ship, not returning Janik's smile. "Too much has happened."

❧ ❧ ❧ ❧ ❧ ❧ ❧

Back on the ship, Dania roamed the deck, checking on the wounded. Janik trailed behind her, offering words of encouragement to the sailors. Auftane had already cared for many sailors but a few were beyond any help. Among the dead,

Janik spotted the first mate. He looked around for the captain and spotted him standing at the prow. Leaving Dania and Auftane to care for the wounded, he went to the captain.

The sparkling ring in the sky was reflected in the waves around them as a scintillating mosaic of light. The ship had resumed its course toward Xen'drik.

They stood in silence for a moment, then the captain glanced at Janik. "Glad to see you made it aboard," he said quietly.

"Thank you," Janik said, looking at the dark water ahead. "It was a devastating attack."

"Yes," Avaen replied, "but not unexpected. And thanks to you and your friends, our losses were far less than they might have been. I am grateful."

"I noticed your first mate among them."

"Eisha, yes." The captain's voice was flat. "She was a good first mate."

"I . . ." Janik hesitated, unsure whether to press the point, but decided to forge ahead. "I get the sense she was more than that."

"She was a good friend, too. And—" His voice broke, and he paused for a moment, wrestling his emotions back under control. "And we were lovers once. Like you and Dania, I suspect."

"Yes, briefly. An ill-fated affair." Janik scowled. "We should have just been friends."

Avaen nodded slowly, staring blindly ahead.

They stared together into the night as the rest of the crew finished gathering the bodies of the fallen and tending the wounded, then finally returned to their posts or their bunks. The quiet of the ocean, filled only with the sounds of creaking ropes and splashing waves, settled around them again.

Three moons set behind the western sea, and the eastern sky was beginning to brighten before Avaen finally clapped Janik on the shoulder and shuffled back to the wheelhouse to prepare for a day of sailing.

❈ ❈ ❈ ❈ ❈ ❈ ❈

By the end of the week, they were in Shargon's Teeth. Rocky islands jutted up from the waters all around them—very much like the sharp teeth of a shark, giving the area its name. Janik knew that the rocks that did not protrude from the water were the most dangerous, for they could tear a hole in the bottom of the ship before the pilot knew there was a danger.

This was where Shubdoolkra's clan was supposed to appear and guide the ship through the treacherous waters. Janik had guessed that the earlier attack meant no guidance would come, but he took no comfort in being right on that score.

"Mathas told me you had secured sahuagin guides for the Teeth," Captain Avaen said to Janik as the nearest islands loomed close.

"I had made arrangements for a clan to guide *Hope's Endeavor*—the ship we were supposed to sail on. I left word for my contact about our change of plans, but I suppose it's possible that he didn't receive my message."

"I think the attack at the start of our journey made that clear," Avaen said, giving voice to Janik's silent thoughts. "It doesn't matter, though. House Lyrandar has good charts of the Straits of Shargon. They're not perfect, and we won't be able to sail at night, but we can get through. As long as we don't suffer another attack like that."

The earlier attack was nothing, Janik thought. We really don't want to see them come in force.

"If the sahuagin do approach," he said aloud, "I can try to negotiate with them. I have made the promise of tribute and I'm still prepared to keep that promise, despite the attack."

"Very well. One way or another, we'll get through the Teeth and safely to Stormreach. It might take a while." The captain returned to the wheelhouse. Janik shortly felt the surge in speed that meant Avaen was back at the helm, using the power of his dragonmark to propel the ship.

The sun was not fully below the horizon that night when the sahuagin made their presence known. A bonfire blazed at the edge of the water on a nearby island, and a voice called out in thickly accented Common, "Breathers in air and dwellers in sun, what tribute do you offer to Baron Yadkoppo? Speak quickly, for you trespass on waters that belong to us!"

Captain Avaen stood on the forecastle, but he looked back as Janik emerged from his cabin and strode toward the bow. Taking a place beside the captain, he called back in the sahuagin tongue.

"Dweller in deep and dark, we have promised tribute to Baron Yadkoppo and his people by the hand of his loyal servant Shubdoolkra in the City on the Dagger's Hilt."

The sahuagin on the shore did not respond immediately, and Janik couldn't tell why. He glanced over his shoulder at Mathas, who stood farther back and watched the sahuagin keenly.

Mathas caught Janik's inquisitive glance. "He is conferring with other sahuagin who are mostly immersed in the water," he said quietly.

After a moment, the sahuagin called back in its own language, its deep voice booming over the water. "The one of whom you speak is dying the thousand deaths in the jaws of the Devourer."

Janik turned away from the sahuagin and slumped to the deck, his back to the bulwark.

"What is it?" the captain hissed. Every eye on deck was glued to Janik.

"Shubdoolkra is dead," Janik said. "Dying the thousand deaths—either a traitor or a victim of treachery." His mind was racing, trying to figure out what this would mean for their chance at safe passage. What was the proper response in this situation?

"Krael again," Mathas said. "Your contact didn't receive the tribute he expected from *Hope's Endeavor* when it sailed through. Either his people killed him as a traitor for promising tribute he didn't deliver—"

Janik finished the sentence. "Or Krael killed him when he appeared to demand the tribute." He stood again and called back to the sahuagin. "One foe rakes with two claws. The one who has broken faith with you has broken faith with us as well. I bring the tribute I promised to Shubdoolkra, and I will swear to avenge his death."

"What are you telling them?" the captain demanded, growing increasingly nervous.

"That we have a common foe, and they're still getting their money."

"Even after they attacked us?"

"That was probably a different village," Janik said. "And unless we want them to attack us again, I'd better pay what I promised."

The sahuagin conferred with its compatriots in the water and called back to Janik. "What is the tribute you bring?"

Janik repeated the offer he had made to Shubdoolkra.

There was no discussion this time—the sahuagin responded at once. "Your tribute is acceptable to Baron Yadkoppo. You will cast it into the waters at your present position. Once we have determined that there are no broken promises, we will lead you through Shargon's Teeth. If promises be broken, the Devourer will judge."

Janik let out his breath, which he hadn't realized he had been holding, and nodded to the captain. "I'll need a few sailors to help me unload the tribute," he said. The captain shouted orders and two sailors followed Janik down into the hold. They emerged with three crates of goods and dropped them over the bulwarks and into the shallow waters off the starboard bow.

A long delay followed while the sahuagin opened the crates and inspected the contents. Janik, the captain, and a number of sailors watched with some anxiety, peering into the water at the dark shapes moving below. Then the one on the nearby shore called out again in its sonorous voice, "Your tribute is accepted! You will follow us through Shargon's Teeth. Baron Yadkoppo promises that no harm will come to your ship or crew while you are in our care."

"Lead on, then!" Janik called back. He turned to the captain. "They're going to lead us. I'll stay up here to keep an eye on them and translate."

"Then I'll follow your lead," Avaen said. "Thank you, Janik." He hurried back to the wheelhouse and, on Janik's signal, the ship started moving again.

❂ ❂ ❂ ❂ ❂ ❂ ❂

They sailed only during daylight. This far south, the beginning of autumn did little to shorten the days, and Avaen managed a good twelve hours of sailing each day. The waters were treacherous, and the captain's dragonmark did little to speed their progress around the dangerous reefs and jutting islands. On the rare occasions that they hit a stretch of open sea, they could sail only as fast as the sahuagin ahead of them could swim—still a respectable pace, but Janik could see captain and crew chafing at the pace, clearly accustomed to faster progress on most of their journeys.

And that was the pace for a week. Around the middle of the eighth day, the sahuagin swimming ahead of the ship called back to Janik, speaking its native tongue. "Water darkens, light fades—your destination lies before you!"

Janik looked outward and saw two large islands looming just ahead. The sahuagin was leading the ship between them, but beyond, he could see no more islands.

"In Stormreach we call them the Kraken and the Hydra." Janik was startled by Auftane's gravelly voice at his shoulder. "They're like a pair of monsters waiting to devour a ship passing between them. From our perspective, they're the entryway to Shargon's Teeth—the first hazard of many on a long journey. I believe sailors from Khorvaire call them the Pillars, or the Way Out. I think our names are much more evocative, don't you?"

"I'm not sure evocative is always good," Janik replied, "especially when the images evoke death and ruin."

"Fair enough," the dwarf replied.

Janik signaled the captain to adjust course slightly. Before the sun moved noticeably in the sky, they had cleared the Pillars and open sea lay ahead.

"We give our thanks to Baron Yadkoppo and his people," Janik called out to the sahuagin, who were now swimming out of the way to let the ship sail past.

"May you return to the dark water with meat on one shoulder and gold on the other," the sahuagin leader said.

"And you," Janik called. Then he walked to the other side

of the ship, where no sahuagin watched, and spat into the water. "It will take me weeks to get the taste of that language out of my mouth," he said to no one in particular.

For the first time in days, the crew unfurled the sails to their fullest extent, and the captain impelled the ship to her top speed. *Lyrandar Dayspring* skimmed over the surface of the water like a skipping stone, bouncing over the waves and swells, occasionally sending huge sprays of water high into the air. The crew's spirits rose noticeably—not until he heard laughter again did Janik realize how scarce it had been while they were in Shargon's Teeth. The weather was fine—the sun shone brightly in the clear sky and glittered on the water.

The captain kept the ship racing during daylight, and the new first mate kept her going at night. By the end of another week, the lookout spotted the coast of Xen'drik. Soon they could all see the land and its mysterious forests, and as the next morning dawned, the city of Stormreach spread out on the coast before them.

CHAPTER 8

Stormreach had once been a city of giants—in fact, Janik's first published paper had described the crumbling ruins that still surrounded the modern settlement. The first human settlers had been pirates who used it as a base for raids on ships bringing dragonshards and other treasures from Xen'drik to Khorvaire. Eventually, the city became a base for trade—a place for explorers, dragonshard prospectors, and treasure-seekers to stock up on supplies, a market where they could trade their finds, and a port for semi-regular routes to Khorvaire. Naturally, the dragonmarked houses—particularly House Tharashk and House Lyrandar—were among the first to establish a presence, and they devoted considerable effort and resources to eliminating the pirates.

In modern Stormreach, house enclaves and supply markets stood in clusters of buildings along with all the ordinary trades found in any small city, crowded in by the huge stones of the ancient ruins. The city was dangerous—partly because many of its residents were little better than pirates, and partly because traveling from one part of the city to another often meant a long walk through barren ruins along a rarely-patrolled road. It was possible, though, never to leave the area nearest the docks, and that was Janik's inclination every time he visited the city.

By midday, Janik and his companions were off the ship, grateful to feel solid ground under their feet again. Mathas and Auftane went into the city to find lodging. Dania went to the local church of the Silver Flame. Janik arranged to meet them for dinner at a restaurant called Forest's Bounty, then went with Avaen into a dockside tavern.

The captain took a deep drink from his ale and wiped the foam from his mouth. "Well, Janik," he said, "I hope your expedition is a success."

"Thank you," Janik said. "What are your plans?"

"There's always cargo to carry back to civilization, and usually passengers as well. And it's rare enough to see a Lyrandar ship here that I can usually get very good terms. But I'm not sure I'm ready to sail Shargon's Teeth again."

Janik nodded. "I know that feeling. Would you like to ferry us down the western coast? I can pay you pretty well, but I can't pretend it's not dangerous."

"And danger is exactly what I want less of," Avaen said. "I appreciate the offer, but I must decline."

"I understand. What will you do, then?"

"I think I'll take a position in my house enclave here, at least for a while. I don't think I can be landbound for too long—perhaps in a year or so, the sea will call me back. In the meantime, Stormreach will be a change of pace, something new to help me—" He broke off.

He didn't need to finish. Janik understood. A change of pace was exactly what he had needed three years ago, after Maija disappeared with Krael. He raised his mug, and Avaen raised his to meet it, his eyebrow arched quizzically.

"To fresh starts," Janik said.

"To fresh starts," Avaen repeated. They clinked their mugs together and finished their drinks in silence.

❀ ❀ ❀ ❀ ❀ ❀ ❀

Janik spent the rest of the afternoon making inquiries around the docks about *Hope's Endeavor*. By sunset, he was confident that the ship had not arrived yet—or someone had paid large amounts of money to keep news of her arrival silent. Janik found no one who was expecting the ship to pull into port, even though many people in Stormreach recognized the names of Captain Nashan and his ship. That the ship was not expected was hardly surprising—had Nashan left in a hurry under pressure from Krael, he would not have sent word ahead. Doing so would have little point, at any rate, since travel through the Teeth was so unpredictable. By the day's end, Janik was satisfied that they had docked in Stormreach before Krael. A minor victory, perhaps, but it was the first in some time, and Janik savored it.

A satisfied smile on his face, he made his way to the restaurant to meet his friends. Forest's Bounty was inland, away from the docks, and it catered to people who were sick of eating fish on long sea voyages. Janik had discovered it on his first trip to Xen'drik and had declared it his customary site for the first meal after coming ashore. Instead of the seafood prevalent in most Stormreach restaurants, it offered venison and tapir, along with a wide variety of vegetables, mushrooms, and fruits.

When Janik arrived, he found Mathas and Auftane already seated, chatting like old friends as they picked chunks of yellow and orange fruit from a bowl with long, slender forks. He nodded at the headwaiter, whose name he couldn't remember, and sat down next to Mathas, his back to the door.

"Ah, good evening!" Auftane said, raising a glass of wine to Janik and taking a drink. "Your elf friend has been telling me about your past adventures in Xen'drik." Mathas looked a little sheepish, and Janik guessed that they had been talking about their last adventure and all the drama that surrounded it.

"And are you still interested in accompanying us?" Janik asked.

"I certainly am, if you will have me."

"Well, Mathas, what do you think? Should we drag this dwarf across the desert with us? Will he slow us down too much?"

Mathas smiled his thin smile. "I think that any slowing of our pace will be more than compensated by the contributions Auftane will make along the way."

"Well spoken, Mathas," Janik said. "In my opinion, you more than adequately proved yourself in our battle against the sahuagin."

Dania's voice floated over Janik's shoulder. "How would you know? You spent half that battle practicing your back stroke."

Janik turned as Dania took the empty seat on his right. "I could tell that you all had the situation well in hand," he said. "I wanted to prevent any further assault from the water."

"Worried the sharks might climb up on deck?" Dania said, and Auftane guffawed.

Janik narrowed his eyes. "You never know," he said in a mysterious whisper. "Especially where the sea devils are concerned." He joined the others in their laughter.

"So I can come along?" Auftane asked.

"Dania, you don't have any objection, do you?" Janik asked.

Dania paused, staring at Auftane a moment. Apparently satisfied, she shook her head. "No," she said, "I agree with Janik. You've more than proven your worth, Auftane. You are most welcome."

"Thank you," Auftane said, getting to his feet. He grabbed Dania's hand and shook it. "I won't let you down, I promise." He did the same to Mathas and Janik before sitting down again.

Janik leaned across the table and looked to both sides, at Mathas and Dania. "Was I ever that enthusiastic about risking my life in Xen'drik?"

"Well, let me think," Dania said. Mathas put his hand to his mouth, barely covering his grin. "There was that first trip, when you pretended to be terrified of the Emerald Claw but couldn't wait to get into the jungle."

"And there was the time with the river shrine," Mathas said.

"Oh, right, with the lobster thing," Dania said. "What did you call it, Mathas? A chewer?"

"Chuul," Mathas corrected.

"Chuul, right. Yes, you were a little excited that trip. And when we found the Temple of Sondar Thaj in the Marsh of Desolation."

"But you've grown much more jaded recently," Mathas said.

"Indeed! When you thought you might have figured out where Mel-Aqat was, I would say your childlike enthusiasm was moderately diminished."

"I think you've made your point," Janik said. "So I like this work."

"And you know we wouldn't be here with you if we didn't share some of that enthusiasm," Dania said, putting a hand on Janik's folded arms.

"Not me," Mathas said. "I hate Xen'drik. I'm only here because someone needs to keep an eye on you children."

"Well, Auftane is coming with us now," Janik said. "He's an adult who can watch over us. Do you want to stay behind?"

"Hmm," Mathas said. "How old are you, Auftane?"

"I have just passed my eightieth summer," the dwarf replied. "I am considered an adult by my people." He turned to Janik. "Surely you are as well?"

"Well, I'm thirty-six," Janik said, "and Dania—you'd be thirty-eight, right?"

"I would have thought you were much younger," Auftane said to Dania.

"I'll take that as a compliment," Dania said with a playful scowl. "My elven ancestry keeps me looking young. Like Mathas here." She gestured at the venerable elf.

Mathas pretended to be hurt. "That was impolite," he said, running a hand over the bald crown of his head. "I'm sorry, Auftane, but until you have completed a century, you're still a child in my reckoning. No, it won't do. I'll have to accompany you once again." They all laughed.

"So it's settled. We're all going to Mel-Aqat," Janik said. "Now let's get down to business. We have an expedition to plan. I want to be out of town before Krael arrives. I want to stay as far ahead of him as we can, so there's no chance of him getting to the ruins before us."

"I agree," Dania said. "So what's our plan?"

Janik pulled a sheaf of weathered parchments from his coat, rifled through the pages, and produced a crude map. He spread it out on the table so all could see.

"Last time, we traveled through a lot more desert than we had to," he said. "Auftane, from clues in several ancient texts, I had determined that Mel-Aqat lay somewhere in the desert here, between the Fangs of Argarak and this smaller mountainous area, the Sun Pillars. We took a keelboat on the river to the western coast and down the coastline here"—he traced his finger on the map to show their route—"to this inlet. We wanted to get as far inland as we could before starting across the desert, but we still had a lot of desert to cover. I think this time, we should come ashore here"—he pointed to a stretch of coast farther north. "That way we can cross this region, the Wasting Plains—"

"Oh, that sounds much better than the desert," Dania said, rolling her eyes.

"It will be," Janik said. "It's dry, but not nearly as bad as Menechtarun. At least something grows there, even if it is mostly brambles. You have to remember that the first explorers of Xen'drik were prone to giving the landscape some fairly dramatic names. So if we cross the Wasting Plains north of the Sun Pillars, we can enter the desert from the north, and have a shorter trek across the sun-blasted sand than we had last time."

"I am definitely in favor of minimizing our exposure to sun-blasted sand," Mathas said, nodding.

"In fact, if we stick close to the mountains to the east here," Janik added, "we might even find water. I suspect that some streams flow down from the mountains before they dry up completely in the desert."

"I don't think we should bet on that," Dania said. "I think most of the water will just flow down the other side of the mountain range."

"You're right—we'll bring water anyway," Janik said. "It's

just nice, sometimes, to find it fresh in a stream instead of drinking it from a skin."

"So we need to find a ship to carry us down the coast," Mathas said.

"Right," Janik said. "I asked Captain Avaen if he would be willing to take us, but he declined. So we'll need to see what our letter of credit can accomplish. Instead of hugging the coast, we could go straight across the Phoenix Basin here, then use a launch to come ashore. The problem is that it's extremely dangerous and the waters aren't well charted. That makes most commercial captains unwilling to try it."

"How much time are we looking at?" Dania asked.

"We'll be stuck with two months of overland trekking no matter what we do, just to get from the coast to Mel-Aqat. But sailing across the Basin . . ." Janik did some quick measurements on the map and some figuring in his head. "We might make it in . . . four months total? Compared to the eight months it took us last time, when we took a keelboat down the coast."

"Trimming four months off the journey sounds like it would be worth a lot of money," Dania said.

"I agree. But I don't know if it will be possible. I'm willing to look into it, if you all agree it's the way to go." He looked around at his friends. "I'm sure this town is full of people willing to risk their lives for a small fortune. Or a large one. I hope the Keeper of the Flame isn't having second thoughts about this letter of credit."

"The wealth of a nation is not easily depleted," Mathas said.

"Though I can't imagine she'd be happy to learn that funds from the Cathedral were going to some pirate captain," Dania added, frowning. "What are the chances of finding someone at least vaguely reputable to take us?"

Janik rolled his eyes. "You might as well ask if we could find an honest merchant in Callestan." The inn district in the lowest reaches of Sharn was notorious for the crooked deals constantly occurring there.

Auftane laughed, but Dania glared at Janik. "You're pretty quick to assume the worst," she said.

"You know this city as well as I do. Maybe the city's not run by pirates any more—"

"Or maybe it is," Auftane interrupted. "Just dressed up to look fairer."

"Fair enough," Janik said. "Like I said, no commercial captain is likely to risk his ship crossing the Basin. And there are no other cities down the coast—a captain can't carry cargo at the same time to make it worthwhile. We're going to pay for this in dragonshards, and we're going to get someone who cares only about the money. The alternative is going down the coast, like we did last time, and taking the eight months."

"Let me look," Dania said.

"What?"

"Let me look for a captain. If I can find someone I trust, we'll cross the Basin and get there in four months. If not, we take the coast and the eight months."

"And let Krael take a pirate ship and get there in four?"

"Just let me look."

"Who do you think you're going to find? A former pirate who's got religion and given up his pirating ways, but can't find honest work because of his checkered past? Or maybe a paladin ship captain who'll take us because he believes in our mission?"

"If I can't find someone, then we'll decide what to do."

Janik threw up his hands. "Sea of Fire, you're stubborn!"

He clenched his jaw, then sighed. "We need a couple of days to get supplies anyway. You can look tonight and all day tomorrow. But if you haven't found someone by the next morning, I'm taking over. And we'll use whoever will give us the best deal. Or really, whoever will take us—I don't think we're in a position to be choosy."

"Just let me—"

"Yes! You can look!" Janik laughed and Auftane was quick to join in. Mathas grinned, and after a moment, even Dania cracked a smile.

"I knew you'd listen to reason," she said.

· ◉ ◉ ◉ ◉ ◉ ◉ ◉ ·

The next morning, as Dania set off on her fool's errand, Janik took Mathas and Auftane to gather supplies for the journey. They planned for four months of food and gear—two months aboard ship, where their only food would be whatever stores they carried with them, and two months in the wilds, where they could supplement their rations with hunting and foraging. They bought two tents, and Auftane purchased a new backpack. They joined Dania for dinner in the evening, and all four of them were exhausted from a long day of scouring the city. Dania had not yet found a reputable captain to take them across the Basin, but she refused to admit defeat.

"I'll look more tonight and in the morning," Dania said. "You gave me that long. And I have a good lead."

"Whatever you say, Dania," Janik replied.

They were all so tired that their conversation during supper was subdued. Janik went to bed early, planning the first places he would look for a captain in the morning as he drifted to sleep.

Janik slept late and stumbled out of bed with the sun already creeping high in the sky. He dressed and went to Dania's room, knocking on her door. She didn't answer, so he went downstairs, hoping to find some breakfast before starting the day's work. Pushing open the inn door, he nearly bumped into Dania.

"Well, good morning!" she said, smiling warmly. "Janik, I'd like you to meet Breddan Omaar." She gestured to the tall hobgoblin at her side. Breddan clasped a fist to his chest and gave a small bow. "Breddan, *fith a'aeran* Janik Martell," she croaked.

"Your Goblin is appalling, Dania," Janik said in Goblin. He returned Breddan's gesture of greeting. "Your ancestors' swords were keen and strong," he said formally.

"Your Goblin is very good, Janik Martell," Breddan said in perfect Common. "It is an honor to meet you. I have heard much about you, even before I met Dania this morning. She, of course, is unstinting in her praise of you."

"Well, thank you," Janik said, looking from Dania to the hobgoblin. He wondered how Breddan interpreted his relationship with Dania. Just for a moment, he wondered what Dania's interpretation was.

"Why don't we sit down and talk, Janik?" she said. "Where were you heading?"

"I was going to look for some breakfast."

"What are you hungry for, Janik Martell?" Breddan said. "I know Stormreach like my ancestral home."

"Well, when I'm at home, I like a pastry."

"I know the best place for pastry, not far from here. Follow me!" Breddan started down the street. Janik arched an eyebrow at Dania, who just smiled and took his arm, pulling him along behind the hobgoblin.

"Breddan has a small sailing ship," Dania said as they walked.

"Do you?" Janik said.

"A miserable vessel," Breddan replied over his shoulder, "but with the blessing of the Flame, he will carry you across the Phoenix Basin."

Janik arched his eyebrow at Dania again, and said under his breath, "So which is he? The ex-pirate or the paladin?"

Dania jabbed her elbow into Janik's ribs, her lips silently forming a "Sh!" Breddan led them around a corner to a small bakery, and Janik nodded his approval. The smells coming from inside made his stomach rumble, and he never would have found the place on his own. He owed Breddan at least a hearing for that. He bought pastries for everyone, and they sat at a small table to talk.

"So you're willing to take us across the Phoenix Basin?" he asked Breddan.

"Well, your friend informed me that you could pay well, and I am in need of income," the hobgoblin replied.

"What's your story? You carry cargo normally?"

"I would, but few merchants are willing to entrust their goods to my care."

"Why is that? Your ship is seaworthy, right?"

"It is not my ship that scares away customers, I'm afraid. Many find it difficult to put their faith in an heir of Dhakaan such as myself." Almost unconsciously, Janik translated the phrase—heir of Dhakaan—into the goblin tongue: *Dhakaan kurrashan*. It was a far more elegant term than the clumsy Common word, goblinoid, and conjured echoes of the ancient glory of the goblin empire. "Many are quick to assume I am a pirate."

Janik looked away from Breddan, glancing out the window.

He was embarrassed at his own hasty assessment of the captain.

"I made inquiries with the local church of the Silver Flame," Dania interjected. "They told me they knew of a captain in need of work."

"The Silver Flame has saved my life, in more ways than one. I was born into slavery here in Stormreach. I did menial tasks aboard a merchant ship, but I watched everything and learned the sailor's craft. A noble paladin who made a fortune fighting the evil of this dark land bought me and set me free. I found work as a sailor and began to learn the captain's craft. Eventually I saved enough money to buy my own ship, but since then I have had little work."

"Let's talk specifics," Janik said. "How long will it take to cross the Phoenix Basin?"

"Where exactly is your destination?"

Janik pulled the worn map from his coat pocket and smoothed it out on the table. "We'd like to make land about here." He pointed to the western end of the Wasted Plain.

Breddan studied the map for a moment. "I do not know the Basin that far south," he admitted. "I'm not sure reliable charts exist for those waters. What I do know is this—the waters of the Phoenix Basin are deep, and many dangerous creatures make their lairs in its depths. Assuming we do not feed a dragon eel, we should make it most of the way in . . . hmm, fifty-four days. Then we must negotiate the shallow waters near your destination."

"I had estimated two months," Janik said. "I'm glad we agree."

"And then what? Will you want me to wait at anchor for you to complete your task and return?"

Janik was taken aback. He hadn't given any thought to what would happen after they returned from Mel-Aqat. He had no idea what might await them in the ruins, no clue how long it would take to find what they were looking for—whatever it was—and no inkling what to do when they found it.

"I . . . don't think so," he said slowly. "It will take us another two months to cross the Wasted Plain, here, to reach our destination. I really don't know how long we'll be gone—and of course, there's always the possibility we just won't come back." He noticed that Dania was listening with keen interest, but he avoided her eyes. "I think it will be best if you drop us off and then return to Stormreach and spend your earnings."

"I am not a spendthrift," Breddan said. "But neither am I excited at the prospect of spending four months or more at anchor in the Phoenix Basin. I will return without you. But if I might ask, how will you get back to Stormreach?"

"How big is your ship?" Dania interjected. "Could we carry a keelboat aboard, use it to put ashore, hide it somewhere, and then use it to come back along the coast?"

"My ship carries a launch already," Breddan said. "We could replace it with something more seaworthy—assuming you are willing to pay for such a vessel."

"Janik, do you think that would work?"

Janik ran his fingers through his hair, thinking for a moment. "I don't have a better plan. We might come back and find the keelboat gone, I suppose, but at least that gives us a chance of not making the journey overland. We could store supplies on it for the trip back."

"Which means less weight on our backs through Mel-Aqat," Dania said.

"Exactly. Well, Breddan Omaar, what price would you ask for this journey?"

The hobgoblin looked distinctly uncomfortable, and

Janik could understand why. He needed money—he had said as much. And he was within reason to ask for a large sum—so large he was embarrassed to name it.

"Wait," Janik said. He pulled a blank scrap of parchment from the sheaf of pages in his coat pocket, and found a quill and a bottle of ink in his pocket. He shoved them across the table toward Breddan. "Why don't you show me your figures?"

Breddan accepted the parchment gratefully, scratched a few numbers in neat columns, and handed it back to Janik. "That amount would cover my expenses and pay for my time."

Janik forced himself to keep a blank look on his face as he looked at the large sum. It was hardly extravagant—in fact, Breddan had allotted a pittance for his own wage, and had not inflated the numbers to account for the danger of the journey. Even so, it was clear to Janik why they had not traveled this way last time, when they paid for the expedition out of their own pockets. He glanced up—both Dania and Breddan were watching him expectantly. He made some further calculations in his head, then tucked the parchment into his pocket.

"I believe we have a deal," he announced. Breddan smiled, showing his sharp teeth, and Dania actually clapped her hands in delight. "How soon can you be ready to leave, Breddan?"

The hobgoblin's smile faded quickly, and he looked down at the table. "Ah, well," he said. "I wonder if I might request some portion of my payment in advance. My ship needs a good cleaning and some maintenance before undertaking such a long and hazardous journey."

"I can give you the whole sum up front," Janik said, shrugging. "I need to pay you at the House Kundarak bank anyway, and I can't do that at the end of our journey. Shall we say, a third of it today, and the rest on the day we leave? How long will you need?"

"A third of that sum will be perfectly sufficient," Breddan said, bowing his head gratefully. "Would a week's time be too long?"

"My friend," Janik said, "your ship will save us four to six months of travel. We can afford to wait a week."

❁ ❁ ❁ ❁ ❁ ❁ ❁ ❁

Janik and Dania delivered the good news to Mathas and Auftane, and they all spent the next several days getting ready for the trip—gathering more supplies, rounding up some rare charts of the waters of the Phoenix Basin, and purchasing a keelboat. Janik supervised delivery of the keelboat to Breddan's ship, *Silverknife*, and got his first look at the ship as the smaller boat was loaded on board. Afterward, he met the others near the docks and they walked together to Forest's Bounty for dinner.

"When he said she was a miserable vessel, I thought it was Flamer humility," Janik said, laughing.

"Oh, no!" Dania exclaimed. "Is it really awful?"

"Let me just say that I'm glad he delayed our departure by a week in order to clean and repair her," Janik said.

"But it's been five days already," Mathas said. "Is the vessel seaworthy?"

"Oh, she's seaworthy. Look, I didn't mean to worry you all. It's just—well, we're not going on a Lyrandar galleon. We're going to spend two months on a small, cramped, dirty ship."

"But we all agree that's better than six months on a keelboat, or eight months on foot, right?" Auftane said.

"Of course," Dania said, and Janik nodded. Mathas looked unconvinced but said nothing.

The sun had faded from the sky except for a line of purple along the western horizon, silhouetting the stone buildings of the modern seaport and the crumbling ruins of the ancient giant city. High above, one moon hung proudly while seven more clustered at opposite ends of the Ring of Siberys, sliver—thin crescents in the darkening west and rounded gibbous moons in the pitch-black east. The golden motes of the Ring shone bright and clear in a wide band across the sky, larger here than it ever appeared in Khorvaire. Torches blazed along the sides of the nearly-deserted street, dancing wildly in the warm wind off the sea.

An eruption of laughter came from a group of people ahead of them, just short of an intersection. Dania's hand shot across Janik's chest as she stopped dead.

"I know that laugh," she hissed.

"Krael." The name was a growl in Janik's throat, and he turned his gaze from Dania to the cluster of people in the distance.

He started walking again, his face set in a scowl as he tried to make out details of the people up ahead. After just a few steps, he spotted Krael, towering above most of his companions by at least a head. One other member of the group was as tall—the warforged assassin. Janik gritted his teeth. At least a half-dozen people trailed Krael—or maybe more like eight or nine. Janik had only four on his side. His heart pounded. His eyes flicked over the others—a few women, one who might have been Tierese—but he did not see Maija. He was only vaguely aware of Dania beside him, grabbing his arm, trying to slow him down, hissing something at him.

"Janik, remember—Krael's a vampire!" she said, and

finally the words penetrated the rage throbbing in his ears.

It was too late. The others had seen him approaching, and Krael's companions were spreading out to form a wide semicircle, with Krael and the warforged, Sever, in the middle. Krael stepped forward and spread his arms in a wide gesture of welcome. His massive flail hung on his back, banging against his plate armor as he walked.

"Well, well!" the vampire called across the distance. "If it isn't my dear friend Janik Martell!"

CHAPTER 9

You got the name right, Krael," Janik shouted back. Even
as his mind screamed about the danger of walking into the
semicircle formed by Krael and his allies, anger drove his feet
forward, closer to his adversary.

Krael Kavarat was an enormous man, as tall and muscular
as any orc, though his bloodline was pure Karrnathi human
as far as Janik knew. He wore a suit of full plate armor which
somehow seemed too small to contain his great bulk. He also
wore the characteristic helm of an Emerald Claw officer,
covering half his face with its stylized clawlike design. He was
clean shaven, but blond hair cascaded over his shoulders from
beneath the edge of his helm.

"And Dania," Krael said. "Back in Janik's company since
your Sentinel Marshal met his end in Karrnath?"

"Sentinel Marshal?" Janik said quietly, throwing Dania
a sidelong glance. She waved her hand dismissively, keeping
her attention focused on Krael.

"It's so nice to see you all together again. Mathas too!
Aren't you going to introduce me to the dwarf?"

"Shut up, Krael," Janik spat. The vampire's words stung, making Janik painfully aware that they were not all together again. He felt Maija's absence as if it were a wound. "You sent your warforged assassin after me twice, you robbed my apartment, and stole our ship. Stop talking like you're some long-lost friend." Janik was close enough that he didn't need to shout, and he could see Krael's allies closing in on both sides. Dania was close on his right, but not close enough to get in the way of his sword arm. He heard Mathas and Auftane right behind him.

"Don't forget that I took your Maija away," Krael said, grinning. Then the smile vanished from his face. "Her, you can have back, as far as I'm concerned."

"What are you here for, Krael?"

Krael gave a small shrug, but a spasm of anger on his face belied his feigned indifference. "Revenge."

"That makes two of us, then," Janik said, pulling his sword from its sheath in a flash of steel. Like a ripple of water, steel flashed all around the ring of Krael's allies. Dania drew her longsword. Only Krael, Mathas, and Auftane stood empty-handed.

"You misunderstand me, Janik," Krael said. "You are not the one I want revenge against. Although I suppose it would be pleasant enough to watch you die."

"This is a bad idea, Janik," Dania whispered at his elbow. "Krael is strong, to say nothing of his friends here."

"Put those weapons away!" Several of Krael's allies turned to see Stormreach guards hurrying up the street toward them. Janik and Krael were frozen, each waiting for the other to make a move. Around the semicircle of Krael's Emerald Claw lackeys, a few swords and flails found their way back to belts. Glancing behind Krael, Janik could see why. Stormreach didn't entrust the task of keeping order in the city to rough-necks pulled from the farms and dressed up in uniforms. The Stormreach guards were highly trained soldiers, mostly former officers from the armies of the Five Nations, and included some real muscle in the form of ogres and an occasional hill giant. One of those giants walked up behind Krael at that moment, and the great hulk of a vampire stood only as high as the giant's waist. Sever, the warforged assassin, tugged at Krael's arm, looking back at the approaching giant and his two human compatriots.

Janik felt sure that the giant and the two humans could wipe the street with him, his friends, Krael, and all the Emerald Claw thugs. But he didn't care. He had nursed this hatred and anger for three long years. He gripped his sword tightly. He wanted so badly to plunge it into Krael's body, to hurt and kill him and make the bastard pay for what he'd done. Janik didn't care what happened to him in the process. It didn't matter that Krael was a vampire, it didn't matter that the warforged next to Krael had nearly killed him twice already, and it didn't matter that a hill giant was standing behind Krael, lifting a tree trunk over his shoulder, getting ready to clear the street with it. He didn't care that he couldn't win—he just wanted to fight.

Dania still clutched her sword and Janik could feel the tension in her. He suspected she was having the same kinds of thoughts. What had happened when she met Krael in Karrnath? He realized he didn't know, but it had stirred up the same degree of hatred in her heart, and her newfound devotion to the Silver Flame had done nothing to diminish the rage she felt toward Krael. He stole a sidelong glance at her and caught a glimpse of the fire in her eyes. She would stand behind him.

"Janik?" Mathas said. "I am inclined to believe this is not the time and place for this confrontation."

Janik didn't respond, but Dania shifted her stance slightly.

"I think the elf is right," Auftane whispered. "I think we could take the lackeys, and you can leave the warforged to me, but I'm worried about the vampire. To say nothing of the giant."

Dania turned toward Janik.

"It would be unfortunate if we were forced to harm well-meaning members of the Stormreach guard in the course of battling our foes," Mathas added.

"They've got a point," Dania said. "We'll have our shot at Krael, I'm sure."

"You're right," Janik said. "Let's get out of here." He shifted his sword to his left hand and slid it into its sheath while raising his other hand to point at Krael. "Some other time, Krael!" he called.

The vampire hadn't moved, but was still staring at Janik and Dania. Janik turned his back on Krael, took Dania's arm, and hurried down the block toward a nearby tavern. Mathas and Auftane followed. Janik refused to look back at Krael—he couldn't stand to see that satisfied smirk again. A group of people had gathered outside the tavern door to watch the confrontation, alerted by the call of the Stormreach guard. Janik ignored their laughs and whispers and pushed through. He led his friends to a table near the raging fire, and they all sat down.

"So tell me about Karrnath, Dania," Janik said when they all had drinks in their hands and the hubbub had died down.

Dania scowled and stared into her tankard. She was silent

for a moment, collecting her thoughts, then took a deep breath. "I went there to work for a friend of my late father's," she said, "an exorcist of the Silver Flame named Kophran ir'Davik. He was a pompous ass, as I believe I might have mentioned before." Mathas grinned and nodded. "Along with a Sentinel Marshal, Gered d'Deneith—"

"Krael mentioned him," Auftane interjected.

"Yes. The three of us tried to fight the influence of evil in Atur." She paused and sighed again. "It was a bit like trying to put out a forest fire by spitting on it. Atur has earned its nickname, the City of Night. Anyway, one evening we went to a house where every inhabitant had been brutally murdered. Blood and bodies were strewn everywhere. Gered determined that two vampires were involved, one a shifter, and one a human—well, that one turned out to be Krael. Gered and I followed a trail away from the house and encountered Krael in an alley. We talked for a little while before Gered and I realized he was one of the vampires we'd been hunting, and then—" She broke off suddenly, swallowing hard.

"He killed Gered?" Mathas said softly.

Dania breathed a deep sigh. "Not quite. He started drinking Gered's blood, but then Kophran came back." She took another steadying breath. "Kophran filled the alley with silver light, and that drove Krael away." Her voice trailed off and a half smile lingered on her lips.

"What about Maija?" Janik's voice was barely audible above the din of the tavern.

"Well, it turned out that Krael and Maija had awakened this old shifter vampire named Havoc as part of their search for the Tablet of Shummarak."

"You mentioned that on the ship," Mathas said. "What is that tablet?"

Janik answered the elf's question. "It's an important serpent text from Xen'drik, dealing with the legendary war between the dragons and the fiends in the first age of the world. Specifically, it describes how the allies of the dragons, the couatls, bound the lords of the fiends deep within Khyber."

"Sacrificing their own physical forms to trap the fiends within their spiritual coils," Dania added, repeating what Kophran had told her. "And supposedly the Tablet of Shummarak goes on to reveal a means by which the bonds of the couatls' coils might be broken, releasing the lords of the demons upon the earth again."

Janik raised his eyebrows, wishing he had discussed the Tablet with Dania earlier.

"So Krael and Maija were hoping to find the Tablet and destroy the world?" Auftane asked.

"Undoubtedly part of some Emerald Claw plot," Janik said.

"So we tried to learn more about this vampire, Havoc. He was rumored to have owned the Tablet some time before the Last War. And we managed to track him down—we found all three of them in a little shrine beneath the city. Havoc, Krael, and Maija." She swallowed hard again. "That's when Gered died. Maija cast a horrible spell, and he just . . . went out. Like pinching a candle." She shook her head. "Kophran killed Havoc—or forced him to turn to mist, or something. I guess you can't really kill a vampire. Maija disappeared—teleported away, I think, and Krael ran as well. Kophran figured Havoc was in charge of the operation, and insisted we take steps to finish him off. We ended up chasing a cloud of mist through half the sewers and catacombs under the city until it reached Havoc's original crypt. Then we were able to destroy him for good, or Kophran said we had. But I didn't see Krael or Maija again. We hunted for them for a long time, but as far as we could tell, they both left Karrnath entirely."

"Did she . . . did Maija say anything?" Janik asked.

"Quite a bit, actually, considering that we were doing our level best to kill each other."

"You fought her?" Somehow this seemed impossible to Janik. Some part of him, he realized, had long assumed that there was just some misunderstanding that would all be resolved the next time he saw Maija. That was why he had rebelled so strongly against Dania's assertion that Maija was beyond redemption. And to imagine Dania actually trying to kill her, so convinced that Maija was lost to evil that she would take her life—his head started to swim.

"Of course I fought her, Janik." Dania's voice was gentle but firm. "Have you heard what I've been saying? She was working with a pair of vampires. She killed Gered—a Sentinel Marshal and a good man. As far as I could tell, she was trying to release the lords of demonkind and set them loose on the world. Of course I fought her."

Janik nodded but turned aside, staring into the fire.

"What did she say, Dania?" Mathas asked.

Dania paused, trying to remember the details of their intense fight beneath the streets of Atur. "She mocked me. Every damned word was a mockery. She was so full of . . . of spite, malice, contempt. She said the vampires had grown tiresome or outlived their usefulness, and I asked her if that was what had happened at Mel-Aqat—whether she just tired of us. That's when she cast the spell that killed Gered—it was like a wave of death crashing over me."

As Dania spoke, a series of memories raced through Janik's mind. They started, as thoughts of Maija always did, with Mel-Aqat—as she took the Ramethene Sword from Janik's hand and ran over to Krael, offering it to him hilt first. Krael had seemed taken aback—he took a defensive stance as she approached, as if he thought she would attack him with the sword. When she handed him the weapon, Janik couldn't hear what they said, but Krael still seemed suspicious. She had been mocking then, too—shouting back at him as she disappeared into the wilderness with Krael.

"Sorry about this, Janik," she had said, not sounding sorry at all, "but when the opportunity for something bigger and better comes along, you need to take it."

Dania fell into silence and no one else said anything. Janik was lost in his memories—remembering that a sardonic edge had crept into Maija's voice before they left the ruins. Mathas had asked in the airship approaching Sharn whether something had happened in the ruins, and now Janik realized that something had. He couldn't identify what it was or when it happened, but Maija had said several things that had irritated him as they departed the ruins. At the time, he blamed the strain of travel and the stress of their days exploring Mel-Aqat. But she had always been the one who bore up the best under pressure—she would soothe their frayed nerves with inspiration and comfort that sometimes seemed to come straight from the Sovereign Host—from Olladra's hearth or Boldrei's embracing arms.

A now-familiar ache seized Janik's chest as he remembered lying in her arms in the ruins at night. The touch of her hands always seemed to soothe away the aches and bruises and hurts of the day even more than her spells of healing did. Her love for him had always felt like tangible proof of the Sovereigns and their divine love. She had been his priest in a very real sense—standing between him and the Host, bringing his prayers to them and delivering their responses, whether in the form of divine magical power or in the soft words she whispered to him at night.

And he had lost that. Their last night in the ruins, she had held him, but her hands had no comfort and her words were biting. Instead of soothing away his worries and fears, she had mocked them—gently, but the words had stung when he needed reassurance and consolation.

"A wave of death," he said into the silence, echoing Dania's words. "Why does that sound like an omen of things to come?"

"Well, thank you for that cheerful thought," Dania said.

"If it's an omen," Mathas said, "perhaps it's a warning of the consequences of failure. If we released something from Mel-Aqat, perhaps that something is the reason that Maija and Krael were looking for the Tablet of Shummarak. Maybe the thing we released is seeking to release something greater. If one fiend-lord were released from its prison, waves of death might be a very accurate description of what would come next. If they were all released . . ."

"They won't be," Dania said firmly. "We're here to make sure of that. I seem to have steered this conversation toward predictions of doom, and I'm sorry. Gered's death was terrible, and Maija will pay for it, but her evil spell is *not* a portent of our future or the world's. The Silver Flame has called me to this work and empowered me for it, and I will not fail." She slammed her fist on the table, a little harder than she intended, and Auftane started in surprise.

"Of course we won't," the dwarf said. "You think it's safe to head to the restaurant now?" Dania and Mathas laughed.

Janik stood up, his face grim. "I'm not hungry. I'll see you all in the morning." He turned and walked out of the tavern, his companions too surprised to call after him.

"Mathas, did I say something out of line?" Dania asked.

"No, no," Mathas said, patting her hand. "You just have to understand that Maija is still a fresh wound for Janik."

"It's been three years!"

"Well, then an open, festering wound. He has never bandaged it or treated it—he's like an animal who keeps biting at a wound so it can't heal. Maija was his healer, caring for his body and soul. Without her, he doesn't know how to heal the wound in his heart."

"I worry about his soul," Dania said softly.

"So do I," Mathas said. "Losing Maija seems to have driven him away from the Sovereign Host."

"And he seems quite uncomfortable every time I mention the Silver Flame."

"Yes, though I suspect that has as much to do with his experience of your church in Sharn as it does with the overall state of his soul."

"The church in Sharn is hardly a fair representative of the church as a whole. I mean, it has its share of corrupt patriarchs—"

"And pompous asses," Auftane interjected.

"And people like Kophran, yes," Dania said. "But I am convinced there is no greater force for good at work in the world. Mathas, when I went to Karrnath, I was as ruined as Janik is. My past felt like an enormous weight on my shoulders. We were hunting these vampires, and for a while I was convinced that I was as bad as they were. I couldn't stop thinking of all the people I killed during the war. Kophran didn't help that, of course—he treated me as though I were not quite a person. But there were two things that got me out of that. One was the realization of what vampires are—they're warped by pure evil stronger than anything that grows in human hearts. And the other was my taste of the Silver Flame, my experience of pure good. I felt it wash over me when Kophran drove Krael away."

"So how do you account for the evil you say has grown in Maija's heart?" Mathas said. "You said she was not a vampire."

"No, but I am not convinced that she is human any more."

"What do you mean?" Mathas's brow furrowed, spreading deep wrinkles over his face.

"I'm not sure. It's possible that she has made a pact with some demon, or one of the Dark Six. Perhaps it is her use of evil magic that has so deeply corrupted her. Maybe both, and those two things could certainly be related."

"But not human?"

"I don't know, Mathas. She's not a vampire. She's still alive, near as I can tell, but she's more evil than anyone I've encountered since. She's the only living person whose evil was almost tangible like that—like what I could feel from the vampires. That's what I mean."

Dania looked at the dwarf beside her, who had been sitting quietly through most of her conversation with Mathas. "I'm sorry, Auftane," she said. "We seem to spend a lot of time talking about the past."

"I suppose it's a good thing I find such topics interesting," Auftane replied with a smile.

"Damn it, why do we spend so much time talking about Maija?" Dania threw her hands in the air. "It's been three years since she walked out on us."

"The topic of Krael, at least, seems relevant to our current expedition," Auftane said.

"True, and it is hard to separate one from the other," Mathas observed. "They left Mel-Aqat together, and you encountered them together in Karrnath, Dania. I'm not sure that Maija is completely irrelevant, either. Perhaps it was only by chance that we did not meet her on the street tonight."

"That would have been ugly," Dania said. "Janik was bad enough after seeing Krael."

⊛ ⊛ ⊛ ⊛ ⊛ ⊛ ⊛

Janik strode along the darkened streets of Stormreach toward the inn. Half of him hoped he would run into Krael again, while the other half knew it would mean almost certain death, at least if Krael was still with Sever and Tierese and his other half-dozen allies. One on one, Janik figured it would be an even match, vampire or no vampire.

Like his friends, Janik wondered if Maija were here as well. But he kept coming back to Krael's scornful comment, "Her, you can have back, as far as I'm concerned." So it seemed likely that Maija was not here with him. But Krael had said he was here for revenge—and not against Janik. Was he looking for Maija to take revenge against her? Had she turned on Krael as well? In that case, perhaps she was here on her own. Perhaps she had taken the Tablet of Shummarak from Krael and brought it to Xen'drik, hoping to release a demon lord. Perhaps she was taking it to Mel-Aqat, the Place of Imprisonment.

But if she was no longer working with Krael, then why was she doing any of this? If she didn't work for the Emerald Claw any more, who did she work for? Why would she be trying to free an imprisoned fiend, if not on Emerald Claw orders? Could Dania be right—that Maija had become irredeemably evil?

"No!" Janik shouted aloud, drawing some alarmed stares from passersby on the street. Scowling, he lowered his head and kept his eyes on the cobblestone street, quickening his pace toward the inn. He gritted his teeth. He simply could not accept that he would never have Maija back, that she was forever lost to him.

He reached the inn, stumbled up to his room, and collapsed in his bed.

* * * ⊛ * * *

Dawn's light and a gnawing hunger woke Janik early, and he looked blearily around his room. He jumped to his feet when he realized that the contents of his pack were strewn across the floor near the door. He couldn't be absolutely certain, but he was fairly sure that they had been neatly in place when he returned to his room the night before.

"Damn you, Krael," he muttered as he knelt on the floor. Without touching anything, he took inventory of the items—the pack was empty, but nothing seemed to be missing. Then he noticed that several items lay right in front of the door, which opened inward. The door could not have opened since the gear was spread over the floor. That meant two things. First, someone had definitely been in the room while Janik was sleeping. Second, that someone had not left by way of the door. Janik drew his sword and thoroughly searched the room. It was small, and there was no place to hide. The window was directly over the bed, which meant that someone using it to leave the room would have had to step right over Janik as he slept. He was a fairly heavy sleeper, but he was confident that would have awakened him.

"Now you're just showing off," he said. Shaking his head, he stowed his gear back into his pack.

* * * ⊛ * * *

"Turned to mist," Dania said. They were walking to the dock—Janik hoped they could encourage Breddan to set sail early, staying ahead of Krael. "Gered told me that vampires can turn to mist, and I saw Havoc do it in Atur."

"That's probably it," Mathas said. "He could have turned to mist outside your door—or anywhere, really—and slipped through the crack under the door. Then he returned to solid form inside your room, spread out your belongings to let you know he had been there, and left the same way."

"He's just trying to scare you," Dania added.

"Well, it damn well worked!" Janik said. "There was a vampire in my room while I slept last night! I made sure to check for bite marks when I got dressed this morning."

"Did you find any?" Auftane asked. He looked genuinely worried.

"No, I did not. And the point is, he could have done anything he wanted."

"That's exactly the point he was trying to make," Mathas said. "He wants you to think he's in control, that he's the one with the power."

"He's driving home the point that I walked away from our little encounter last night, not him," Janik said. "Rubbing his victory in my face."

"That wasn't a victory, Janik," Dania said. "And walking away from a confrontation in the street is not a defeat. We have more important work than brawling with Krael, Janik. Don't let him intimidate you."

"I'm not worried about him intimidating me. I'm worried about him drinking my blood while I sleep! But he can't do that while we're sailing across the Phoenix Basin . . . can he?"

"No," Mathas said, "he won't be able to move as fast as the ship travels. Unless he's stowed away on the ship."

"Or Breddan's ship is more of a wreck than you let on," Auftane said, drawing laughter from everyone.

"Janik, if he had wanted to kill you, or drink your blood, he would have done it last night," Dania said.

"Maybe he got in there and realized he wasn't hungry," Janik said. "It doesn't matter. I just want to leave town as quickly as we can, whether Krael has any designs on my blood or not. The fact that he's here means he has caught up to us. We need to stay a step ahead of him, so we need to leave now. And," he added, pointing at Mathas, "we need to make sure he isn't stowed away on the ship. I know it sounds crazy, but I'm going to inspect the ship's stores crate by crate before we weigh anchor. If you would help me, I'd appreciate it—I'm not sure I'd recognize a vampire who had turned to mist."

"He would have a hard time concealing his presence from me," Dania said. "The stink of his evil is as strong as Maija's. I'll help you look."

"Thank you. Oh, look at this." They reached the docks, and Janik was leading them toward Breddan's berth. But he pointed now at a different ship—*Hope's Endeavor.* "It's Nashan's ship—the one Krael stole out from under us. Let's have a word with Captain Nashan, shall we?"

"A word," Dania said firmly. "There's no need to hurt him."

"You don't think so?" Janik said, but he smiled. "Don't worry, Dania. I am capable of restraining my temper. We'll just have a civil conversation." He stepped onto the gangplank leading up to the ship's main deck. "Ho there, *Hope's Endeavor!*" he called. "Permission to come aboard!"

No one moved on the deck or in the rigging. Janik looked at his friends, then walked up the gangplank to the deck. "Anyone here?" The ship creaked and water lapped at its sides, but no one answered Janik's call.

"They must have all gone ashore," Auftane said, making his way slowly up the gangplank.

"And left the ship unguarded?" Dania replied. "Unlikely. I'd say something is definitely wrong."

Janik moved to the forward cabin and pushed the door open. "Sea of Fire! Nashan!" Ducking his head, he rushed into the dark cabin.

Shutters were closed over all the portholes, and the cabin smelled of illness and death. The ship's captain lay on the floor, his legs and arms spread-eagled, blank white eyes staring up at the ceiling. Janik knelt beside him, and Nashan took a long, painfully slow, rasping breath.

"Should've . . . waited . . . for you," he wheezed. His skin was chalk-white, and as Janik looked him over he quickly noticed the angry red wound at his neck. The skin was puckered and the twin punctures were white inside.

"He bribed you to take him instead, then killed you instead of paying you," Janik said quietly. "Nashan, you were the spawn of a sea devil, but you didn't deserve this."

A flicker of a smile passed over Nashan's face, but he said no more.

CHAPTER 10

Dania appeared in the doorway, casting a long shadow into the room. "There's no sign of the crew," she said. "Nashan is dead?"

Janik nodded, pushing the captain's eyelids closed. "Send Auftane to tell the wharf guard, will you?" he said. "I want to look through Nashan's log before they get here." Dania stepped away from the door and Janik stood up. He opened all the shutters to let in the daylight, then began rustling through the parchments scattered across the desk and floor.

When Dania returned a quarter hour later, she found him sitting beside Nashan's body, a neat stack of parchments beside him and the leather-bound captain's log open in his lap, showing two blank pages. He was staring vaguely toward a porthole.

"Janik?" she said.

"He fed on Nashan every day for the month it took them to get here," Janik said, still staring toward the porthole. "His lackeys killed off the sailors one by one. Apparently the Emerald Claw agents with him could sail the ship by themselves, at least well enough to get them here once they were through Shargon's Teeth. Nashan was the last one alive, the only one to see port. And Krael left him in no shape to get off the ship." He shook his head. "And for no reason. He writes that they just seemed to enjoy killing people—the war-forged most of all. Nashan seemed unsure whether to be more afraid of Krael or Sever. But he was powerless—he wrote that whenever Krael looked at him, he just went limp."

"I know the feeling," Dania muttered.

Janik looked at her for the first time. "What do you mean?"

Dania sank down to the floor beside Janik. "The first time we encountered Krael in Atur," she said slowly, "we were talking, exchanging barbs like we did here last night. But closer, face-to-face—the point of my sword was at his neck, even. I didn't know yet that he was a vampire. And then the next thing I knew, he was in my head, his voice right in my mind, commanding me—and I couldn't resist. He made me attack Gered, made me stand by while he drank Gered's blood. He wanted me to watch my friend die. If Kophran had not returned when he did . . ."

"You didn't mention that before," Janik said quietly.

"Can you blame me? It still hurts to admit it—that I stood by helplessly while my friend nearly died. I know it wasn't my fault, but . . ." She shrugged. "Well, I have no intention of doing that again, standing by while a friend dies."

They sat in silence for a moment, then heard the heavy tramp of feet along the dock that signaled the arrival of the wharf guard. Janik jumped to his feet, and offered a hand to Dania.

"Thanks," Dania said softly, squeezing his hand before letting it go. She walked toward the cabin door as the sound of feet came up the gangplank and onto the deck. "In here," she said, and the guard captain came in. A gnome, he had no need to duck through the doorway, and he strode over to Nashan's body. Two human guards stood outside the doorway, craning their necks to peer in.

"What happened here?" the gnome said, and Janik gave him a quick summary, finishing by handing over the captain's log. He gave the gnome a description of Krael, though he had little hope of the wharf guard finding the vampire or having the strength to overcome him. An hour later, they were allowed to leave.

"Well," Janik said, "now it's even more important that we get underway as soon as possible. Krael is unlikely to stick around for long with that mess in his wake."

"Let's find Breddan," Dania said. "Where's this wreck of a ship you told us about?"

"Just up there," Janik said, pointing vaguely ahead. "Unless Krael has sabotaged her."

"Don't even joke about it," Mathas muttered. "I wouldn't be surprised at this point."

They quickened their pace and reached Breddan's ship, *Silverknife*. To Janik's relief, the ship was crawling with sailors and shipwrights making repairs, and he quickly spotted Breddan on the poop deck.

"Janik! Dania!" Breddan called out. "Come aboard!" He jumped down to the main deck and met them at the top of the gangplank.

Janik was impressed. The money he had given Breddan had clearly been put to good use. *Silverknife* looked worlds better than the last time he'd seen her. More than that, Breddan looked better. When they had first met, the hobgoblin seemed awkward and a little slow. Now he was sprightly and agile.

Janik wasn't sure whether the money had put the spring back in Breddan's step, or whether he was simply more at home on the deck of his ship than he was on land. Perhaps both factors were at work, but the improved appearance of the ship and her captain made Janik feel much better about his chances for success on this journey.

"To what do I owe the honor of this visit?" Breddan said with a small bow.

"You've done a fine job fixing up the ship," Janik said.

"Thank you. I am proud of my ship, and proud to be able to maintain him as he deserves."

It took Janik a moment to remember that ships were masculine in the goblin tongue. He smiled, casting his eyes on *Silverknife* again, imagining her as a hulking male bugbear.

Dania hadn't missed a beat.

"You haven't met our other companions," she said. "This is Mathas"—the elf bowed—"and Auftane." Auftane extended his hand with a wide smile, and Breddan shook it.

"Welcome aboard my vessel. I hope you find him comfortable on your journey."

"Breddan," Janik said, "about that journey. You said you'd be ready to leave in two more days, right?"

"The day after tomorrow, yes." Breddan looked a little nervous, anticipating Janik's next question. "That was our agreement."

"What are the chances we could leave earlier? *Any* earlier. Tomorrow if we have to, or even today? The ship looks great, we've got supplies packed and ready to be loaded, and we can help with anything more that needs to be done."

"Is there trouble?"

"No. No, it's not like that. Well, not exactly. See, we need to get where we're going before a rival of ours does. We just learned he has arrived in Stormreach, and he's not likely to stay long. We want to make sure we set sail before he does and lessen his chances of getting there before us."

"Hmm." Breddan did not look happy at this, and he stroked his stringy beard for a moment. "Let me ask my boatswain. Make yourselves at home." He hurried toward the aft ladder and disappeared into the hold.

Janik looked around. Not seeing any place where he could get comfortable, he stayed on his feet. Mathas sank into a kneeling position, resting his hands on his knees and closing his eyes. Dania leaned against the bulwark behind her, and Auftane stood beside Janik, shifting uncomfortably.

"What do you make of that?" the dwarf asked Janik. "Is he up to something?"

"No," Dania and Mathas said at once. Mathas did not open his eyes.

"I trust Breddan completely," Dania said. "He's got a good heart, and he wants to be treated right. He knows that if he wants fair treatment, he's got to give it."

Auftane nodded. "Mathas, what's your explanation?"

Janik laughed. "You have to understand Mathas," he said. "He can read volumes from the way someone holds his hands while he talks."

"At the risk of perpetuating this endless joke, which Janik seems to enjoy so much," Mathas said, opening his eyes long enough to give Janik a sidelong glare, "when Breddan was not speaking, his eyes were flicking around the ship. They came to rest on each item still needing attention. He was checking off a list of things to do and worrying that he might not be able to get them done in time, even for our original departure time."

Auftane nodded. "Makes sense to me." He held his hands

behind his back and rocked on the balls of his feet.

A moment later, Breddan returned from the hold, and Mathas rose smoothly to his feet. The hobgoblin was shaking his head, which they all could read as a bad sign.

"To be blunt," Breddan said, "one week was a hopeful estimate. I think we can still set sail the day after tomorrow, but we will still be making repairs during our first few days of travel. I cannot imagine leaving any earlier than that." Janik scowled, but said nothing. "There is one thing I wonder about," Breddan continued. "This rival of yours—is he a very large man with long blond hair?"

"Krael," Janik said. "Have you seen him?"

"My boatswain tells me that he was here last night, making inquiries about our work. I was not aboard, or I would have sent him on his way."

"So he knows we're taking this ship," Dania said. "Breddan, you are in danger."

"Cavaan said he seemed dangerous," Breddan said, stroking his beard.

"He is dangerous," Dania said. "He's a vampire. Breddan, listen—we just saw the ship he took from Sharn to get here. He killed every man aboard, the captain last of all. Krael is extremely dangerous."

Breddan's eyes were wide, and he fixed them on Dania. "Why don't you destroy him? Isn't that the call of the paladin?"

"If an opportunity arises to destroy Krael, be assured that I will take it," Dania said. "But I know his power, and he is surrounded by many allies. To attack him in his strength would be suicidal, and the Silver Flame calls no one to useless death."

The hobgoblin nodded. "Perhaps it was a mistake to

accept this mission. But I cannot return the money you have given me, and I will not break my word to you. I think . . ." he paused, and this time Janik noticed the way his eyes scanned the ship, "I think we will sail before the sun sets tonight. It will be difficult, and I'll need your help. We'll need to work through the night as well, but at least we will be out of port. And with the help of the Silver Flame, we will not be food for sharks or vampires."

"Put us to work," Janik said. "Mathas, I'd like you to get our things together—anything left in our rooms, and the supplies we need loaded aboard. Then, please go to House Kundarak and get the rest of Breddan's payment. I assume you'll prefer running errands around town to hard labor on the ship." He smiled, and Mathas nodded. "The rest of us are under your command, Breddan."

The day went by in a frenzy of activity. Janik mended sails and spliced ropes and could never quite shake the feeling that Breddan gave him those jobs because he thought Janik was useless for anything else. Janik also made periodic sweeps of the ship, checking for any sign that Krael had infiltrated.

Dania spent a great deal of time in the water, demonstrating an amazing ability to hold her breath while exerting herself, and before long, the sailors were calling her *kak-darzhul,* the Goblin name for the warforged. Auftane proved his value once again. He spent most of the day in the hold while Janik worked on the deck under the blazing sun. Janik heard the sailors whisper in awe about the dwarf—how he excelled at every task though he professed no experience. They said he chanted spells as he worked and wove magic into the wood of the ship. In only a few hours, Auftane had significantly increased the morale of the ship's crew, an accomplishment not to be taken lightly.

As the sun barely slipped behind the tops of the highest buildings in the city, casting long shadows over the docks and the harbor, Breddan declared the *Silverknife* ready to sail, and the sailors gave a mighty cheer. Janik looked around the deck at the crew—his first look at all the sailors together. They were a motley bunch—a number of hobgoblins and goblins, a big bugbear covered with matted fur and missing one eye, an assortment of bedraggled humans, a halfling who looked like a recent immigrant from the Talenta Plains, and a surly half-orc with no tongue. Breddan was not a former pirate, but clearly, many of his sailors could not make the same claim.

Despite the strange blend of crewmen, they worked well together. On Breddan's orders, they moved into action as if they shared a common mind and a single will. They were boisterous, to be sure, yelling more than was necessary and chanting songs in Goblin that Janik felt sure would make Dania blush—and it was rarely easy to make Dania blush. In fact, Dania seemed caught up in the spirit of the crew and contributed some soldiers' marching songs in Common that made the goblins screech with laughter. Auftane joined in the high spirits as well, and bellowed as loud as the human crewmembers in Dania's call-and-response chants. Janik was too tired to do more than grin as Dania clambered in the rigging like she'd been born on a ship. Mathas sat beside him, clearly worn out from his day's activities.

"Another departure," Janik said with a sigh. "You ever feel like you're always leaving places and never really arriving anywhere?"

"What do you mean?" Mathas said. "Every journey has its end. We set sail from Sharn and landed in Stormreach. Was that not an arrival?"

"But as soon as we arrived in Stormreach, we starting getting ready to leave. When we get to Mel-Aqat, we'll turn around and leave. We'll come back to Stormreach, go back to Sharn. And then what?"

"Then what, indeed?"

"I don't know," Janik said. "I just wish that I could arrive somewhere and feel like I had come home."

Mathas nodded, smiling as he looked at Dania. Janik turned and watched Dania laughing with Breddan in the bow, saw Auftane slapping the bugbear's back, and he felt the quiet presence of Mathas beside him. In a way, it wasn't the departure or the travel he minded so much, and the presence of his friends was a comfort not too different from the feeling of home. But something was missing—someone was missing, and he could almost feel the brush of her hair against his face.

* * * * * * *

They sailed through the night, the sailors continuing with repairs to ensure *Silverknife* stayed afloat. Breddan dismissed his passengers from further work, urging them to sleep, but Janik and Dania both stayed up, pitching in where they could. Despite his insistence that elves don't sleep, Mathas was exhausted from the day's work and retired to his cabin shortly after they set sail. Auftane said he wanted to help but needed his sleep so his magic could be fresh for the next day.

Their course took them east for at least a week, then north around the tip of the Skyfall Peninsula—the northernmost stretch of the vast continent of Xen'drik, the area most familiar to explorers and adventurers. As the sun rose over the sea ahead, Janik stood at the bow, watching the sky brighten and then the light dancing on the sea like gold leaf. He went below to his bunk just as Auftane was getting up.

The days flew by. Janik enjoyed the night shift at first, when the ship was quiet and the sailors spoke little. He often found himself working beside the mute half-orc, sharing each other's silence. But he woke up earlier in the afternoon each day, talked with his friends at the evening meal, and by the end of the second week was back to a normal schedule of work and sleep. *Silverknife* was just beginning to bend her course southward—she was approaching the Phoenix Basin.

Janik found a new reason to like the daylight hours. Sailors had long told stories of the Phoenix Basin, and the lack of exploration in its waters suggested truth in the tales. Legends said that when the civilization of the giants fell, the entire continent of Xen'drik was torn asunder by the powerful magic the giants had wielded against invading nightmare demons, the quori. Both Shargon's Teeth and the Phoenix Basin were said to have been solid land that sank beneath the waves in that cataclysm. Indeed, as the ship glided over the still waters of the Basin, Janik occasionally caught glimpses of towering structures deep beneath the surface. The water was not deep and some of the ruins might have gouged holes in *Silverknife*'s hull, but the water was so clear that the crew easily steered clear of these hazards.

Janik spent as much time as Breddan would allow—for the hobgoblin remained a driving taskmaster as the journey continued—standing on the prow and gazing down into the deeps.

"It's good to be doing this again," he said one day to Mathas, when the elf joined him at the prow.

"To be out of the city and back at work?" Mathas asked.

"Yes. I've been so. . . inactive these past few years. I mean, I kept busy and told myself I was doing important work. But writing scholarly articles isn't who I am, you know?"

"I know."

"It took a lot to even consider going back to Mel-Aqat. But I'm starting to think about doing more once we're done with this. Sea of Fire, what would it be like to explore these ruins here?"

"Wet," Mathas observed.

"Yes. That's why, as far as I know, nobody has done more than draw sketchy maps of these ruins from above. What must be down there? What secrets of the giants are just waiting for the right team to discover? What treasures there must be!"

"I would think the sea devils of the straits have plundered the ruins already."

"Maybe you're right. Well, maybe I'll ask the sahuagin what they know about this area."

"You always did enjoy an insurmountable challenge, Janik."

"I always surmount them, don't I?"

"Up until about three years ago."

Janik ran his fingers through his hair. "What are you saying? That I let Maija defeat me?"

"Hmm." Mathas chose his words carefully. "I'm saying that it's good to see you facing those challenges again, and looking forward to new ones."

"I haven't given up on Maija."

"You did already, Janik. For three years you sat in your office at Morgrave University assuming that she was lost to you. Maybe you should accept defeat where she is concerned without giving up on life altogether. You need to get past her."

"I will, Mathas. One way or another, when we leave Mel-Aqat this time, that challenge will be over."

"You expect to see her there?"

"Of course not. It's just—well, I keep thinking about what the Keeper of the Silver Flame said, and what you said about it."

"What was that?"

"She told me that what I had lost was still in Mel-Aqat, remember? And you said that it seemed I had lost a great deal. I know I didn't take that well at the time, and I was saying that all the things I had lost weren't to be found in Mel-Aqat. But I might have been wrong."

"You? Impossible. I have a great deal of respect for your scholarly work, Janik." Mathas was smirking.

"And I have a great deal of respect for your wisdom and insight, Mathas. Thank you for telling me the truth about myself, even when I wouldn't listen to you."

"You're welcome."

* * * ☀ * * *

Crossing the Phoenix Basin, they were soon out of sight of land. The bright blue-green water stretched out to the horizon, reflecting the sun in a brilliant wash of dancing light. At night, the Ring of Siberys, the moons, and the constellations were mirrored perfectly in the still water, so it seemed they were sailing through the middle of an endless sky. Autumn turned into winter, though they felt little difference crossing the tropical sea. Each day, the sun rose and set a little farther ahead of them, but the air remained pleasantly warm during the day, turning a little cooler at night and allowing comfortable sleep.

Janik noted the passage of days in his journal, but found little else to record. He fell into a comfortable rhythm of work and rest that did much to keep his mind off Maija and Mel-Aqat. But both haunted his dreams, solidifying his sense that resolution awaited him in the ancient ruins.

The easy rhythm came to a crashing end as the sun rose on their sixth week of travel.

"Sail ho!" the lookout shouted, rousing Janik from a deep sleep. He hurried to the deck and joined several sailors on the poop, peering into the distance behind them. He couldn't see anything, but the lookout—a human so small she looked like an oversized halfling—was still up in the rigging, training her spyglass on the distant ship. "Two masts—can't see anything more yet," she called down.

"What are its colors?" Breddan demanded as he emerged from his cabin and started climbing the rigging.

"Give me a moment, it's gaining slowly. I think—yes, Stormreach, same as ours."

Breddan grunted. "Which means nothing. Any pirate with a shred of sense would hide his colors at this range. All right, everyone, back to your stations! There's nothing to see!"

The sailors obeyed instantly, but Janik noticed he was not the only one who kept stealing glances aft. A sense of dread began gnawing at him throughout the day. As the sky started to redden in the west, he stood on the poop deck again, staring at what had become a speck on the horizon. Mathas stood beside him, Dania on his other side.

"I suppose you two with your elf eyes can see it perfectly," he said, turning his gaze from the ship to his companions for a moment.

"Indeed," Mathas said.

"See what?" Dania feigned ignorance, but her smile betrayed her.

Janik turned his eyes outward again. "Krael's on board. I'm sure of it."

"Of course," Dania said with a sidelong glance at Mathas, "can't you see him there on the foredeck, staring at us with grim determination?" She pointed vaguely. "Look, he's got a crumb in his hair. Slob."

Despite himself, Janik laughed hard. "I needed that."

"I know," Dania said.

"All right, you two," Janik replied, "stop it!"

"I didn't say anything," Mathas protested.

"You know what I mean. So what do we do?" He jerked his head toward the distant ship.

Dania shrugged. "What can we do? He's gaining on us, even though we're riding the same wind. We can't do anything until he's closer. And even then—well, it might just be a race for the last three weeks."

"Three weeks. What if he sails right past us? Gets there ahead of us?"

"Well, then we'll have to make up for it overland."

"We might have an advantage there," Mathas said. "He cannot travel during daylight." Janik gave him a quizzical look.

"Because he's a vampire," Dania explained. "Janik, please don't ever forget he's a vampire."

"I won't. But maybe you experts should give me a refresher lesson about exactly what that means. He drinks blood—I got that. Something about a stake through the heart springs to mind. Hates sunlight, I knew that." He looked at Dania. "So I know you didn't really see him on deck. Oh, and you said he took over your mind."

Mathas arched his eyebrow and Janik realized he had not been present when Dania told that part of her story. Janik bit his tongue, but the elf said nothing and Dania didn't seem to notice.

"He'll be difficult to kill," Dania said. "His body heals incredibly quickly. But even when it reaches its limits, his body just dissolves to mist. I think I told you that's what happened to the shifter vampire the first time we confronted him. The good news is that Krael isn't likely to have his coffin nearby—once he dissolves into mist, he has to get to his coffin to rebuild his body. He can't do that if his coffin's too far away. Even if it's on the ship with him, I doubt he'll bring it across the desert with him."

"You've made quite a study of vampires," Mathas observed.

Dania blushed slightly. "I've been a little single-minded myself this past year and a half."

"Wait," Janik said, his voice rising a little. "Is that what this is all about? You getting your revenge on Krael? So was all that business about some spirit we released just for show? To make me feel like I had a responsibility for the good of the world to come and sort things out?"

"You've got no business getting angry at me, Janik," Dania said, her voice still calm. "That's the same reason you're here. You and I both have personal motives for our involvement, but that doesn't change the purpose of our mission. The Keeper of the Flame has no grudge against Krael, and she wouldn't give us so much of the Church's money just to help us get revenge. Besides, my study of vampires isn't just about revenge."

"Of course it's not," Janik said, a little quieter, but still biting.

"It's not. My encounter with Krael made it very clear to me that vampires in general—and Krael specifically—are a blight on the world. I don't know any greater evil, and it's worth making sacrifices to fight them, to exterminate them if possible."

"So you're going to launch a new crusade, like when the

church wiped out all the werewolves? And if a lot of innocent people get staked in the process, like last time, that's a
worthwhile sacrifice, is that it?"

Mathas had quietly stepped back, out of an awkward
position between Janik and Dania as their argument grew.
Now the two of them were face to face, and Janik punctu-
ated his last point by jabbing a finger at Dania's heart. Dania
drew back and slammed her fist into Janik's chin. Her
gauntlet drew blood, and Janik staggered backward before
sitting down hard on the deck.

"Sea of Fire!" Janik swore, clutching his chin. "That's
what happens when people get in the path of your crusades? I
guess I'm lucky it was just your gauntlet and not your sword—
or your wooden stake."

Despite the fury that clearly raged in her heart, Dania
extended a hand toward his chin but he flinched away. "Hold
still," she said, her voice gentle. This time he let her touch
his wound, and warmth spread from her touch. "I shouldn't
have hit you," she said, though her voice was still sharp with
anger. "I'm sorry."

Janik didn't answer. He looked down and rubbed his
chin, which showed no sign of a cut or bruise. A faint,
pleasant tingle was all that remained. A jumble of memories
bubbled up inside Janik that hurt far more than the punch
had—the feeling of Maija healing his wounds, an earthier
sensation somehow, where Dania's touch was fire. But Maija's
touch had always held more than healing. It was also full of
love, and often passion. Bonded to that thought, competing
with it, was the memory of the night when Dania had held his
chin and kissed him for the first time. He had thought at the
time how different her touch felt from Maija's, but now they
seemed more alike than different.

"When I speak of sacrifice, Janik, I don't mean plowing over innocent people." The angry edge was fading from Dania's voice, but Janik turned away, looking back at the tiny ship far behind them. "You will understand before this is over."

Janik heard her footsteps thumping away across the deck. When he turned around again, Mathas had gone as well. He leaned on the bulwark, staring out at the distant ship until darkness shrouded it from his eyes. Then, for a long time, he watched the moons make their way across both sky and reflective sea.

LANDFALL

CHAPTER 11

I can't see her any more," Dania said, and Janik slammed his fist into the bulwark.

The four companions were perched at the prow, less than a week from the end of their journey across the Phoenix Basin. Two weeks had passed since the ship appeared behind them. A week ago, she had come even with them, though she kept her distance. For all their apprehension, the passing of the other ship had been uneventful. Dania and Mathas could see figures moving on the deck, but even when Dania borrowed the lookout's spyglass, she was unable to identify them.

The other ship never closed within hailing distance or showed any threat. Janik even entertained occasional doubts that Krael was on the other ship—maybe it was a Morgrave or Wayfinder expedition to Mel-Aqat or some other site in the great desert Menechtarun. Maybe she was keeping a safe distance out of fear of pirates. Most of the time, though, he listened to his dread, and as the ship sailed out of sight ahead of them, he felt a crushing defeat.

"How long until we make land?" Janik asked no one in particular.

"I just checked with Breddan," Auftane answered. "We'll probably wake up on the fourth day from now in sight of land, and once we choose our harbor, we should drop anchor by midday."

"And how much faster is Krael going?"

"Well, it took him two weeks to gain about twenty miles on us," Auftane said, furrowing his brow in concentration. "So he'll probably make landfall sometime during the night, just before we arrive."

"So his head start will depend on how much darkness he still has once he lands," Janik said. "If he gets to shore only a little before dawn and he needs to stop, then we could easily catch up and pass him in our first day's travel."

"Assuming we get to shore well before sundown," Dania said.

"And passing him might not be that simple," Mathas said. "If he has soldiers with him, they could set up patrols around their camp. We would have to give it a wide berth to avoid them."

"And are you vampire experts sure he can't travel during daylight?" Janik said, looking from Dania to Mathas.

"I'm not sure of anything," Dania said, even as Mathas shook his head.

"No?" Janik said, his eyebrows raised.

"He has enough people with him to crew a ship," Mathas said. "In theory—"

"That's enough people to carry his coffin through the jungle?" Janik said.

"If not his coffin, then maybe an urn holding his mist form—or something," Dania said.

"But the living ones need to rest, too," Auftane pointed out. "They can't travel night and day."

"But it's possible they could take the lead early on and keep it," Janik said. "That's exactly what I didn't want to hear."

"You worry too much, Janik," Dania said, putting a hand on his shoulder. "We can't know how it will turn out until we're there. Let's concentrate on getting to shore and getting to Mel-Aqat as quickly as we can."

"You're right," Janik said. He sighed, then smiled. "As much as it pains me to admit it."

A playful push from Dania sent Janik off balance, and he stumbled a few steps, laughing.

● ● ● ◉ ● ● ●

The sun rose on the fourth day and no one needed the lookout to point out the ship's masts rising in the distance ahead of them—or the land rising gently from the water ahead of her. The ship's sails were furled, and even Dania and Mathas could see no one moving on deck. A rocky beach stretched out beyond the ship, giving way to a line of low bluffs crowned with dry, brown scrub.

Janik spent the morning on the prow, unable to eat, watching the miles between them and the shore diminish with agonizing slowness. His stomach was clenched in a knot—the reality was sinking in at last that he was returning to Mel-Aqat. Last time they had passed this very stretch of coast, but had continued farther to the south, making land at the edge of the desert. He couldn't say he remembered this place, but it was familiar—its shape, its looming shore, the sense of untamed wilderness, and the heat weighing on him. Just for a moment, he was sure he saw something large and predatory lumbering along the top of the bluffs, solidifying that sense of utter wildness. Stormreach, in many ways, felt like just another city, though the hill giants working with the city watch were exotic—not something you'd see in Sharn, let alone Fairhaven. But this was Xen'drik, and everything Janik associated with it. Ahead lay new land to be discovered . . . and one old defeat he had to face again.

Breddan approached the shore slowly. He didn't have charts to show the dangers that might lie in the water—Janik doubted such charts existed—and the wash of sand from the beach ahead clouded the water so they couldn't see any reefs, rocks, or sandbars that might obstruct their path or tear the hull. Breddan also tried to avoid getting too close to the other ship, which the lookout had identified as *Hope's Endeavor*.

How Krael had managed to leave Stormreach on that ship was a mystery to them all. Janik had expected the Stormreach watch to keep a close eye on that ship above all else, but it was possible that Krael and his allies were strong enough to fight their way onto the ship and sail out of the harbor. Neither the lookout nor Mathas and Dania, with their sharp elf eyes, could see any sign of life aboard that ship, but that only made the crew of the *Silverknife* more uneasy about getting close to it.

About half a mile from land and roughly even with *Hope's Endeavor*, Breddan declared that they would go no closer, and gave the order to drop anchor. Dania and Auftane had been getting the keelboat ready to launch, moving all their supplies onto it and checking it for any damage it might have sustained.

"We part ways here, Janik Martell," Breddan said, joining Janik on the prow.

"Yes, this is it," Janik replied. "I am most grateful for your work, Breddan Omaar." He shifted to the Goblin tongue and clasped his fist to his chest. "Your ancestors' swords were keen and strong," he said with a small bow.

Breddan returned the gesture and the Goblin phrase, then added in Common, "I pray that the Silver Flame will bless and guard the rest of your journey."

"Thank you," Janik said stiffly. "I hope that your return journey to Stormreach is completely uneventful, and that you find more work before your payment for this trip is completely exhausted."

"Thank you, Janik Martell," Breddan said. "I feel as though this is the beginning of a new time in my life, when work will not be so hard to find. The Silver Flame smiles on me for helping you—I feel it in my heart."

"I hope you are right, Breddan. You're a good man, and you deserve better than you've had so far."

"Janik!" Dania's voice came from the main deck. "We're ready!"

"Goodbye," Janik said, extending his hand.

"Goodbye, Janik." Breddan clasped his hand firmly and shook it. "I will take my leave of your companions as well."

They walked together off the forecastle to where Dania, Mathas, and Auftane stood, along with many members of Breddan's crew. Breddan shook Auftane's hand vigorously, bowed deeply to Mathas, and extended a hand to Dania—which she brushed aside as she threw her arms around him. The reddish skin of the hobgoblin's face deepened to purple, but he returned her embrace. The rest of the gathered crew wished them well—even the mute half-orc clapped Janik warmly on the shoulder. They lowered the keelboat into the water, climbed down into it, and began to paddle their way slowly to the shore.

"The wilds of Xen'drik," Auftane said quietly, wonder in

his voice. "I can't believe we're really here."

"I can't believe we're back," Janik said.

"Have you been into the wilderness before, Auftane?" Dania asked, peering closely at the dwarf. "You grew up in Stormreach, right?"

"I did, but I'm as much a child of the city as you can be in a small city like Stormreach. We used to dare each other to go into the uninhabited ruins around Stormreach, but that's as much as I've ever seen of Xen'drik's wonders. I've traveled quite a bit in Khorvaire, of course, but I've stuck mostly to the cities. Remember, we're farther from Stormreach now than we were in Sharn, if I'm not mistaken."

"Are we really?" Dania exclaimed.

Janik pulled his rough map from his coat and measured with his fingers. "A little bit, yes," he said. "Huh. I never thought about that."

"Which is another way of saying we're more than twice as far from civilization as we were in Stormreach," Mathas said with a scowl, and the others all laughed.

"So the cities of Khorvaire were like my neighborhood," Auftane continued. "This is the wilderness!"

"That's right," Janik said, his voice suddenly serious. "It doesn't get more wild than this, and we all need to remember that. This is not the city, where danger is predictable and lurks in dark alleys. Some of the animals here will try to eat us. Some things lurk here that should not exist in a sane world, and they'll try to do worse than that. Be on your guard, starting now."

As if emphasizing Janik's point, a large, smooth rock jutting just above the water suddenly began to rise. Water streamed down a hulking, crustacean form and two huge claws reached out toward the keelboat.

"In case you thought I was exaggerating," Janik muttered, his sword springing into his hand. "Dania, get us to shore! We can't let this thing tip us."

"What is that?" To his credit, Auftane sounded genuinely curious rather than panicked, and he gripped his huge mace. "What's the best way to kill it?"

"It's a chewer," Dania said, pulling hard on the oar while keeping a close eye on the creature.

"Chuul," Mathas corrected, thrusting his hand toward the creature and sending a blast of frigid cold toward it. It slowed momentarily as the water pouring off its shell crystallized into ice, but the thing kept coming, spraying tiny shards of ice around it.

"Stay out of its claws!" Dania shouted.

"I could have guessed that," Auftane said, and then the creature was upon them. Auftane swung his weapon, smashing it into one of the chuul's claws. Janik drove his blade under the carapace just above the other claw, drawing a gout of greenish blood. Above them, a mass of slimy tentacles writhed like a nest of worms, dripping thick slime into their boat. Dania kept rowing and they surged forward, but the creature leaped toward them again, landing on an oar and snapping it.

"I guess I'm done rowing," Dania said as she drew her sword. The chuul was behind the boat where only Dania could reach it, and its momentum brought its tentacled head down within her reach. In a flash, she cut a gash just above the tentacles, spraying herself with a mix of blood, slime, and seawater.

"Hold still a second, Dania," Auftane said just behind her. She felt his hand on her shoulder.

"Hold still?" she shouted, dodging to her right as the

chuul's claws came down on either side of her. Even as she dodged, she felt a surge of strength and knew Auftane had augmented her armor with his magic.

Mathas reached out to touch Janik's sword. "It will cut deeper," whispered the elf, and he patted Janik's shoulder. "Good luck." Janik gave Mathas an incredulous look and then turned to the chuul.

The creature slammed the rear of the keelboat, lifting the prow out of the water and propelling it forward a short distance, where it plowed into a sandbar, turned sideways, and lodged firmly. Janik jumped out of the boat, landing in water about knee-deep. He splashed toward the chuul, shouting in a vain attempt to frighten the monster away.

He got the creature's attention and it edged along the boat to reach him, giving both Dania and Auftane the chance to land more blows on its back. Auftane managed a solid blow, crushing the hard shell on its back and causing blood to ooze freely around it. The creature turned away from Janik and grabbed Auftane in one of its claws, lifting him into the air. Janik jumped forward and drove his sword toward the chuul's underbelly as it raised both claws, but its belly was as heavily plated as its back, and his sword glanced aside.

The chuul raised Auftane toward the writhing mass of tentacles at its head, and they twisted like giant, slime-covered worms around his limbs, neck, and torso. The dwarf's dark skin paled as the slime penetrated his skin, sending a paralytic venom into his muscles. As Janik jabbed in vain at the creature's legs, the dwarf struggled and then froze. The tentacles drew him closer, and beyond Auftane's stiff body, Janik could see a set of mandibles beginning to open and close in anticipation of tasting the dwarf's flesh.

Janik thrashed with his sword, hoping to distract the

chuul again, but he couldn't land a solid blow from where he stood.

"For the Flame!" Dania's cry turned Janik's head, and he saw her leap from the keelboat onto the creature's back. She had sheathed her sword and pulled out a dagger, and as she landed on the thing's shell, she found a spot to drive the thin blade between the armored plates, drawing a fresh gout of blood. Janik saw a stream of green join the water dripping from the chuul's mouth as the thing's mandibles started tearing at Auftane's flesh.

"Hold on, Auftane!" she called out. "I'm coming for you!" Dodging the chuul's claws as it reached over its back toward her, she scrambled to the tentacles that held Auftane and started hacking at them with her dagger. Each slash of the small blade sliced a few tentacles, cutting some off and making others recoil, loosening their hold on the dwarf. As Janik watched from below Auftane, fell into the water with a splash that drenched Janik.

Janik's relief at seeing Auftane freed disappeared in an instant when he realized that the paralyzed dwarf was lying still, completely submerged in the water, right between the chuul's front limbs. Carefully, Janik advanced, on guard against the creature's pincers, which flailed wildly in the air.

Then the claws stopped flailing and Janik dove forward to grab Auftane and pull him out of the water. The dwarf wasn't moving, but Janik could tell he was breathing properly. Janik looked up at the chuul just as a cluster of glowing blue bolts of magical energy sped over his head and into the creature's carapace. Mathas had chosen his spell carefully, for Dania was now wrapped in the creature's tentacles.

She was not yet paralyzed, and she struggled fiercely, prying tentacles off with one hand as she slashed with the dagger in her other hand. The pincers that had caught her had left ugly marks—the right side of her armor was torn open and Janik could see blood in it—and the chuul was using both pincers in a frantic attempt to keep hold of her.

Janik started to circle the beast, looking for the right place to drive his sword for a killing blow. He kept one eye on Dania to make sure she was still fighting—and still occupying the chuul's attention. Mathas cast another spell, not enough to distract the creature from Dania.

Maybe this will finish it, Janik thought as he plunged his sword deep into the joint where the chuul's rear leg joined its body. The creature gave a bizarre howling screech and Janik wrenched the sword hard, hoping to hit some vital organ inside its monstrous body.

Dania took advantage of the creature's pain to plunge her dagger into its tiny eye, causing it to squeal. This time, the sound was weak and short, and the chuul's legs gave out and its body dropped into the water, splashing Janik with water, green blood, and slime.

Janik slogged to the boat while Dania extricated herself from the tentacles and rushed over to check on Auftane. Janik watched as she crouched beside the dwarf, cradling his cheek in her palm. As if in response to her touch, the dwarf's frozen face seemed to melt. He moved one stiff hand to his chest, pounding his fist against his breastbone as he coughed out a mouthful of water. He took a deep, uneven breath and smiled up at Dania.

"You are a true paladin," he said hoarsely. "Quite a hero."

"Nonsense," Dania said. "Are you badly hurt?"

Auftane started to get to his feet, but the dwarf struggled badly. "I'm all ri . . . ouch!" He touched one hand gingerly to his side, where the chuul's mandibles had torn his skin.

"Here, let me have a look at that," Dania said, reaching toward him.

"No," the dwarf replied, reaching for a wand tucked in his belt. "I can take care of myself. You've got a nasty wound of your own, there." He gestured toward Dania's own torn side.

Mathas called down from the boat. "Why don't you all come up here before anything else attacks? There could be more chuuls in the water, Sovereigns forbid."

Janik watched as Dania helped Auftane climb onto the boat. Mathas reached over the side to help pull him up as Dania pushed from below. Then Dania turned to Janik, ready to help hoist him up as well.

"Are you hurt, Janik?" she asked, scanning him from head to boot.

"No, just wet."

"Good," Dania said, helping hoist Janik so he could reach Mathas's outstretched hand. She climbed up easily behind him.

"So what's this I hear about the legendary fortitude of the dwarves?" Janik said, smiling at Auftane.

The dwarf shuddered. "I guess it's nothing compared to the protection of the Silver Flame," he said, nodding toward Dania. "Or maybe all the slime rubbed off on me." He brushed idly at the sleeves of his coat, and the others laughed.

"That's it, Auftane," Dania said, "you took all the slime with you, so I was safe." Smiling, she laid a hand on her torn side, bathing it in warm silver light as the flesh knit itself together. Remembering the wand in his hand, Auftane did the same to his own wounds.

Janik shook his head. "I don't know, Mathas," he said. "Looks like we're lacking in some key survival skills that these two possess. Ever consider taking up the path of the artificer?"

"I'm more likely to finally listen to Aureon's voice nagging at the back of my mind and take up the cleric's call," Mathas replied seriously.

* * * * ◉ * * *

Dania retrieved a new oar from the hold and managed to work the boat free of the sandbar. As she rowed the rest of the way to shore, they watched over the stern as Breddan's ship disappeared into the haze. No more chuuls reared up from the water, to their great relief. They found a small inlet and pulled the keelboat in, then tied it to a stunted tree leaning over the water.

"Let me look around a bit before we start unloading supplies," Janik said. "I don't want to leave the boat right outside a rampager's lair and come back in four months to find it reduced to splinters."

"A lot can happen in four months," Dania said. "It's hard to imagine we'll find it intact regardless."

"That might be true, but remember, we're not leaving it in the harbor at Stormreach unguarded," Janik answered. "The dangers around here are likely to be wild animals, or monsters that might as well be wild animals. The animals will smell us on it and leave it alone, assuming we don't leave food lying around that they'll smell. The monsters might smell us on it and think it's food, and that's the risk I want to minimize." He jumped off the boat to the bank of the inlet, and crouched to look at the soft earth.

"What about Krael?" Auftane asked.

"If he hangs back to wreck our boat after we leave it here, we'll have some comfort," Dania said. "At least we'll be ahead of him."

"Any sign of his passage there, Janik?" Mathas called out.

"Not here, no. I don't see any sign of big beasts around here, either. I'm going to look around more—see if I can find where Krael came ashore and which way he went."

"Let me come with you," Auftane said.

"All right—come on. Dania and Mathas, stay with the boat." He thought for a moment. "You could start loading our packs for the long walk, if you want."

"Will do," Dania called as Auftane jumped off the boat, landing hard on the bank. Janik and the dwarf started walking toward the beach.

"Thank you for pulling me out of the water," Auftane said as they started climbing a dune.

"Of course."

"You put me in a position where I could see Dania fighting the thing, but I couldn't see you. Couldn't move my eyes, you know."

"I know. That happened to me the last time we fought one of those things."

"It paralyzed you? What happened?"

"Same thing that happened to you. Dania cut me out."

"She is quite a warrior," Auftane said, his admiration clear in his voice. "Empowered by the Silver Flame, I suppose."

"No, she's always been quite a warrior," Janik said. "Since long before she started talking about the Silver Flame all the time. There's Krael's ship." They crested the dune and could see the masts and furled sails of *Hope's Endeavor*. The decks seemed deserted. Scanning the shore nearby, they couldn't see any sign of Krael or his troops. "I don't see anyone, do you?"

"No."

"Let's head that way." He pointed toward an area of shore nearest to Krael's ship. "We'll look for tracks, see if we can figure out what they're doing." They made their way slowly up and down the dunes that fronted the beach.

"Dania was in the army in the Last War?" Auftane asked, picking up their conversation.

"Yes. She's about a finger's breadth away from one of those soldiers you read about in the chronicles, who endured so much in the war that they lose their grip on reality. Come to think of it, maybe less than a finger's breadth, now that she's following the Silver Flame."

"I don't know. She seems quite sane to me."

"I'm not sure I can call it sane when she jumps on the back of a chuul, brandishing only a dagger."

"I call it heroic."

"I suppose. But that doesn't make it any less crazy."

"You didn't fight in the war?"

"Not in the regular army, and not on the big battlefields. But the King's Dark Lanterns, like the Order of the Emerald Claw and the Royal Eyes of Aundair, are an army in their own right. The battles I fought might have been much smaller, but sometimes I've thought that the armies clashing on the battlefield are just a distraction from the spies and guerillas who are fighting the real war."

"An interesting theory," Auftane said, nodding.

"What about you, Auftane? What did you do during the war?"

"Mostly I avoided it, I'm embarrassed to say."

"Nothing to be embarrassed about," Janik said. "It's what any really sane person would do."

"Dania volunteered, didn't she? She said that her father could have kept her out of the army."

"Yes. Proof, I suppose, that she wasn't quite sane even before the war." Janik pointed to marks in the sand where a small launch had obviously been pulled out of the water. "Look, here's where they came ashore," he said. "Let's find that boat."

They followed the trench in the sand to where it curved between two dunes. Janik held up his hand to stop Auftane and looked around, scanning the tops of the dunes. Sure enough, he saw the top of a helmet glinting in the sun. Just as he silently pointed it out to Auftane, a shout came from the crest of the dune. "Now!"

Two crossbow bolts sprayed sand right where Janik had been standing, and a third one glanced off Auftane's armor as he tried to see what Janik was pointing at. Janik was already running up the dune, hoping to close with the crossbowmen before they could reload. Auftane hurried after him, sinking into the sand with each step.

Janik crested the dune and found himself toe to toe with three soldiers wearing the bright green symbol of the Emerald Claw on their tabards. Two were pointing crossbows at him, while the third was already swinging a flail toward his head. He knocked one crossbow aside just as the bolt flew free, sending the shot wild. The other bolt bit into his upper arm, but fell out as Janik drove his sword hard into the belly of the soldier swinging the flail. The flail's momentum carried it into Janik's shoulder, but the strength behind it had failed. Clutching his stomach, the man with the flail sank to the ground.

Janik stepped back, trying to keep the other two soldiers in front of him as they dropped their crossbows in the sand and drew their flails. Out of the corner of his eye, he noticed another soldier on the next dune, pointing a crossbow behind Janik—at Auftane, he assumed.

All right, he thought, three more, one down. That's not too bad.

He smiled as he saw the soldier on the next dune fall to the ground, one of Auftane's crossbow bolts sticking out of his throat. Two and two, he thought.

"What did you do to make Krael hate you so much?" he said, seeing a nervous glance pass between the two who faced him. "Or did you figure that staying behind and watching the boat for four months would be the easy job?"

The soldiers—a man and a woman—didn't respond. Swinging their flails menacingly, they tried to maneuver to flank Janik, but he kept moving to keep them in front of him. The longer he could keep them occupied, he figured, the more likely Auftane would even the odds.

Just as that thought crossed his mind, Auftane crested the dune, running at the nearest soldier with his mace drawn back over his shoulder. Janik waited, then just as Auftane caught the soldier's attention, he leaped at her. His weapon and Auftane's connected at the same time, and the woman sprawled in a hollow of wet, red sand.

The other soldier howled in anger and ran at Janik. Janik dodged—and managed to put his back between the flail and his head. The blow knocked the wind out of him and knocked him to the ground, but Auftane jumped over him and beat the soldier back. The man was in a fury, swinging his flail so fast Janik could barely tell where the head of the weapon was. Janik scrambled to his feet again, fighting to catch his breath. The soldier regained the offensive and was pushing Auftane back.

"Watch your step, Auftane!" Janik called out, but too late—the dwarf stepped backward and tripped on the fallen soldier. He landed hard on his back, his legs draped over the dead woman, her eyes staring accusingly at him. Janik sprang at the last soldier and slid the point of his sword between the back of his helmet and the shoulder plates of his armor, killing him instantly. The man landed on top of Auftane.

Auftane extricated himself from the dead soldiers, leaving the two of them in a grisly heap. Janik found himself wondering if the two had been lovers, and he was briefly tempted to leave them together like that, intimately entwined in death as he supposed they had been in life. But as he looked around and his eyes fell on the boat nestled between the dunes, he thought of a more fitting end for them.

"We'll load the four of them on the boat," he said to Auftane.

The dwarf was still catching his breath, but he shot a quizzical look at Janik.

"Then we'll set the boat on fire and push it out to sea," Janik continued. "And with any luck, it'll hit their ship and set it on fire as well. But really, we're just giving these four a fitting funeral."

"We'll keep them from continuing to serve Karrnath as zombies, too," Auftane said.

"Exactly." Janik grabbed the arm of the dead man and started to drag him down the dune toward the boat.

CHAPTER 12

Janik and Auftane stood at the crest of a dune, watching the blazing boat drift out to sea. It missed the anchored ship, to Janik's dismay, but served its other purposes. Janik knew that Dania wouldn't approve of simply hacking a hole in the boat's hull, so this let them get rid of the boat without resorting to simple sabotage. It also provided the dead soldiers with a dignified end, rather than leaving them to rot on the beach and be picked apart by crabs.

"Now to find Krael and the rest of his soldiers," Janik said as the blazing boat floated out past the ship.

"We're not going to follow them all the way to their camp and fight them alone, are we?"

"No. All I need is to see some clear tracks, and I should be able to get a sense of how long they've been gone. With any sense of the land, I can figure out what course they're taking. Once we get that, we can meet up with the others and plan our own course." He started back down the dune to the place where the boat had been stowed.

"If you don't mind my saying so, you and Dania have

an . . . interesting relationship."

Janik grunted.

"You care a lot about each other."

"You are the most inquisitive dwarf I've ever known. Aren't your people supposed to be more, I don't know, taciturn?"

"I suppose I've never been an exemplar of my race," Auftane said, looking away. "I'm sorry if I've pried."

"No, it's all right, Auftane. Everyone else on this trip knows all about it, and you've been with us all these months and held your tongue this long. You've got a right to understand. Especially since she and I seem to have such a tendency to blow up at each other."

Janik walked in silence for some time. Auftane chewed on his lip, waiting for Janik to answer the question.

"Maija and I were married just before we all took our first trip to Xen'drik, fifteen years ago. I had been in love with her for years, since long before she introduced me to Dania. So Dania was always just a good friend—a very good friend, even more than Mathas, and in some ways, more than Maija. At least that's how I looked at our relationship. I always had Maija, my true love, my wife, and I had a wonderful friendship with Dania. The best of both worlds, you might say.

"Well, Dania's perspective is a little different. She's a couple years older than I am, but she's never been married, she's never really had anyone—anyone except this group of friends and allies. I get the sense that when she was in the army, she felt like she needed to be tougher than all the men in her unit, and that put off any possible suitors. Plus, she comes from a noble family, which almost certainly was not true of her comrades-at-arms. Anyway, when I met her, she'd never really been in love or had a lover.

"Look, there are some tracks." They had reached the place

where the boat had been hidden, and Janik pointed at the sand nearby. He led Auftane to the spot and knelt down to examine the tracks more closely. After a moment, he got to his feet. "Let's follow them a little way. I want to see where the tracks go into the scrub—that'll make it easier to judge how old they are."

Janik led Auftane around the dune and farther inland, then picked up his story where he left off. "So it sounds bad for me to say this, but Dania pretty much fell in love with me as soon as Maija introduced us. It was terribly awkward for her, because Maija was probably her best friend up to that point. And to her credit, she hid it quite well. I don't think Maija or I ever knew until she told me later." Janik heaved a sigh. "So after our first expedition to Mel-Aqat . . . you know what happened there?"

"I think I've pieced together most of the story," Auftane said. "Maija betrayed you to Krael and left with him?"

"I took that pretty hard. Sea of Fire, we all did, Mathas and Dania, too. I guess it was natural for me to look for comfort from my best friend, and it was natural for her finally to confess the love she'd kept inside for twelve years. But what we did—well, it was a mistake."

"You became lovers?"

"Exactly. My feelings for Maija didn't change—they still haven't. And when we got back to Sharn, well, I just sort of disappeared. I don't think she took that very well. Eventually she left Sharn and went to Karrnath. So the first time I saw her since we got back was just before we started this expedition. Which might explain why there was some tension between us at the start of the trip."

"Right," Auftane said. "Good thing that tension is completely dissipated now."

"Right," Janik said through clenched teeth.

By the time Janik and Auftane returned to the keelboat, Dania and Mathas had loaded the supplies for the overland journey. Four heavy backpacks were piled on the bank beside the boat. They had seen no sign of monsters or Emerald Claw agents. Janik related the story of finding the boat and killing its defenders, and explained what they had done with the boat—and the bodies of their foes—after the fight.

"I hardly expect they'd give us the same consideration," Mathas said.

"No," Janik said. "If Krael ever gets the upper hand on us, I fully expect to end up as a zombie marching at his command."

"If not a vampire," Dania said.

Janik scowled. "Promise you'll kill me before that happens."

"I promise," Dania said, without a hint of a smile. "I'm sure you'd do the same for me."

Auftane interjected, "We also figured out which way they went into the plains—or Janik did, right?"

Janik scowled briefly at Dania before responding. "Right," he said. "There's a seasonal riverbed running parallel to this inlet. They started following it eastward."

"How long ago?" Dania asked.

"During the night, as we expected. It's hard to say for sure, especially since everything's so dry once you get away from the beach, but I'd guess they set out about eight or ten hours ago."

"What's your recommendation, Janik?"

Janik ran his hands through his hair, thinking for a moment. "I think we should follow this inlet east—chances are it turns into another dry riverbed pretty soon."

"Can't your map tell us that?" Auftane asked.

"My map is my best attempt to sketch the shoreline as we rowed along it last time. No other maps of this area exist, unfortunately. Anyway, we've got a good six hours until nightfall, and I don't think they could have traveled more than four hours before dawn. If they stopped and camped at dawn, we'll pass them—hopefully at a good distance, assuming the riverbeds run parallel for a while and don't meet up right away."

"It's a plan," Dania said.

"Not to say it's a good plan," Janik said, frowning. "But I guess it's the best we have." He sighed heavily as he bent to pick up his pack, and grunted as he settled it on his shoulders. The others did the same, and with a last look at the keelboat—which Dania and Mathas had tried to cover with loose foliage—Janik led the way eastward along the inlet.

Just as he had predicted, the inlet quickly dried up into a seasonal riverbed. While Khorvaire was enjoying its summer and autumn, the winds off the ocean would bring endless rain to this part of Xen'drik, and these riverbeds would churn with water rushing to the sea. Now, in Khorvaire's midwinter, the beds were dry as bone, the shrubs on their banks parched and dry.

The group walked mostly along the bottom of the riverbed, but Janik climbed the bank every half-hour or so to survey the surrounding plain. It was easy to see how the Wasting Plain had acquired its name: nothing grew that seemed at all vibrant or healthy. Blackened grasses stood in thick clumps above a layer of brown thatch that was occasionally interrupted by more of the same dry shrubs that dotted the riverbanks. The sky was obscured by a brownish haze that hung over the ground, as if the earth were emitting some vile gas that clouded the air.

After about four hours of trudging along the dry bed, another branch joined it from the left. Janik presumed it was the route that Krael's party had followed, and after a short time scanning the ground, he spotted sure signs that his group was now following the trail of the Emerald Claw force.

Janik was uneasy. "If I'm right," he said, "and they traveled about four hours before the sun came up and they were forced to make camp, then we could stumble on their camp around the next bend." He cast his gaze at the banks above, alert for guards.

"Right," Dania said. "As long as we're following their path, there's no easy way for us to get past them. That could mean they're in the lead all the way to Mel-Aqat."

"Unless we find their camp and attack first," Auftane said.

"There's too many of them," Janik said, shaking his head.

"I'm not convinced of that," Auftane retorted. "The two of us took four of them down and barely broke a sweat."

"That's a bit of an exaggeration," Janik said. "I was sweating pretty hard, and my back is still sore from where that flail hit me. Besides, four is a lot different from fourteen—or twenty, or thirty. I'm not sure how many they have."

"Don't forget Krael," Dania muttered.

"I'm not forgetting Krael," Janik shot back, "or that warforged friend of his. We could probably handle fourteen of his soldiers, but they'd distract us from the real threat. No, I don't think we can risk attacking them."

"Won't we have to deal with them at some point?" Auftane said. "Whether it's here or at Mel-Aqat, sooner or later we'll have to face them, won't we?"

"No doubt," Janik said, his face breaking into a grin. "But the later we do it, the more likely the hazards of the journey will whittle their numbers down."

"I don't like the sound of that," Auftane said. "What if the journey whittles our numbers down?"

"So far, we're four bodies up on them," Janik pointed out. "And as much as I hate having them ahead of us, they'll be more likely to stumble into danger than we will."

Mathas broke his silence. "I'd rather have them ahead of us than behind us. They won't have any qualms about attacking our camp."

"You're right, Mathas," Janik said. "So we'll keep traveling until dark. But if we see their camp, we back off, keep our distance. And we won't try to pass them."

"Again, a plan," Dania said.

The sun followed its westward course as Janik led the way east. By the time the sky turned red, they still had not seen any sign of a camp. Janik began to worry that Krael had found some way for his soldiers to carry him on their march during daylight, as Mathas and Dania had speculated. The red light faded from the sky and darkness crept up the riverbed to cover them. They made their way slowly along the riverbed a little longer, until two of the larger moons rose up before them in the sky, just past full, large and bright enough to cast faint shadows on the ground.

Janik pushed them a little farther, but by the time the moons had fully cleared the horizon, his friends were lagging.

"Be kind to an old man, Janik," Mathas groaned at last. "We've had well more than a full day of travel. I need rest."

"But elves don't sleep, Mathas," Janik said.

Mathas didn't respond, but stopped walking. Glancing

around, he set down his pack in a smooth, clear area of the riverbed and rummaged in his pouches.

"What is he doing?" Auftane asked Janik.

"Setting up camp."

"Camp? What's he going to do, conjure us a campfire?"

Janik grinned. "You have to understand, Auftane. You described yourself as a child of the city—well, you're a wild animal next to Mathas."

Mathas had begun gesturing and chanting, and unseen forces began to move around them.

"Coming to Xen'drik is like being thrown in prison for Mathas," Janik continued. "But he tries to make the best of a bad deal."

"I'll gather some fuel for a fire," Dania said, smiling at the look of bewilderment on the dwarf's face.

"So he's not conjuring a campfire?"

"No, we'll make that ourselves," Janik said. "But 'campfire' never seems like the right word."

Dania climbed the bank to gather woody brush, while Janik and Auftane watched Mathas cast his long spell. Janik continued to smile at Auftane's open-mouthed wonderment.

A short time later, a large, sturdy cottage made of sod stood before Mathas. He pushed the door open and invited his friends inside.

Seeing Auftane's face, he said, "What's the matter? Haven't you ever seen a magical shelter before?"

Auftane shook his head.

"Strange," Mathas said, frowning. "Your knowledge of magic is otherwise quite impressive."

"Oh, I've heard of the spell," Auftane said, "and I've read about it, but I've never actually seen one. Not much call for them in the city, is there?"

"Maybe not," Janik said, "but House Ghallanda makes them even in the middle of Sharn once in a while. They tend to blend in with the towers."

Auftane shook his head and stepped inside the cottage. Eight bunks lined the side walls, eight stools surrounded a trestle table, and a small writing desk stood near the door. Opposite the door, a fireplace stood empty, but Dania squeezed in past Auftane to set a load of branches in it, then started working on setting it alight.

Mathas groaned as he settled himself into one of the bunks. "Miserable, as always," he said. "Someday, we'll really camp in style. We'll walk through a shimmering portal into an extradimensional space appointed like a mansion."

"So do you conjure food for us as well?" Auftane asked, clearly impressed.

"What do you think is in that pack on your back?" Mathas said. "No, for cooking, I rely on—" he broke off.

"Hmm?"

"Oh." Mathas looked uncomfortable. "Well, you see, Maija was quite a cook. I confess I hadn't even thought about preparing our food."

"I'll take care of it," Janik said, but Mathas looked pained.

"I don't suppose you cook, Auftane?"

"Oh, I've had dwarf cooking," Janik groaned. "Let me handle it."

"Actually, I'm quite a good cook," Auftane protested. "We'll do it together, Janik. You can steer me away from anything that doesn't appeal to you."

Mathas caught Auftane's eye and whispered, "Don't listen to him!" The look on his face made his opinion of Janik's cooking skills quite clear.

Dania had a fire raging, and she stepped toward the door again. "I'll see if I can get us some fresh meat."

"Careful out there, Dania," Janik called after her.

❂ ❂ ❂ ◉ ❂ ❂ ❂

An hour later, they had devoured a pair of scrawny rabbits and were asleep in the hard bunks. Mathas assured them that the magic of the shelter would alert him if anyone tried to enter, but they all slept fitfully, waking at any sound outside. A few times, Dania rolled quietly out of her bunk and stepped to the door, sword in hand. One time she caught sight of a large, crouching form—a plains lion, she guessed—clearly silhouetted against the moonlit sky, but it stalked quickly away from the cottage. She never saw any sign of Krael or his soldiers.

Janik roused them all early to start the day's travel, eating jerky and dried fruit as they walked. With a wave of Mathas's hand, the sod hut melted into the earth behind them. As the morning mist burned off, Janik led them up the side of the riverbed to look around and get their bearings.

He pointed to a small range of mountains far in the southeast, purple and white against the clear blue sky. "Those are the Sun Pillars," he said. "East of them are the Fangs of Angarak—the main mountain range at the eastern edge of the desert. So that's our gateway—we'll go past the Sun Pillars on the north, then turn south between the mountain ranges and enter Menechtarun."

Dania shaded her eyes against the morning sun to gaze across the plain before them. "Do you think we can just follow this riverbed all the way?"

"Probably," Janik said. "I expect that most of the rain falls on the mountains and flows down this way. As long as it doesn't rain now—and it shouldn't, since it's not the season for it—this should be as good as a road."

"And a good thing, too," Auftane commented, surveying the nearby plain. "I wouldn't want to cut our way through all these brambles."

"Right," Janik said, leading them down into the riverbed.

As the day went by, Janik stopped frequently to kneel on the ground and look for tracks, and his curses grew increasingly vitriolic with each passing hour.

"They're getting farther and farther ahead of us," he said around midday. "I haven't seen any sign of a camp—it looks like they marched through the night and all day yesterday as well."

"What's Krael going to do, march them to death?" Auftane said.

"Quite possibly," Dania said grimly.

Janik urged them to keep walking after the sun had set and the moons had risen in the sky, but he held little hope of catching up to Krael. Exhausted, they repeated the previous night's routine, collapsing into the hard bunks after a simple meal.

The days wore into a week. In the soft earth of the riverbed, the tracks of Krael's party were easy to follow, but clearly, the tracks were getting older. Worse, as the eighth day dawned, the sky did not lighten as it had on other mornings. Climbing to the crest of the bank again, Janik looked to the southeast as he did at the start of every day—and saw a mass of gray clouds towering in the distance, near the Sun Pillars, shrouding the morning sun.

"If I didn't know better," he muttered to himself, "I'd say it looks like rain."

Janik hurried them along in the riverbed, but he kept

their course near the southern bank. Around midday, his caution was rewarded. He heard the rumble of an approaching flood in time to guide them up over the bank, where they stood and watched the torrent sweep down the riverbed, a mantle of branches, dry brush, and other debris draped over its head.

"What is the rainy season in this part of the world?" Dania said.

"Lharvion to Sypheros," Auftane said blankly, staring at the water.

"Midsummer to mid-autumn," Janik said, shaking his head. "It should have been over three months ago. I admit I don't know this area as well as the northern peninsula, but I was almost sure—"

"You were right," Mathas said. He was not watching the water raging past them, but gazing to the southeast. "This is not a natural storm."

"From bad to worse," said Janik. "Could it be Krael, trying to shake us off his trail?"

"It could be anything," Mathas said. "Could be Krael, could be one of the hundreds of random magical effects left over from the end of the Age of Giants. It could be an elemental storming in the mountains, or even a giant."

"Whatever it is, it's damned inconvenient." Janik kicked a loose stone into the churning water. "It means we're traveling on the riverbank now, which means scrub and brambles. It also means we're more visible, without the cover of the banks on either side."

"Maybe," Dania said, "but we're also less vulnerable. We could have been ambushed by archers on the banks at any time in the last week." She smiled. "I'm actually a little relieved that I can stop looking up every five steps."

"Great," Janik said, rummaging in his pack. He pulled out a short, thick sword, not ideal for combat but designed for cutting through the growth of a jungle. He held the leather scabbard and extended the heavy hilt to Dania. "You can put all your extra energy to use in clearing us a path."

It was slow going compared to the relatively open river-bed, but Dania cut through the brittle scrub and led them at a steady pace, without showing any sign of tiring. They camped before the sun went down, since the moons no longer offered much light and their path was harder to see in the pale golden light of the Ring of Siberys. Around midnight, Janik woke to the sound of rain pelting the thatched roof of Mathas's conjured hut. He rolled out of his bunk and stood in the doorway, watching the huge drops of rain making tiny craters in the dry ground, quickly turning the dust to mud.

Somewhere far in the distance, a horn blew one long, low note. It barely reached the edge of his hearing, so Janik felt it more than heard it, below the splattering of the raindrops on the ground.

"Mathas is right."

Dania's soft whisper at his shoulder startled Janik, but he recovered quickly and did not turn around.

"This is not a natural storm," she said. "It has a malign air about it, as if . . ." she trailed off, searching for a way to explain it.

"Now rainstorms have the stink of evil about them, too?" Janik demanded, his voice a harsh whisper as he turned to face her. "Aren't all destructive storms the work of the Devourer? That's what my mommy always told me."

Dania just looked at him, her face draped in shadow. Her red hair stuck out from her head at all angles, a mess that had always appealed to him—particularly on their last trip through Xen'drik, when he would awaken in her arms every morning. But there was a set to her jaw that he had not seen before, a sternness that hadn't been present in the younger woman he had allowed to love him those years ago. What had she become? A paladin stood before him—he could see it even in the little hut's darkness, full of strength and righteous fury and conviction.

Conviction that, to Janik, seemed utterly misplaced.

He shook his head and turned to look at the rain. An evil storm! he thought. He almost envied Dania the simplicity of her vision. The storm was evil. Krael was evil. Maija was evil. All that evil—as if it somehow gave a larger meaning to their conflict. Dania believed she stood on the side of good, opposed to all this evil. As if she were part of some great, cosmic struggle.

"No," Janik whispered more quietly, almost to himself. "This isn't about some war between the light and the darkness, Dania. It's us against Krael. A hatred born out of fifteen years' rivalry. We hate him, he hates us, we'll each do anything in our power to destroy the other. That doesn't make us right and him wrong, us good and him evil. We're human, that's all."

"No, Janik, he's not human."

"Right, he's a vampire. And he drinks the blood of ship captains for his nightly cordial. But he was always that kind of a bastard. He's got fangs and spooky powers now, but as far as I can tell, he's the same damned bastard. He hates my guts as he always has—and fair enough, the feeling's mutual—only now he's got a little more muscle to back it up."

"His soul is gone, Janik," Dania's voice grew slightly louder. "In its place is a shred of the Endless Night, a shard of pure destruction. He is not like us—he is most certainly not like me."

"Because your soul's been bathed in the Silver Flame now? Which makes you pure and perfect, holy and righteous. You're good and he's evil."

"I'm not saying I'm perfect, Janik."

"We're all just bastards at each other's throats," Janik said. "Predator and prey, or lions fighting over territory. You fought in the Last War, Dania, you know what I'm talking about."

"This isn't the same."

"Why? It's still us against Krael, just like it was during the war. Only now he's a vampire and you're a paladin, is that what you're saying? Seems to me you changed and he changed, but I don't see how that means our conflict is suddenly all about good and evil."

Dania thrust a finger toward Janik's chin and opened her mouth to speak, but stopped herself. She drew a deep breath, slowly lowered her hand to her side, and lowered her voice to a whisper. She took Janik's arm and led him out into the rain, pulling the hut's door almost closed behind her.

"Look, Janik," she said calmly, "I know you're having a hard time accepting what I told you about Maija."

"We're not talking about Maija. We're talking about Krael, and I'm not even sure how we started that. We were talking about the weather until you turned it into a force of evil."

"You've been talking about Maija since the word 'evil' first came out of your mouth. You think I'm lying to you about Maija's aura of evil, or trying to make more out of this whole thing than it deserves. And I tell you, I'm not."

Janik opened his mouth, but she held up her hand and cut him off.

"Listen! You're right that most of the war and hatred in

the world boils down to human stupidity. We can be a lot like animals, fighting over territory or mates or—or nothing in particular, just for the sake of fighting. Nobody knows that better than I do, Janik, nobody. Like you said, I fought in the Last War—I know this—anyone who was part of the army knows it. For a hundred years the Five Nations tore themselves apart over idiocy and vanity and pride. You're right, Janik, you're right—that wasn't about good and evil. That wasn't about anything more than people being stupid and killing each other because it seemed like the thing to do at the time.

"But this isn't." She emphasized her point by slamming one fist into her palm. "Look, you're even right that for fifteen years we've pursued this thing with Krael largely out of the same damned pride and hatred. But that changed in Mel-Aqat, Janik. You haven't seen it yet—maybe Krael hasn't even fully realized it, and he's still pursuing his idea of revenge. But we're not here just to beat Krael to some ancient ruins, just to get one up on him or pay him back for beating us last time."

"That's exactly why I'm here," Janik interrupted. "You think I give a damn what the Keeper of your Flame says about evil spirits and saving the world?"

Dania looked like she'd been stabbed in the stomach. Her mouth hung open, her brow furrowed as she stared at him, her eyes flicked back and forth between his. Then she closed her eyes, shaking her head sadly.

"I guess I hoped you did," she said, and turned back to the door. She did not turn around as she walked, dripping with rain, into the hut, but quietly said, "Good night, Janik."

Janik stood in the rain, puddles forming in the mud around his bare feet. He glanced at the sky, then looked at the water on his arms. He held up one hand and rubbed his thumb across his fingertips. The water felt oily.

"That doesn't make it evil," he said to himself. "Just unnatural."

He cast another dark look at the sky and followed Dania into the hut. He crawled back into his bunk, but did not sleep any more that night.

THE FIEND-LORD'S DOMAIN
CHAPTER 13

For three more weeks they marched through the rain along the river, which swelled more and more with each day. Dania's task grew more difficult as the once-dry scrub drank up the foul rain and sprouted prickly leaves. The mud sucked at their boots, slowing them. They mostly walked in silence, and sat down to eat in the evening sullen and soaked to the bone.

They saw no further sign of Krael and his allies until they reached the Sky Pillars and turned away from the river, south toward the great golden desert called Menechtarun.

During the last week of their journey along the river, the mountains drew nearer and nearer on their right side, and the Fangs of Angarak rose up on the horizon ahead of them. Eventually, the river bent away from the Sky Pillars, veering due east toward the distant Fangs, and Janik led them south. Around mid week, the rain stopped, then the sky grew clear, and by the next morning, the sun shone hot on their skin and dried their clothes. The vegetation was dry, brittle scrub again, and it became more widely scattered across the dry earth.

Early the next morning, Mathas spotted a crumbling tower rising above the foothills to their right, as if it had been built to watch the narrow passage they were following between the two mountain ranges.

"I think I saw someone up there, moving around," he said. He seemed older with every passing day as the strain of the journey took its toll on him, but he never complained—and he remained alert.

"If you saw him, he probably saw us," Auftane said.

"You underestimate Mathas's eyes," Janik said. "And we still have some cover here, as long as these bushes hold out."

Dania pointed into the hills above the ruined structure. "We could head up here and circle around above it. You can see there used to be a wall that would have blocked our way, but it's long gone."

Janik tried to follow Dania's pointing finger, blinking several times as he tried to make out the wall she was talking about. "I'll take your word for it," he said. "But we need to stay out of sight of the tower as much as we can. Let's start by getting behind that ridge." He started walking, crouched low in the bushes, and the others followed, doing their best to stay out of sight.

They reached the cover of the ridge and heard no suggestion that they had been spotted. Mathas slowly climbed the ridge and peered up at the tower, and even his keen eyes saw no one moving there. They kept the ridge between themselves and the tower as they made their way up into the hills.

"Churning Chaos!" Dania exclaimed. "What is that?"

Janik's eyes had been fixed on the top of the tower, just coming into view over the ridge, and he turned around to see Dania. She was looking up and ahead of them, and he followed her gaze to a stretch of level ground at the base of a short cliff. For a moment he had no idea what had prompted her exclamation. Then he noticed that what he had taken for rubble collected at the bottom of the cliff was not rubble at all.

It was a field of bones. Skulls, helmets, breastplates, swords, arm bones, leg bones, and ribs made a jumble of death and ruin.

Dania rushed ahead and Janik followed close behind, keeping one eye on her and the other on the tower. He crested the rise, pleased to see that Dania was crouched near a large boulder, keeping out of sight of the tower as she surveyed the field of death before her. Janik crouched beside her. Behind him, Mathas and Auftane stayed under the cover of the ridge, looking up at the scene.

Janik quickly noticed what Dania had seen from below. These were not the sun-bleached bones of a centuries-old battle. Many of them still hung together, sprawled as they had fallen in battle. Cloaks, boots, the leather straps of armor—all lay intact. And the armor bore the insignia of a grasping green claw.

"The Emerald Claw?" he breathed. "What in the world?"

Dania pointed toward the base of the cliff, and Janik saw a piece of fabric stirring in a slight breeze. Carefully moving closer, he saw broken beams of wood, more of the Emerald Claw skeletons, and a single hand jutting up from the wreckage of what he guessed had been a palanquin. Unlike all the other bones in this place, the hand was still clothed in flesh, dry and shrunken, but otherwise intact.

With a glance at the tower, Janik picked his way over a few skeletons and leaned over where the corpse lay. He was startled to see a face grinning up at him, its eyes wide open but dark. Its lips were shrunken back from its teeth.

"Sea of Fire," he muttered.

The dead man was draped in robes of emerald and black, with a sparkling ruby and onyx amulet around his withered neck. The hand Janik had seen from afar was outstretched in front of the body, while the other was folded beneath its owner's back at an unnatural angle. The legs and lower torso were crushed beneath the palanquin, while the upper body was nested on sumptuous black cushions.

"Mathas," Janik called, "would you come here, please?"

"What is it, Janik?" Dania asked as the elf started toward them.

"I'm guessing we've got a cleric or necromancer here, and I want Mathas to check him out."

"Is it possible that whatever killed these soldiers somehow stripped the flesh from their bones? Some vile spell?" Dania asked.

"Anything's possible." Janik turned to Mathas as the elf reached them. "Mathas, would you take a look at that body? Tell me anything you can about him and the spells he might have been casting."

As Mathas bent to examine the robed man's corpse, Janik turned his attention to the ground around them.

"Well, it's easy enough to see the prints of the soldiers' boots," he said. "They fought in close ranks, but their opponents pushed them all around the field. They were clearly overpowered, but that's not a big surprise—the four of us would probably have overpowered this rank and file." He looked more closely at the ground near the shattered palanquin. "Their foes did not wear boots," he pronounced. "Looks like clawed toes . . . and fur."

"Some kind of animal?" Dania asked.

"Two legs. Not very big."

"Based on the scrolls in his pouches, this gentleman was clearly a necromancer," Mathas announced. "I would hazard a guess that these soldiers were dead long before they reached this place."

"Dead before?" Janik said, looking up at Mathas. "Undead?"

"Krael and the necromancer probably killed them all at the first dawn," the elf answered. "So they could keep marching day and night."

"Carrying the necromancer in the palanquin," Dania added. "And probably carrying Krael as well, at least during the day."

"And the warforged could walk forever without getting tired," Janik said, "just like these poor bastards." He kicked absently at a shield near his feet. "I guess the ones we killed on the beach really did have the easy job."

"So now we know how they got so far ahead of us," Auftane said, still hanging back at the edge of the carnage. He looked at Janik. "We should move along now, shouldn't we?"

Janik laughed. "Why, Auftane! What are you doing back there? Come on into the thick of things."

"Well, you didn't give me any instructions, so I figured I'd . . . keep watch?"

Nearly drowning out the dwarf's last words, a horn blasted a loud, low note from the ruined tower. At the same time, two brawny figures leaped down from the cliff above them, heavy swords flashing in the sunlight. Janik recognized the sound he had heard in the rain three weeks before. But he had little time to think about it as a sword flashed toward him.

Dania sprang forward and interposed her shield between the scimitar and Janik's head, and Janik reeled backward, getting his first good look at their attackers. They stood a hand's length taller than him, and were clad in heavy armor formed of overlapping metal scales. Their swords had cruel teeth along one edge, and their shields bore spiked edges, making them as much weapons as defensive tools. Beneath their pointed helmets, the faces of tigers snarled in a blood fury.

Janik glanced at Mathas and saw that the elf was deep in concentration on a spell. Dania's sword was dancing furiously with the blade of one creature, and she seemed to have the duel under control. Meanwhile, the other had charged toward Auftane, who was startled and stumbling backward, away from the creature's assault. Janik raced to help the artificer.

Despite his reluctance to enter the field of bones and his initial surprise at the creature's charge, Auftane recovered by the time Janik reached him and was battling in fine form. He swung his mace hard at the creature's head just as Janik arrived, and Janik drove his short sword into a gap in the creature's armor at its shoulder.

The blow should have drawn a huge gout of blood and crippled the creature's sword arm. Janik felt his thrust pushed back, however, almost as if some magic within the thing's body repelled the metal of his sword. It bled, so Janik knew it was a living creature, but he could tell he would need more than a few well-placed blows to take it down. Auftane's hard swing also seemed less damaging than it should have been.

As the creature roared and sidestepped away from him and the dwarf, Janik stole a quick glance over his shoulder at Dania. She was having a little more luck piercing her foe's hide, but not much. Mathas seemed to have done better—the other creature looked a little scorched from one of the elf's spells.

"What are we dealing with here?" Auftane called out.

The faces of tigers. Something fell into place in Janik's mind, and he shouted, "These are fiends of Khyber!"

As he turned his attention back to the fiend nearer to him, Janik heard Dania say, "Then let's see how you like a taste of holy power, fiend!" Her sword struck like a peal of thunder against her opponent, and the creature roared in pain and rage.

Janik dodged a great sweep of his foe's sword, but the clawlike spikes on the creature's shield raked his arm as he tumbled out of the way. "Damn!" he muttered as he thrust his sword toward the fiend's shield arm. His blow was almost an afterthought and barely grazed the creature's orange fur.

"Holy power, eh?" Auftane murmured, stepping backward out of the creature's reach while its attention was focused on Janik.

"Got any of that in your wands there, Auftane?" Janik said. Even as he spoke, though, he saw the dwarf using his fingertip to trace symbols on the wooden shaft of his mace. As Janik feinted and parried the fiend's much heavier sword, Auftane stepped forward again, swinging another powerful blow at the creature's tigerlike head.

This blow mattered, Janik was sure—the dwarf's mace crackled with power as it connected, and Auftane carried his swing through in a stream of crimson. The fiend staggered and snarled. It kept its feet, but Janik had the clear sense that it lacked the strength to roar.

He took the opportunity to drive his sword into its gaping mouth. He placed the strike perfectly, and the blow should have killed the fiend in an instant, but somehow, the blade refused to cut. He might as well have been stabbing the creature with a feather.

Snarling, the fiend bit down on Janik's blade, holding it tightly between its teeth. In the instant before Janik realized what was happening and he released his grip on the hilt, the fiend swung its shield into Janik's ribcage with crushing force, sending him sprawling backward to the ground. It spat the sword onto the ground and stepped forward, raising its cruel blade over its head.

A blast of brilliant light engulfed the fiend, accompanied by a deafening clap of thunder. When Janik's vision cleared, he saw the fiend still standing over him, but its sword had slipped from its hand and its eyes were rolled back in its head. Behind it, he could see Mathas standing near Dania, looking with satisfaction at the result of his lightning spell. The fiend slumped to the ground, joining its companion in oblivion.

"Sea of Fire," Janik muttered, struggling to his feet. "Let's not do that again. Suppose there are more of those?"

"Someone blew that horn," Auftane said, handing Janik his sword.

"You're right," Janik said as they walked over to Mathas and Dania. "I think I heard the same horn three weeks ago, if that's possible."

"Low sounds like that can travel quite far," Mathas said.

Dania looked puzzled. "Could Krael have been that far ahead of us?" she asked.

Janik buried his fingers in his hair. "If they were really traveling day and night without ever stopping, I suppose they could."

Dania used her foot to roll the nearer fiend onto its back, looking at its tigerlike face matted with blood. "So these things attacked Krael and his party here, probably three weeks ago, when you heard that horn, Janik. The skeleton soldiers probably fell quickly, and the necromancer died."

"But Krael and the warforged escaped," Janik said, scowling.

"That seems most likely," Mathas said. "Although perhaps they were captured."

"What I most dislike about this," Dania said, "is the horn. Somebody blew it, obviously, which means more of these fiends are probably in that tower. But more to the point—"

"Somebody was meant to hear it," Auftane said.

"Exactly," Dania said. "Which suggests we've just found an outpost of a little fiend kingdom."

"Janik," said Auftane, "how far are we from Mel-Aqat?"

"From Mel-Aqat?" Janik pulled the sheaf of parchments from his pack and produced his map. He held his little finger up to the map, then compared it to the map's scale. "About a hundred and fifty miles," he said.

"A hundred and fifty miles of barren desert," Mathas added. "Probably three weeks of travel."

"Three weeks . . ." Auftane mused. "And you heard the horn three weeks ago, right?"

"You think the horn could be signaling someone in Mel-Aqat," Janik said. "I think you might be right."

"You recognized these fiends?" Auftane asked. "From your last visit there?"

Janik took a deep breath and let it out slowly, rubbing his hand over the stubble on his chin as he collected his thoughts. "I recognized them from texts," he said, "not from experience. The earliest descriptions of Mel-Aqat describe giant statues of people with the heads of tigers, so naturally I've done some research about what those were supposed to depict. You remember in Stormreach, when we were talking about the Tablet of Shummarak? About the great war that supposedly raged between fiends and dragons in the first age of the world? Well, the legends describe those fiends—or at least some of them—as having the heads of tigers."

"Rakshasas," Mathas said. "I have read of them as well."

"Exactly," Janik said. "The most powerful of these rakshasas were called rajahs, their rulers, and they were ultimately bound within the earth—"

"By the couatls," Dania interrupted, "the allies of the dragons. They sacrificed themselves to bind the fiends forever."

"Right," said Janik. "But the servitors of the rajahs were not all bound or destroyed. Several ranks or breeds of these fiends served the rajahs. Some wielded powerful magic. A black-furred variety served as scouts and assassins. And there was a warrior caste, called zakyas. I'm guessing that's what we have here."

He paused, running his hands through his hair. "It is possible that Mel-Aqat was a place where one of the rakshasa rajahs was imprisoned."

"What?" Dania turned to face Janik.

"I'm beginning to see some of the pieces of the puzzle here," Janik said, staring at the tiger-headed demon on the ground. "I don't know how they fit together yet, but I think I see some pieces."

He furrowed his brow in concentration.

"Some of the most ancient texts that mention Mel-Aqat—the same ones that describe the statues of these demons—call it the Place of Imprisonment. I'm certain that the ziggurat at the heart of the ruins is the locus of that imprisonment. That ziggurat is the one structure still standing in the city, and we could not find a way inside it on our last visit. So I have considered the possibility that your church is correct, Dania, and we released this rakshasa rajah from the Place of

Imprisonment on our last visit. But I don't think that's the case, partly because we never got into the ziggurat."

Dania's face was flushed. "Unless the Ramethene Sword was a key of some kind," she said, "and removing it from its place opened the prison."

"That might be possible—if it weren't contradicted by every extant text about the Ramethene Sword," Janik snapped. "If your carefully reasoned theory had any validity, you would expect to see descriptions of the sword as a key, or a linchpin, or a keystone, maybe a cornerstone. Instead, it's described—as one would expect for a weapon of war—in terms of its capabilities as a weapon. It's the Sunderer, the Fleshrender, the Axis of Destruction. You are too hasty to assume the worst, Dania. But the most important reason I don't believe we released the rajah is that the world would have noticed by now. By all accounts, these creatures possess power to rival the Dark Six, and little subtlety. If one had been released into the world three years ago, I'm fairly confident that Stormreach would not still be standing, at the very least."

Dania looked unconvinced, but Janik ignored her to continue his train of thought.

"That said, I suspect that the possibility of Mel-Aqat being the Place of Imprisonment for one of these fiend lords is not irrelevant to what we're doing here. Dania said that Krael and Maija were looking for the Tablet of Shummarak in Karrnath. I told you before that the Tablet is an ancient inscription that describes what we've just been talking about—the fiends that ruled the world in ancient times, and the couatls that imprisoned them in the earth. Thanks to Krael stealing the most important books from my library, I have no idea whether there's a specific connection between the Tablet and Mel-Aqat, but it seems pretty obvious there's a general connection. Both of them are connected to these ancient fiends."

Auftane interrupted. "So you think Krael and Maija were looking for the Tablet so they could use it to free the fiend imprisoned at Mel-Aqat?"

"I think that's possible, yes," Janik said. "Although I still have no idea how much Maija is involved in all of this. I only know what Dania told me."

"We have no evidence that she is here with Krael," Dania said. "Assuming she's still alive, she would have slowed the party down."

"Unless she was also riding in the palanquin with that necromancer," Mathas added.

"Not very likely," Janik said. "No, I don't think Maija is here. But the other piece is these zakya warriors. Again, I think there's some connection to Mel-Aqat, but I'm not sure what it means. We're relatively close to Mel-Aqat, close enough that the horn might have been meant for someone there. But we didn't see any fiends there last time. So does that mean that the imprisoned rajah has been freed, and these zakyas are serving him? But then what's Krael doing here?"

Janik heaved a deep sigh. "Oh, it makes my head ache. This is the sort of problem best addressed in a quiet library, not out in the wild."

"And what are we going to do about that horn?" Dania added, casting a wary glance toward the tower nearby. They were mostly shielded from the view of anyone in the tower, but they had hardly been careful about hiding since the first attack of the rakshasas. "Do you think we should attack the tower, Janik?"

"I think it all depends on what's in there. Mathas?"

"Of course, Janik," Mathas said. "I will require some

time." He turned toward the tower and closed his eyes, beginning a low chant and tracing complex symbols in the air with his hands.

Janik turned to Auftane. "You did something to your weapon that made it more effective against them. What was that? I felt like I was stabbing them with a spoon instead of my sword."

"Like many creatures of evil," Dania said before Auftane could answer, "these fiends are susceptible to holy might. Without that power behind your blows, your sword could not pierce their defenses."

"So we know Dania's black-and-white interpretation of events," Janik said, looking at Auftane. "I want to hear yours, Auftane. You're no paladin. What did you do to your mace?"

"Well, Dania's interpretation is correct," the dwarf replied. "More or less. The world is full of opposing powers, and it's simple enough to find one power to use against another. When you're fighting a creature of cold, you make your weapon fiery. And when you're fighting fiends, you make it holy."

"But how do you do it?"

Auftane laughed. "That's what I do. Everything has magic in it—it's just a matter of adjusting it to get the effect you want. It's relatively easy to do, if you only need it to last a short time. With enough time and the right materials, you can make it permanent."

"So you could do it to my sword?"

"Sure," the dwarf said, "for about an hour and a half."

"Long enough for us to clear out that tower."

Mathas made a last dramatic gesture and fell silent, standing like a statue with his eyes closed. The others watched him in silence for several moments, then he began to speak.

"I didn't see anything between here and the tower," Mathas announced. "There's not much to the tower at all—from this side it looks mostly intact, but if you go around the other side, the walls are crumbled away. There's one more fiend by the doorway, it looks like—yes, there's another one perched on a ledge higher up, looking toward us. With an enormous horn. I think that's all, just those two."

"Go ahead and send the eye around in a wider circle," Janik said. "Let's make sure there aren't more hiding in the hills."

"Very well," the elf said. After a short silence, he said, "No, nothing. Looks like we're clear."

"Great," said Janik. "Let's go get those two."

"Wait, Mathas," Dania said. "Can you see if there's a way for us to approach the tower under cover? Can we circle behind somehow?"

"Hold on," Mathas said. "I'm not sure . . . yes, perhaps. If we start going that way—"

Without opening his eyes, Mathas pointed away from the tower, to where a shallow gulley ran down from the level spot where they stood.

"—we should be able to come around more or less from behind. I think we can get fairly close before we come into view."

"Excellent," Dania said.

"Good thinking, Dania," Janik said. "Are we ready?" Mathas's eyes fluttered open, and he nodded.

"Here," Auftane said, "let me have your sword."

Janik's left hand dropped to the scabbard at his belt before he realized that he still held the blade in his right. He wiped it clean on the dead necromancer's robe before handing it, hilt first, to the dwarf.

Auftane took the sword, holding it gingerly in his hands. He dipped his thumb into a small jar he had produced from one of the many pouches at his belt, and began tracing glyphs and symbols on the blade.

"It was faster when he did it before," Janik said with an apologetic glance at Mathas, who grinned.

"I can do it faster, but it takes a lot out of me," Auftane said, continuing to trace symbols on the sword and sounding a bit distracted. "In the thick of battle, it's worth it. Since we have the time, I might as well take it."

"Fair enough," Janik said.

❖ ❖ ❖ ◉ ❖ ❖ ❖

A quarter of an hour later, they were making their way up another gully toward the back side of the tower. As Mathas had described, the ancient tower was now little more than a single, curved wall facing the north. The fiends had erected a wooden ladder leading up to a small ledge marking what must once have been the tower's roof. There was barely enough room for the creature that stood up there, and it kept one hand on the wall as if ready to catch itself in case the ledge crumbled beneath its feet. The zakya kept its eyes glued to the north, clearly still expecting Janik's party to emerge from hiding in that direction.

They came into view of the tower within a stone's throw of the two fiends. Mathas started the battle by engulfing them in a white blast of frigid air. Frost caked their armor and fur as they roared in surprise and pain. Janik and Dania rushed forward and the zakya on the ground ran to meet them, while the one on the upper ledge made its way quickly but carefully down the ladder, the rungs slick with ice.

Before the second one finished its descent, Janik and

Dania had flanked the first zakya and sent it sprawling on the ground. Janik gave an admiring glance at his sword, which no longer felt like a blunt implement. Whatever Auftane had done had proven quite effective—his second blow had pierced straight to the fiend's heart, killing it instantly.

Seeing its companion felled so quickly, the second fiend checked its headlong charge and approached more warily, careful to avoid getting between Janik and Dania. Auftane reached them at the same time as the zakya, swinging his mace into its hips as it focused on Dania, hacking with its sword and slashing with its shield. Roaring in fury, the creature turned its full attention to Auftane, pushing him backward—but leaving its own back exposed to Janik's sword. Janik aimed his next blow carefully, finding his opportunity when the zakya overextended its arm to hack at the nimble dwarf. He slid his blade into a gap in the creature's armor at its shoulder, and it stumbled, roared weakly, and collapsed.

"You said something about making this magic permanent?" Janik said to Auftane, admiring his sword once more.

Auftane laughed. "Time and money," he said. "Unfortunately, we're not likely to have the time or the right materials until we're back in Stormreach."

"Too bad," Janik said. He wiped the blade on the fur of the second rakshasa, still crusted with frost, and slid it back into its sheath.

❖ ❖ ❖ ◉ ❖ ❖ ❖

With the tower cleared of its guards, Janik led his friends out of the tower and into Menechtarun, the great golden desert. The dry scrub that had been growing more sparse since they left the riverbank disappeared completely. The dry earth became sun-blasted sand, and they found their footing much less stable. With each step, their feet sank and slid in the sand, slowing their progress to a crawl. The Fangs of Angarak rose up on their left, and Janik steered their course toward the more solid—and, he hoped, less arid—ground of the foothills.

They saw no more towers and no more zakyas. The sand crawled with snakes and scorpions—some of them almost as large as Auftane—but most of them slid or scuttled away as Janik drew near at the front of the group, and the more aggressive specimens were quickly dispatched. After fighting armor-clad demons, even a dwarf-sized snake did not seem threatening.

Each night, Mathas erected his magical hut, its walls seemingly formed of sand bricks. The quiet desert grew noisier at night as unseen creatures emerged from their hiding places to hunt in the cooler air and cover of darkness. Janik continued to sleep fitfully, spending hours lying in his bunk listening to the sounds outside and the slow breathing of his companions. He rarely rose to look out the door any more—partly because he doubted any serious threat, and partly because he didn't want to risk another confrontation with Dania.

Mel-Aqat loomed larger in his mind with each passing day. They would reach the ruins in a matter of weeks. What would they find there? Had they indeed released or awakened some ancient fiend that had reestablished a kingdom of demons in the ruins and the surrounding desert? Would Krael be there, perhaps already engaged in the ritual that would shatter the spiritual bonds of the couatls and release the rakshasa rajah from the Place of Imprisonment? Was it possible that Krael had already succeeded?

And what about Maija? He did not expect to find her at Mel-Aqat, of course, but he held on to the possibility that he might find some clue there about what had happened to her.

Perhaps even a way to bring her back to him.

❦ ❦ ❦ ❦ ❦ ❦ ❦

Passing days stretched into passing weeks, and then . . . they arrived. Just as the days seemed to blur, one into the next, in a haze of desert heat and endless sand, Mathas spotted giant stone blocks half-buried in the desert sand.

"Those are only the remnants of the city's outer wall," Janik said, "and they're still miles away. We should make camp here, out of sight and out of reach, and plan to approach the ruins tomorrow."

"If you're serious about being out of sight, we should move farther away," Dania said. "If we can see the walls, they've got some chance to see us—especially once Mathas has erected our campsite. And there are still a few hours of good light."

"Agreed," Janik said. "But Mathas, why don't you send your eyes ahead and give us some idea what we can expect?"

"Of course. Should I do that now, or after we make camp?"

"Why not do it now?" Janik said. "The information might be useful in choosing where we camp."

Mathas began the long chant that would let him extend his senses as far as the ruins, and Auftane dropped down on the sand, sitting awkwardly with his short legs spread in front of him. Dania crouched beside him, but Janik paced in the sand around them. After walking all day for six straight weeks, he had a hard time stopping while the sun was still in the sky—especially with their destination in sight.

As Mathas cast his spell, Janik kept gazing toward Mel-Aqat, half expecting some answer to all the questions that had haunted him for three years to rise up like a plume of smoke from the ruins. He stared until his eyes burned in the dry desert air, then turned abruptly, resuming his pacing for many moments before beginning to stare again. He was dimly aware of Dania and Auftane engaging in quiet conversation, and even half-heard his own name once or twice, but he could not tear his attention away from the ruins.

When Mathas began to speak, though, Janik turned at once and listened raptly.

"By the Host," the elf croaked, "the city certainly has changed since we've been away." Mathas stood entranced, eyes closed, leaning slightly toward the ruins.

"What?" Janik demanded, moving to stand right at Mathas's shoulder. "What do you see?"

"First of all, they've been doing some building. It looks mostly like stacking blocks, with no mortar, but some of those blocks are quite large. They have erected some semblance of a wall around the city—as far as I can see, it follows the line of the original city wall."

"By 'they,' I assume you mean the tiger-fiends," Janik said.

"Yes, the rakshasas. Quite a number of them are posted along the wall. They're the soldiers, the zakyas, like the ones we fought at the tower."

"Quite a number?" Dania called, still crouching on the sand behind Mathas. "Can you be more specific?"

"They are in groups of two or three, spaced along the wall. But the groups are close enough to each other that it would be hard to fight them one group at a time—reinforcements would be quick to arrive."

"Organized resistance," Janik muttered. "That little fiend kingdom you suggested, Dania. I don't like this."

"Nor do I," Dania said. "Mathas, what's inside the wall? Have they rebuilt more of the city?"

"One moment. I need to send the eye over the wall."

"Sort of makes you wish he could have sent the eye all the way here from Stormreach and saved us all the trouble, doesn't it?" Auftane said. "We could be resting by a roaring fire in a fine restaurant somewhere while Mathas investigates the ruins with magic."

"Believe me, my friend," Mathas said, opening his eyes just long enough to glance back at the dwarf, "if such a thing were within my capabilities, I would have been the first to suggest it. I think I can rightly claim the distinction of despising travel more than any of you."

"What's that?" Auftane pointed up where a dark shape was silhouetted against the bright desert sky. Janik and Dania looked up, following the dwarf's short finger.

"Is it a dragon or something?" Janik said. "Dania, I'm counting on your elf eyes."

"That's no dragon," Dania said. "By the Flame, what is it doing here?"

"Is it some kind of winged snake?" Auftane said.

"You're not far off, Auftane." Dania's voice was a whisper, and Mathas opened his eyes, distracted from his spell by her awed tone. "That's a couatl."

CHAPTER 14

The four companions stared into the air, watching the winged serpent snaking across the sky. Its wings shimmered with rainbow colors in the bright sunlight, and its movements were stunningly graceful, as if it were dancing. It drifted slowly over them, tracing a wide arc across the sky, centered above the ruined city. If it saw them, it showed no sign—it did not seem to linger above them or slow its progress as it passed over them. Janik watched it until it was a tiny speck and then vanished from his sight, then his gaze fell on Dania.

She was still spellbound, her eyes fixed on a distant point in the sky where her keen eyes could still make out the couatl's writhing dance. Tears streamed down her cheeks, past the upturned corners of her mouth. Janik watched her face for a long time, saw her smile brighten as she observed some new nuance in its movements. She looked radiant—her expression struck him as a softer, warmer version of the holy flame that had wreathed her sword in battle against the fiends. It was an expression he had seen on Maija's face in rare moments when she was deep in prayer, and it stirred something in his soul that he had not felt in a very long time.

He watched Dania while she stared up at the couatl. When she finally lowered her gaze, it fell on Janik, and he quickly averted his eyes, embarrassed to have been caught staring at her. His embarrassment grew when he realized that Auftane and Mathas had been watching him, and he found himself wondering how much of his feelings had shown on his face. Mathas had a mild scowl on his face, but Auftane was grinning broadly.

Collecting himself quickly, Janik barked at Mathas. "Is that eye of yours still in the ruins? Or are all three of them staring at me?"

Mathas started, then closed his eyes again. "Back in the ruins. Just coming over the . . . Sovereigns!"

"Now what?" Janik demanded.

"They have rebuilt more than the wall," Mathas said. "And they are still building. Like the wall, they are simply stacking pieces of the ruins on top of each other, in random fashion. The ziggurat is still standing, of course, right at the center of the wall's circle. Then it looks like mounds of rubble are heaped up here and there around it. Hmm. They appear to be random, but I wonder—What?" His eyes popped open.

"What is it, Mathas?" Dania asked, putting a hand on the elf's shoulder.

"Someone canceled the spell. That means—"

"They know we were watching," Janik said. "Do they know where we are?"

"No way to know," Mathas said.

"I think I know," said Dania, pointing toward the ruins.

Janik followed her finger, but couldn't see anything. "You know, I'm getting tired of this. Why didn't my mother marry an elf?"

"They're coming," Dania said. "In strength."

Janik led their retreat toward the foothills, skirting the ruined city. At first, he made a half-hearted attempt to hide their tracks, but soon he decided that getting to the cover of the hills was more important than hiding their footprints in the shifting sand. Dania brought up the rear, turning frequently to look for signs of pursuit. As the sky darkened, they made their way up into the parched hills, and Dania announced that their pursuers were out of sight.

Janik called a halt and everyone fell onto the sand in exhaustion.

"We need rest," he said, "but I'm not sure we should use your shelter, Mathas. Too easy for them to spot from a distance."

"You could be right," Mathas said, sounding as if he doubted it. "They'll certainly spot an open campfire more easily. And the shelter offers a degree of protection that is not insignificant—solid walls and magically locked doors."

"I understand," Janik said, "and I'm not immune to the lure of a comfortable bunk and a warm fire. But if they find us during the night, I don't like the idea of being locked inside a tiny cottage, no matter how secure it is."

"You'd rather be able to run," Dania said.

"Well, yes," Janik said. "I guess I don't believe that little cottage is completely impervious, or I'd be happier being trapped inside it. But if you start from the presumption that they're going to break through its defenses eventually—when the spell ends in the morning, at the latest—then I don't want to be surrounded in a small space when they do."

"You're right," said Dania.

"And—" Janik was ready to escalate the conversation into a heated argument, but stopped abruptly. "I'm right?"

"Yes, Janik, I actually agree with you."

"Well. So we'll make camp—here, unless you think there's a better spot nearby, Dania."

"This is good. Plenty of cover, but also good vantage points for the watch."

"No fire—we'll need to break out the blankets. It'll get cold here within a few hours."

"I'll take the first watch," Dania said.

Mathas grumbled at Janik. "I suppose now you're going to gloat about insisting that we'd need tents."

"Gloat?" Janik said, feigning shock. "Why yes, I suppose I am."

Janik and Dania quickly erected two small tents in a secluded hollow. As Auftane and Mathas settled themselves into both tents, Dania climbed the side of the hollow and selected a high point to keep watch. Janik followed her and sat down beside her on the dry ground.

"You should rest, Janik," Dania said. "I'm not going to stay up through your watch."

"I'll turn in soon," he said, but he sat there, staring toward the ruins.

"Something on your mind?" Dania asked.

Janik shook his head and ran his fingers through his hair. "Yes," he said, "I suppose. I just . . . wanted to ask you something."

"What?"

"That couatl—was it . . . how . . . oh, Sea of Fire, I don't know what I'm asking."

"Wasn't it beautiful?" Dania said, and for a moment Janik saw something on her face again.

"Dania, it's . . ." Janik sighed heavily. He stared at the tiny crescent of Nymm, the largest moon, following the sun down below the western sky. "It's been a long time since I allowed myself to believe that anything like that could exist, in this world or any other."

Dania nodded her understanding, but did not answer.

"I felt something, watching it," Janik continued. "And then I saw your face, and I could see that you were—I don't know, you were swept up in it. To me, it was like a faint memory of some childhood happiness, but it seemed you felt it vividly, immediately."

Dania rested a hand on his knee and looked at the ground between them. "It was a very powerful experience for me, Janik." She looked up, right into his eyes.

Janik fought the urge to look away and let the subject drop.

"Do you really want to hear about this?"

Janik hesitated a moment, then nodded.

She smiled. "Well, to me the couatl embodies everything that's good in the world. Even more than the Silver Flame. At some level, I understand the Silver Flame in my head as a manifestation of the spirits of the couatls who bind the fiends in Khyber. But seeing a couatl—a real, live couatl flying free across the sky—struck something deeper in me. When I first heard the legend you repeated back in Stormreach, about the couatls binding the demons, I was stunned."

She looked down, avoiding Janik's searching gaze. "I guess it sounds sort of stupid," she said, "but you have to understand what was happening at the time. I don't think I ever fully realized the extent of the war's effects on me. I left the front lines and sailed to Xen'drik with you, feeling like the worst sort of killer, like one of those madmen who hunts women in the towers of Sharn, or a lunatic who tries to build a magical device powered by souls. I killed so many people, Janik. So many."

Janik saw an echo of the haunted look that came over her face every time Dania talked about the war, and he finally began to understand it.

"That didn't really change when I started traveling with you and Maija," she went on. "We were still fighting the war, just on a different scale."

Janik nodded. "I've often thought that we were fighting the real war, and all the great battles were just a distraction."

"They were more than a distraction," Dania said, "but you're right. We were just as caught up in the killing and madness and stupidity as the troops on the front lines, and just as blind to the futility of it."

She got smoothly to her feet and started pacing.

"I think part of the reason I was able to hide my feelings about you for so long was that I honestly didn't believe that I deserved any affection from you. I was convinced that even though you and Maija claimed to be my friends, you despised me as much as I loathed myself. I don't think I ever could have put that feeling into words, but as I look back on it, I'm pretty sure that's what it was. I was a killer! How could you truly care for me in any way? How could I care about myself?"

She stopped pacing and looked out at the setting crescent moon.

"Then I finally revealed my feelings to you, after Maija left. To my surprise, you made love to me, and for those months of travel I actually felt worthwhile." She shrugged. "Then you dumped me in Sharn and disappeared, which left me . . . devastated."

"Dania, I—"

"No, Janik," she interrupted, dropping to her knees in front of him, grabbing his hands and looking earnestly into his face. "Please understand, I'm not trying to place blame.

Like I said back in Thrane, it's all past. It's forgiven. Please. I'm just trying to explain something to you that's very . . . complicated."

She took a deep breath, smiling. "To understand where I am now and what that couatl means to me, you have to understand where I was when I got to Karrnath and started working with Gered and Kophran. And that was not a happy state. I remember the night in Atur when we first witnessed the handiwork of Krael the vampire—there were bodies everywhere. And Kophran started going on about how these poor people had brought this fate on themselves by practicing the religion of the Blood of Vol."

Janik gaped at her.

"I know—I wanted to strangle him. But I remember saying to him that I deserved death at least as much as they did, that I was far more guilty than they were."

"What did he say?"

"The bastard agreed with me." Dania got to her feet and resumed her pacing.

"But hunting the vampires—Krael and the shifter, Havoc—it changed me somehow," Dania continued. "I came to see them as something different from all the killing of the war. To them, the people they killed weren't adversaries, they were food. They didn't even pretend at the sort of honor that soldiers use to cover the murders they commit. And then when Krael intruded my mind, I felt so . . . violated." She shuddered.

"So my first taste of the Silver Flame came right then. Krael was controlling me, using his powers to make me watch, helpless, as he drank Gered's blood. And as much as I dislike Kophran, I have to give him credit—he saved Gered's life right there, and probably mine as well, by coming at just the right time and driving Krael away. We were standing in an alley—Krael and Gered and I—and Kophran came to the entrance of the alley, behind me, and sent waves of holy power toward Krael—power that washed right through me. I had never felt anything like it before."

She stood still and fell silent for a moment, her head bowed and her eyes closed. Janik said nothing. He looked up at her, anxious for her next words. He thought he recognized the feeling she described—it was the same holy power he had felt in Maija's touch, both when she laid her hands on his wounds to cure him and when she caressed him in love. His heart was aching more strongly now than it had in months—as if, somehow, what he had lost in Maija was within his reach again. Not in Dania, but in what she was telling him.

Dania sighed. "You know, Janik," she said, "I'm no priest. I don't know whether I could express the doctrines of the Church of the Silver Flame in a way that would mean anything to you or help you at all. All I can tell you is what happened to me."

"Please," Janik whispered. "Please do."

"Later that night, as we were talking about Krael and Havoc, Kophran told me about the couatls. The piece of it that leaped out at me was that the couatls sacrificed their own freedom in order to bind the demons. They had been waging war for a million years. And it seems to me that they finally realized something—victory would never come through more war. They and the dragons could never beat the demons by force. The only way to end the war was for the demons and the couatls—both of them, spirits of good and spirits of evil—to leave the battlefield. The demons would never do it willingly, of course, but the couatls were willing to make that sacrifice."

Janik nodded but his brow was furrowed in concentration— he still wasn't hearing what he was looking for.

"Look, Janik, I saw a lot of people lay down their lives in the war. A lot of them did it because they wanted to be heroes. They thought that their deaths would help Breland somehow. In my mind, they were just more casualties of war. But the couatls made me think of the people I saw who weren't motivated by their own pride or their belief in the nation—people who gave up their lives to save their friends. Covering their squad's retreat. Shielding their buddies from a magical blast. Utterly selfless, willing to die—not so their friends could go on fighting, but out of some small, tragic hope that maybe their deaths would allow their friends to live in a better world some day. Like they knew that some day the war would be over, and some people would still be around to enjoy whatever world was left. And maybe their deaths would make it possible for their friends to be there at the war's end."

Tears were starting in her eyes again, and she tried to brush them away.

"The vampires taught me that there is very real evil in the world, Janik. Terrible evil, willing to consume the world to feed its own hunger. To me, the couatls are the embodiment of the wonderful good that is also in the world. That good is the only thing preventing evil from devouring all life."

Dania sat down on the ground beside Janik, looking very tired. It seemed to Janik, for a moment, that she felt the weight of that responsibility very keenly, as if the burden of saving the world from destruction rested on her shoulders alone.

She put her hand on his folded hands and looked into his face. Janik glanced down at her hand and covered it with one of his own.

"I think I know what I saw when the couatl flew by today—the pure good you're talking about."

Dania nodded.

"And if it's possible for such a thing to exist, then perhaps what you've been saying about Krael and . . . and even about Maija is all true. Maybe they are utterly evil and beyond all hope. But I still don't want to believe it."

"I can't pretend that I have it all figured out, Janik. The truth is that I still haven't found the one thing I want most."

"What's that?"

"Peace. I want peace. I want to stop raging and fighting and killing and worrying. I wouldn't mind a chance to stop thinking. I want to sleep without fear, without setting watches. I want to rest in the warmth I felt in the alley, and never have it fade away."

She shook her head and stood up, trying to hide the tears that had formed in the corners of her eyes. She walked to the edge of the ridge and looked out at the setting moon again.

"I just want peace, Janik."

As she spoke, she slowly drew her sword from its sheath. Janik sprang to his feet, afraid of what she planned to do with it. As he reached her side, she pointed the tip of her sword into the desert beyond their camp.

"They're coming again," she said. "They've found us."

❂ ❂ ❂ ❂ ❂ ❂ ❂

Janik and Dania raced into the hollow to rouse Mathas and Auftane. They abandoned the tents, which stung Janik bitterly but seemed to give Mathas great satisfaction, and hastily packed up the rest of their gear.

Janik chose a rocky path away from the hollow, counting on the difficulty of tracking them over such ground. He set a quick pace and steered them away from the approaching rakshasas and toward Mel-Aqat.

"Why are we going toward the ruins?" Auftane asked.

"We need to get there eventually," Janik said. "And given the number of zakyas out looking for us, I'm hopeful that the ones remaining in the city will be caught off-guard."

Their brisk pace staved off the chill of the desert night, and five nearly full moons lit their way across the barren land. They traveled well into the night, until the disks of the moons silhouetted the walls of Mel-Aqat in front of them. They approached the walls under a cloak of shadow. Moving slowly and as quietly as they could manage, they crept up to the ruins without hearing any sign that they had been detected.

Janik led them to the base of the wall. He ran his hand over the stone, looking up. It appeared that the rakshasas had, as Mathas described, simply rearranged the crumbling stone blocks of the ruins, forming them into a ring around the city and then stacking another layer on top of the first. From where he stood, Janik thought he could see a gap between the blocks forming the upper layer above him, allowing access to the city—if they could get over the lower block.

"I'm pretty sure I can climb this," he said, turning to his companions. "If I get up there and drop a rope down, will the rest of you be able to make it up?"

"Of course," said Dania. Mathas nodded, though he looked almost too tired to speak.

Auftane looked uncertainly at the stone block, but then he nodded as well.

"Up I go," Janik said.

He slid one hand up the wall until he found a good handhold in the worn rock, then did the same with one foot. A moment later he was sliding up the side of the wall like a spider. He only slipped once and caught himself quickly. He reached the top of the block and squeezed into the gap between the two upper ones. He checked above him, still not seeing any guards, and peered down the length of the gap. It narrowed considerably at the other end.

"Wait there," he hissed down to the others. "I want to make sure we can get through the other side before you all climb up here."

Turning sideways, he crept along between the two stone blocks until he was sure he could fit in the gap all the way through. He peered out the narrow space at the far end and gasped as he got his first look at Mel-Aqat in over three years.

It had changed considerably, as Mathas had said. On their last visit, only the merest suggestion of ancient buildings marked what had once been a great city, with the exception of the towering ziggurat in its center. Janik and his companions had dug away some of the parched earth to reveal more of the crumbling walls in places, and they had found one ancient vault underground that was almost completely intact—and there they had found the Ramethene Sword. But above ground, nothing had stood—barely two stones stacked on top of each other.

This time, in addition to the reconstruction of the wall, there were strange, crumbling towers erected in various places around the central ziggurat. They were nothing more than huge stone blocks in haphazard stacks, like the constructions of a young child's toy blocks, but on a much larger scale. Some leaned far to one side, while others buckled in the middle and then righted themselves. For a moment, Janik almost thought he saw some pattern to their arrangement around the ziggurat, but it escaped him and he made a mental note to consider the question later. He needed to help his friends over the wall—and quickly, before any guards appeared.

He pulled a coil of fine silk rope from his backpack and

looked for a good place to tie it as he moved back to the outside edge of the wall. The worn stone surface offered no large protrusions—barely more than the narrow fingerholds he had used to climb the lower blocks. He reached the outer edge and threw one end of the rope down.

"Wait another second," he whispered. "I need to secure this end."

He tied a large knot in the other end of the rope as he made his way back along the narrow gap. On the inside edge, he crouched down and worked the rope in between the upper and lower blocks so that the knot would catch in place. He pulled hard on the rope to make sure it was secure, checked one more time for guards, and, seeing none, went back to the other end of the gap.

"Come on up," he said.

Dania tested the rope with her weight and then handed it to Mathas. The old elf glanced at the rope, then handed it back to Dania.

"I'll do it my way," he said, and cast a quick spell. Looking up at Janik, he started to float upward. At the top, Janik reached out and pulled him over to stand on the wall, laughing quietly.

"I don't think there's room for you to get past me," he said to Mathas.

Janik backed into the gap, making enough room for Mathas and Auftane, who was walking up the wall, pulling himself along with the rope. Dania held the rope at the bottom to keep him from swinging. Mathas tried to help Auftane clamber up over the edge, almost causing them both to tumble back down onto Dania.

Dania came up last, pulling herself quickly hand over hand and easily finding her feet on the top of the wall. She pulled the rope up behind her and handed it to Auftane, who passed it to Janik. Janik led the way through the gap and pulled the knot free from the crack where he had wedged it.

"Uh-oh," he said, ducking his head to the side just as an arrow whizzed past his ear. Mathas cursed in pain behind him. Janik pulled his head farther into the gap while searching the ground below for the source of the arrow.

Mathas spotted the rakshasa first, ignoring the arrow's cut and sending a blast of magical fire to engulf a figure crouching in the shadows below them. The zakya roared and loosed another arrow, which clattered harmlessly off the stone block behind Mathas.

"Well, I'm no use up here," Janik muttered. He dropped the rope behind him and jumped to the ground, landing on his feet and running over to the zakya. It dropped its bow and pulled out a heavy, toothed sword. Too late, Janik remembered how the other fiends had resisted the bite of his blade, and he wished he had been less impulsive.

The zakya's fur was partly burned away by Mathas's fiery blast, and Janik saw pink, blistered flesh beneath it. He could see the pain in its eyes, but its mouth was twisted into something like a snarling grin as it anticipated cutting into Janik with its sword.

Good, Janik thought, it expects me to be easy.

The fiend led with a sweeping blow that would have knocked Janik flat on his back while it opened a gash in his belly—if Janik had been in its path. He tumbled down and to his right, staying ahead of the blade and enticing his foe to extend the swing, reaching too far out. Planting his feet at the end of his roll, Janik hurled his whole body at the zakya, leading with the point of his sword. The blade entered the fiend's body below its arm and bit deeply despite the creature's preternatural toughness. Janik ended his roll facing the wall, where Mathas was floating to the ground, and he saw Auftane fumbling with the rope to get himself safely down.

The fiend wheeled to face Janik and adopted a more cautious stance, holding a blood-drenched hand to the wound beneath its sword arm and snarling in anger.

"Janik, watch out!"

Janik was barely conscious of Mathas's shouted warning, but instinctively dodged to the side just as another rakshasa's blade swung down where his head had been. In the same instant that Janik dodged, a massive bolt of crackling lightning stretched from the elf's fingertips to engulf both fiends. The one in front of him fell, tiny arcs of lightning flaring in its fur. The second fiend roared and charged past Janik toward Mathas, beginning to raise its sword for a deadly blow.

"Ignore me, will you?" Janik muttered. As the zakya passed him, his sword darted out and sliced into the fiend's leg, sending it sprawling on its face on the dusty earth. Janik sprang forward to kill it before it could rise, but it rolled over and slammed its shield into Janik, knocking him aside. He tried to roll with the blow and come up on his feet, but the blow had upset his balance and he joined the rakshasa sprawled in the dust, staring up at the sky.

The fiend didn't bother trying to get to its feet. It used the momentum of its roll to carry itself to where Janik lay. It planted its sword hand on Janik's shoulder to pin him to the ground, and lifted its shield so its sharpened edge was positioned right over Janik's neck.

THIRD REUNION

CHAPTER 15

The fiend paused for only a heartbeat. Janik saw its feline mouth curve into a wicked smile and the muscles of its shoulder tense to drive the shield down.

Something hit the rakshasa like a stone from a catapult, knocking it off Janik completely. Janik leaped to his feet and saw Dania on the ground, tangled with the fiend, which looked more like a fierce tiger locked in a death struggle than a warrior in armor. It roared as it tried to roll Dania onto her back, and it ignored its weapons in favor of trying to bite her neck.

Janik took a deep breath as he picked up his sword from the ground, trying to calm his pounding heart. He moved as fast as he could to the zakya and Dania, but he felt like he was running in a dream, as if his feet were mired in swampy ground.

"Get it off her, Janik!" Mathas was yelling. He was poised to cast a spell, but he didn't want to risk catching Dania in the blast. Dania was struggling, but she seemed unwilling to loose her sword, even though she couldn't possibly bring it to bear in such close quarters.

Janik reached them. With his left hand, he grabbed a

fistful of the zakya's fur and skin between its helmet and its armor, pulling with all his strength to draw its head back. It snarled and tried to twist its head around to bite his arm, then Janik drove his sword up under its chin.

Again he felt that his sword had grown blunt, that it couldn't bite through the unnatural flesh. But it didn't matter. Dania broke free of the zakya's grasp, found her feet, and stepped backward, swinging her sword with all her strength. Her weapon hit the creature and erupted in a burst of silver flame, then cleaved through its neck as the flame seared its fur and flesh. Janik pulled his hand back from the flames in surprise, leaving his sword embedded in the zakya's chin. The sword landed, impaled in the fiend's severed head, at Janik's feet. Its body slumped to the ground.

"Thanks for getting it off me," Dania said.

"Thanks for keeping my head on me," Janik replied. He bent to pull his sword free, and tested the point with his finger. "Auftane?" He looked around for the dwarf, finding him beside Mathas.

"Give me the sword," Auftane said, anticipating Janik's request. He took the blade and traced symbols on it as he had done before, then handed it back to Janik. "That ought to help."

"Thank you." Janik checked the point again out of habit, then slid the sword back into its sheath. "On second thought," he said, pulling it out again, "I expect I'm going to need this again soon."

"I can't quite believe we're not still fighting," Dania said. "Those two certainly made enough noise to draw attention."

"Well, we don't know how many of these things are here," Janik said. "The party that came after us was large, so maybe they didn't leave many behind."

"Sounds pretty optimistic," Auftane observed.

"It's a pleasant enough fantasy," Janik said. "But it's probably a trap."

"Now that's the Janik I know," Dania said with a wry smile.

"Where now?" Auftane asked.

"A place to talk about this that's not out in the open," Janik said. "It would have been good to come in here with a plan."

"We were making our way toward a plan," Dania said, "but they caught us off guard. Sneaking up on our camp in the middle of the night—honestly, they have no respect for the way things are supposed to be done."

Janik laughed quietly and pointed to a heap of rubble nearby—evidently one of the efforts to rebuild the ruins. They moved quietly into its shadow and huddled together to plan their next steps.

"I see two possible approaches," Janik said. "One would be to retrace our steps from our last journey. I have the map I made then, though I don't know how helpful it will be with all the building they've been doing." He pulled the sheaf of parchment out of his coat and rustled through it. "The other option would be to head straight for the ziggurat, assuming that whatever is going on here has its origins in that structure." He found the map he was looking for, checked the positions of the moons to orient himself, and pulled a small, smooth stone from another pocket. The stone glowed with a dim white light, and he held it near the map so he could read it.

He pointed to a spot at the edge of his map. "I think we're about here," he said. "Last time we came from the west and only made it about this far."

"May I see the map?" Mathas asked, extending a hand.

"Of course." Janik placed it in the elf's wizened hand and held the glowstone so it illuminated the map.

Mathas studied it for a moment. "A typical scholar's scratches," he sighed. "You can read these notations, can you?"

"You know I can. What are you looking at?"

"Well, I can't make out a word of it, but if my memory serves—and I have no reason to believe that its efficacy has been dimmed by my advanced age—then we must be almost directly above the place where we located the Ramethene Sword, and not far from the entrance to that underground vault."

"Let me see that," Janik demanded. He snatched the map from Mathas and held the light close to it. "Of course," he said. "You're right. And we had thought that we might be close to finding an entrance to the ziggurat down there."

"I'm sorry," Auftane interrupted, "but could you back up a little bit? I'm having a hard time following you."

"Forgive me, Auftane. I forget you weren't with us last time. On our previous expedition, we came in from the west, over here." He pointed to the map and trailed his finger over it, showing their route through the ruins. "None of this was here—there was no wall, and none of these stacks of blocks. We went straight to the ziggurat and searched for a long time, hoping to find a way inside. We made wider and wider circles around it, and right here—" he pointed to a spot just west of their current position—"we did some digging. We managed to uncover the outline of a large chamber. It was boring work, though, and we gave up on uncovering any more of it—especially once we stumbled onto a passage leading down into the earth, still clear enough for us to pass through. That led us down into a large vault that was pretty much intact, and that's where we found the Ramethene Sword."

"When we brought the sword up to the surface, Krael met us," Mathas said, "and after that defeat we lost interest in exploring the site any further. But we believed that if an entrance to the ziggurat were found, it would likely be connected to that underground vault."

"And that passage is near here?" Auftane asked.

"I admit that my mapping suffered in the excitement of discovery," Janik said. "But I believe Mathas is correct. It should be close."

"Then it could very well be that your two approaches are one," Mathas said. "By retracing our steps to the vault where we found the sword, we might be able to reach the ziggurat and get to the heart of this."

"That reminds me," Janik said. "Mathas, what do you make of the arrangement of these towers, these stacks of rubble?"

"What do you mean?"

"When I was up on the wall, it struck me for a moment that there might be some pattern to their placement around the ziggurat. Does that suggest anything to you?"

"Hmm," the elf said, stroking his chin. "I had a brief impression of a similar thought when I was scouting the ruins with my spell. But I didn't discern anything specific."

"A pattern?" Auftane said. He rested his hand on the nearest block of stone and closed his eyes for a moment. Janik and Mathas exchanged a quizzical glance. "Yes . . ." The dwarf almost sang the word, surprisingly high and clear, but quickly resumed his normal low rumble. "There are lines of power pervading this place."

"Binding the rajah?" Dania said.

"I can't tell their exact purpose, but binding is possible.

On the other hand, this structure seems to be designed to focus the power lines. Why would the zakyas be building these towers up if they're making the rajah's prison stronger?"

"Maybe something else is going on," Janik said. "Could they be arranging these lines of magic power in a different way, maybe to weaken the bonds of the prison?"

"Anything's possible," Auftane said with a shrug. "I would need to examine more of the structures, try to get a sense of the larger pattern to determine exactly what's going on."

"So what should we do?" Janik said. "Should we check out the rest of the towers, or head underground and look for a way into the ziggurat? Dania, what's your opinion?"

"Underground."

"Mathas?" Janik said.

"Underground, I think," the elf said. "While I admit to some curiosity, I also cannot deny a feeling of urgency. I think we should try to get to the heart of the matter as quickly as possible."

"Auftane?"

"I agree with Mathas. Curiosity be damned."

"Then we're agreed," Janik declared. "Let's find the way underground."

● ● ● ◉ ● ● ●

They crouched low amid the rubble, trying to stay out of sight of any guards that might be stationed on the wall or patrolling the ruins. They rounded a heap of jumbled stone, and Janik pointed to another crooked tower ahead.

"That tower should be at or near the passage entrance," he said. "Let's hope they haven't covered it."

"Quite the contrary," Auftane observed as they neared the tower. It displayed the most complete construction they had seen in the ruins: a carefully built keystone archway leading between two large blocks. Beyond the arch, they could see a stairway descending into the earth.

"Oh, there are stairs now?" Janik said. "And I was looking forward to scaling that drop again."

"Stairs probably mean guards," Dania warned. "If this is a well-used route, it will be watched."

"Weapons ready, everybody," Janik whispered, and he saw Auftane shift his grip on his mace. "I'll go first."

Janik stepped up to the archway and peered inside. He produced the glowstone from his pocket and shone its dim light ahead of him into the dark tunnel. Seeing no sign of guards, he motioned the others forward and stepped through the arch.

Janik felt his foot tug a tripwire and he jumped forward in a flash, keeping just ahead of a dozen gleaming metal blades that arced out of the wall. He hit the floor in a roll and crouched low, ready to jump again if the trap had more to offer.

"Wait!" he hissed. Auftane came up short just before crossing the tripwire. The blades slid back into the walls, disappearing so smoothly that Janik could see the slits only because he knew where to look.

"There's a tripwire," he whispered to Auftane, "just in front of you." He took a cautious step back toward the dwarf, who crouched down to look for the wire.

"Ah, I see," Auftane said. "Back up, out of reach of the blades. I'll cut the line."

Janik took four steps back, checking carefully to make sure he was beyond the reach of the blades' deadly arcs, and nodded to Auftane. The dwarf was examining the wire carefully and checking the walls around it.

"If you want to do it right—" Janik began.

"Tie off the ends so the tension isn't released, I know," Auftane interrupted. "But that's a lot more work. Still," he added, "best to be safe. Would you hold one side?"

Janik stepped beside the dwarf, keeping his eyes on the wire in Auftane's hand.

"Hold it here and don't let it move," Auftane said. Janik grabbed the wire where the dwarf indicated. Auftane grabbed the line near the opposite end and used a small pair of clippers to snip it in the middle.

Janik slowly let out his breath.

The dwarf's nimble hands quickly tied off one end of the wire against the wall, then he took the other end from Janik and did the same.

"Should be safe now," he announced, getting to his feet.

Janik advanced carefully down the hallway, then turned and nodded to Auftane. "Well done," he said as the dwarf followed him, waving Mathas and Dania forward.

"Thank you."

Janik advanced cautiously down the stairs. Several times he tensed, ready to spring, before realizing that the movement beneath his feet was just the hasty workmanship of the stairs rather than a sophisticated pressure-plate trigger to another death trap.

The stairs led them far underground, and before long Janik called a halt, set his pack on the stairs, and produced a lantern, stowing the glowstone in his coat pocket. He opened the lantern's shutter just wide enough to light the width of the stairs ahead of him, shouldered his pack, and continued to the bottom.

The stairs gave way to a huge vault, a grandly impressive chamber that remained well preserved through the centuries.

It showed clear signs of its age, particularly in the stylized bestial faces carved in the walls—they were worn and barely recognizable as tigers. In places, the walls had crumbled away, and darkness hinted at open spaces beyond.

Four archways sculpted to resemble the gaping mouths of tigers led into passages extending farther beneath the ruined city. Above them, a number of small balconies overlooking the chamber suggested another level of passages higher up. Janik stood in a fifth archway, looking across the room at an elaborate sculpture. Set in an alcove, the statue depicted a dragon sprawled on its back, an expression of pain contorting its features. Janik reflected that he had barely looked at the statue the last time he was here—he had been completely focused on the blade that had been embedded in the stone dragon's breast, the Ramethene Sword.

Seeing this chamber stirred his memories powerfully, more so than simply reaching Mel-Aqat had. The room was exactly as he had left it three years ago, when he had wrested the sword out of the statue and carried it out of the chamber and up to the surface. Where Maija had abandoned him. Lost in his memories, he turned and looked behind him, toward the fateful spot where he had faced off with Krael. From the expressions on their faces, he could tell that Dania and Mathas were also feeling those memories rushing back.

"Watch out!" Auftane yelled, his eyes wide. The dwarf grabbed Janik and pulled him to a crouch just as two arrows pierced the air where his head had been. The arrows clattered against the wall as Janik rolled backward into the chamber, gripping his sword tightly as he moved.

A zakya stood in one of the archways, nocking two more arrows to a massive bow and beginning to draw the string back. Two more of the creatures started pushing past the first, swords and shields in their hands. Janik and Dania met them side by side. Mathas sent bolts of flame hurtling toward the archer.

Janik fought almost automatically, his mind still swimming in his memories. His sword bit deep, thanks to Auftane's magic, but in his mind it became the Ramethene Sword, an instrument of pure destruction flashing like lightning as it cut and jabbed. He could almost see the image of a grasping Emerald Claw on the shields of the fiends he fought, and he let out all the rage he had bridled for three years, let it empower his blade and give strength to his blows. Past and present flowed into one—but where he had been powerless before, standing dumbly as Maija took the sword from his hand, staring bewildered as she gave it to Krael, now he was powerful. He was fury given flesh, and the rakshasas felt his wrath.

He was not aware of Mathas and Auftane, and only dimly aware of Dania as she moved beside him, maneuvered around their foes with him, gave him openings. Her sword flashed again and again with holy power, which felt to Janik like an elemental expression of the rage he felt.

Only when he faced Dania over the kneeling form of the zakya archer, which had dropped its bow and hastily drawn a sword, did he see her face and realize that his face, too, was streaked with tears. Janik wrenched his sword out of the dying fiend's shoulder and stepped back, giving Dania room to cut its head from its neck.

Janik blinked several times at the zakya's helmet as it bounced on the floor, rolled drunkenly, and stopped. The fury still pounded in his chest, beat like a war drum in his temples, clenched in his jaw, and set his face like stone. But his stomach churned with something else—a disgust at this bloody work, a deep weariness that began to spread as an ache to his bones. Dania's words surfaced in his storm-tossed mind.

I just want peace, Janik.

Dania's gasp shook him from his reflection. Her wide eyes were focused on something over his shoulder, and he wheeled to face whatever new threat was upon them.

A woman stood on one of the balconies, her hands clenching the stone railing in front of her as she leered down at them. "Hello, old friends," she purred.

Janik's voice was hoarse in his throat. "Maija!"

CHAPTER 16

Dear Janik," Maija said into the deafening silence. "How have you been? Getting along without me?" Her voice grated on the stone and scraped across Janik's heart, mockery oozing from every syllable. "Dania told me you were perhaps a little heartbroken. Poor thing."

"Damn you to the Outer Darkness, Maija Olarin," Dania swore through clenched teeth.

"Tsk. Didn't your fat exorcist friend teach you not to use such strong language, Dania? Or if not him, then perhaps that sweet boy Gered?" Maija's expression of feigned innocence twisted into a cruel smile. "Or did he die before he could teach you much of anything?"

Janik saw Dania step in front of him, but she held her sword at her side. She stared up at Maija in silence, then staggered backward as if some invisible force had struck her. Roused from his stupor, Janik caught her before she fell on the floor and held her up as she struggled to regain her feet.

"What did you do to her, Maija?"

"Do? I did nothing." Maija sneered. "Perhaps she asked a

question and couldn't handle the answer."

"What happened to you, Maija?" Janik cried. "What happened to the love we shared? Where is the touch of the Sovereigns in you?"

"I very much doubt you can handle the answer to those questions, dear Janik."

"I can't handle not knowing. I need to know. Damn it, I deserve an answer!"

Maija's smile stretched to a thin line. "I lied."

The words were barely more than a whisper, but the force of them nearly knocked Janik off his feet. His arms grew weak and Dania began to slip from his grasp, but she found her feet and lifted her sword.

With a wordless shout, Dania ran forward, leaping into the air to grab the edge of the balcony where Maija stood. As she pulled herself up, Maija stepped back in surprise. She recovered quickly, though, and made a forceful gesture with her hand, as if to push Dania off the balcony.

The effect was far more dramatic than a physical push. Dania flew backward over Janik's head and landed behind him in a clatter of steel.

"And so the end begins," Maija whispered.

Curling her hands into twisting arcane gestures, she reached toward Janik, purple-black lightning sparking around her hands. Zakyas appeared in four of the archways around the chamber, and zakya archers stepped onto the other balconies, pulling back their bowstrings and taking aim.

Janik heard roars and shouts, the clamor of weapons and shields, the rattle of arrows hitting stone and armor. But he saw only Maija, her hands extended to him and her eyes locked on his. He felt as if her hand were locked around his throat.

For a moment, he thrilled at the imagination of her touch as he stared into her eyes—his mind could almost imagine it as a loving caress. He stared into her eyes as the edges of his vision went black. A glint of red in her brown eyes was the last thing he saw before the darkness swallowed him.

❂ ❂ ❂ ❂ ❂ ❂ ❂

He was lying on his back. The first thing he became aware of was the hard floor beneath him, and then a throbbing pain slammed through his head. His eyes struggled to open and he became vaguely aware of a face bending over his own. Then he recognized the face and rolled away from it, finding his back against a stone wall.

"Krael!"

"About time you woke up," the vampire said, grinning. "I'm not sure how much longer I could have held off my hunger."

Janik looked around. They were in a small stone chamber with a heavy iron door—no windows, not even a grate through which light or fresh air might come. His lantern lay in the middle of the floor, its bright beam casting weird shadows on Krael's face. Krael's warforged lieutenant stood impassively behind Krael. The still forms of Janik's three companions were heaped on the floor around them.

Without a word, Janik turned his back on Krael and knelt beside Dania. She was battered and coated in dried blood, but he surmised that much of the blood was not hers, for her breathing was steady and her pulse strong.

"They're all alive and reasonably healthy, Janik," Krael said. "But I find it touching that you checked on Dania first. I'm sure your concern would warm her heart."

Ignoring Krael, Janik moved beside Mathas next, then

Auftane. As the vampire had said, they were alive and seemed all right.

"You know, the whelp she found in Karrnath was nothing at all like you, Janik," Krael went on. "He was a Sentinel Marshal, definitely a step up on the social ladder, but so very bland. Even his blood lacked spice. I told her as much when I first met him."

Janik clenched his jaw and pretended to study Auftane's wounds more closely, though they were obviously not serious. He wanted to leap on Krael and rip out his throat with his bare hands to shut him up, but he decided that ignoring the vampire was the more prudent course.

For the moment.

"As for you—well, I have to say, I always thought far more of Dania than of your bitch Maija. I was pleasantly surprised by Maija when she gave me the Ramethene Sword, but she definitely took a turn for the worse after we—"

Janik couldn't contain himself any more. "Stop it!" he roared, lunging at Krael, grabbing at his throat and clawing at his eyes. "Shut up!" His fingers were useless against the vampire's cold flesh, so he began pummeling Krael's face and head with his fists, punctuating each word with a blow. "Don't ever defile their names with your mouth again!"

It struck him as strange that Krael didn't fight back, and his rage began to subside. As his head cleared a little, he realized that Krael's hands were bound behind him, and the vampire had been completely unable to defend himself from Janik's furious assault. Neither had the warforged moved, though Janik could not see any restraint on him.

Janik got shakily to his feet, leaving Krael prone and smirking on the floor. He turned his back on the vampire and the warforged.

"Janik?" Dania murmured, and Janik rushed to her side.

From the corner of his eye, Janik saw the warforged step forward to help Krael get upright again. He caught a glimpse of strange blue manacles binding Krael's hands, but he turned his full attention to Dania.

"I'm here, Dania," he whispered, clasping her hand.

"Is Mathas—? I saw him fall."

"He's fine, Dania, we're all alive."

"What's that—" her nose wrinkled and her brow furrowed as she blinked several times to clear her eyes. Then she sat upright. "Krael!"

"Dania," the vampire said, flashing his sharp teeth in a wide smile.

Dania's hand grasped wildly at her belt before she realized her sword was not there. Krael shrugged to emphasize his own helplessness, and Dania calmed somewhat.

"What's going on?" she said. "Where are we?"

"I'm not sure—" Janik began.

"Look around," Krael interrupted. "We're in a cell in the ziggurat at the heart of Mel-Aqat. Doesn't it stagger the imagination? This very room might have been used fifty thousand years ago to hold prisoners of the giants before they were sacrificed."

"Any idea where our weapons are?" Dania growled, provoking a harsh laugh from Krael.

"How do you know we're in the ziggurat, Krael?" Janik said.

"Unlike you lot, I was awake when they dragged me in here," Krael said with a sly grin. "Which means I know the way out."

"So why haven't you pulled your cloud of vapors trick and slipped out under that door?"

Krael scowled and turned his body so Janik could see the manacles clasped around his wrists. They were forged of a strange blue steel, and Krael's movements made small blue sparks crackle around them.

"A particularly fiendish invention," Krael said. "They prevent me from altering my form in any way. Sever's tried everything he can think of, but he's been unable to get them off me."

"I've heard of such things," Auftane said, sitting up and pressing a hand to his battered head. "But I've never seen them. I'd very much like to examine them . . . once my head stops spinning."

Krael laughed. "If you can figure out how to get them off me, you can examine them all you want, dwarf. You know Janik, you never did introduce me to your new companion back in Stormreach. Very rude of you."

"His name is Auftane," Janik grunted.

"Auftane Khunnam," the artificer said. "I've heard so much about you, Krael."

"I expect you have," Krael said. He sighed. "And I'm sure none of it was good."

Auftane looked reflective. "Yes, that's true."

"Auftane," Janik said, "will you look at Mathas and see if you can do something to wake him up?"

"How neglectful of me," Krael said. "I haven't introduced my lieutenant here," he jerked his head at the warforged. "Well, Janik, I gather you have met Sever, but I don't think your friends have. Sever, the lovely Dania ir'Vran, the unconscious Mathas Allister, and our new acquaintance, Auftane Khunnam."

"How pleasant to see you again, Martell," Sever said, the sarcasm in his voice sharply contrasting with his emotionless face.

"You're quieter when Krael's around," Janik said to the warforged. "Or is it because you don't have a sword in your hand?"

"Take your pick, Martell."

"Well," Janik said, getting to his feet, "if we're cooped up here and forced to talk to each other, we might as well make it productive. I want to know what in the Nine Seas is going on with Maija."

"By the Flame, Janik," Dania said, "her evil overwhelmed me. I have never encountered another creature so strongly stinking of it. Not even Krael—"

"That's enough, Dania."

"Janik," Dania insisted, "not even Krael makes my senses reel the way she did. She commands these fiends! Can't you see it? Do you still not believe that she's beyond redemption?"

Janik sighed deeply. "Do you remember what you said to me back in Stormreach? That you wouldn't stand by and watch a friend die, ever again? That's what this is to me, Dania. I can't turn away while Maija dies. I can't give up on her. I've got to fight for her, even if I have to fight a legion of fiends under her command, even if it means fighting her. I can't just accept it, damn it. I will not be a bystander to her destruction."

"You'll have to hold me back, then," Krael said.

"That's what I was going to say," Dania said, glaring at Krael while looking a little uncomfortable at sharing the vampire's opinion.

"Why, Krael?" Janik asked, wheeling on the vampire. "What did she do to you?"

Krael snarled at Janik, baring his long fangs, for a moment looking like a ravenous beast furious at being caged.

Janik didn't flinch, but held Krael's stare. After a moment, the vampire spoke.

"All right, Janik. Let me tell you a story. I believe you know the beginning—or shall I go over it for the benefit of those who weren't present?"

"I've heard it," Auftane said over his shoulder. He was busy tending to Mathas, but clearly paying attention to the conversation. Janik noted that Mathas's eyes were open, but he looked very weak.

"As have I, Captain Kavarat," the warforged said.

"Well, then," Krael continued. "Maija traveled with us back to Stormreach and from there directly to Korth by airship. Along the way, she played with my affections, as I presume she did with yours, Janik. Except I did not fully trust her, so I was not swayed by her charms. Her *considerable* charms."

Janik almost leaped at Krael again, but the vampire's grin told him Krael was trying to provoke him, and he didn't want to provide that satisfaction.

"She made up a story—that another Emerald Claw agent had contacted her and swayed her to our side, and worked out a deal in which she'd hand a treasure over to me in order to prove her loyalty to the Emerald Claw. She kept up the lie for quite a while. Once we reached Karrnath, she claimed to have had another meeting with this agent, who told her to keep working with me. I knew she was lying, and my superiors confirmed my suspicion, but they ordered me to play along, to find out what she was trying to accomplish. I admit to some curiosity about what she was doing, trying to bluff the Order of the Emerald Claw."

Krael cracked his neck before continuing.

"That went on for about a year," he said. "We spent most

of that time in Karrnath, sneaking around the agents of the damned king to get the work of the Order done. She seemed genuinely committed to working with the Order, and I was just starting to believe that she was really on our side. Then she came to me and announced that she'd been assigned to look for the Tablet of Shummarak. You know what the Tablet is, Janik?"

"Of course."

"Well, that caught the interest of my superiors, and they told me to keep working with her. They assigned a priest to accompany us, a simpering idiot named Mudren Fain. They wanted me to get the Tablet if we managed to locate it. Well, it took us a year of searching, and the hunt led us around Khorvaire, briefly to Xen'drik, and finally back to Atur in Karrnath—which is where I saw Dania, of course."

Janik was getting sick of Krael's sarcastic grin and mocking tone, but the vampire was telling him new information—new pieces of the puzzle were taking shape in his mind. He glanced at Dania, who seemed to be keeping her anger in check by thinking hard about what Krael was telling them.

"We returned to Atur because we had traced the Tablet of Shummarak to its last known owner, a shifter vampire called Havoc. Mudren finally proved himself useful by discovering the location of Havoc's crypt. We found him in his crypt, where a bunch of idiots had left him for dead before the Last War. They drove a stake through his heart and left, figuring the job was done. Well, when Mudren Fain pulled the stake out of the shriveled remains of Havoc's heart, we quickly discovered that the job was not done."

"Havoc came back," Dania said blankly.

"Havoc came back," Krael repeated. "He grabbed Mudren Fain by the throat and drank every last drop of blood out of the damned fool's body while dear Maija stood there, licking her lips. Oh, and did I mention? I would have stopped Mudren from pulling out the stake, but Maija had cast a spell on me to hold me helpless."

"Licking her lips?" Dania asked.

"Licking her lying, cheating, blasphemous lips," Krael said. "And then she struck her deal with Havoc. Anyone want to guess what she gave him in exchange for his help in finding the Tablet?"

"You," Janik and Dania said at the same time.

"Exactly. Havoc grabbed me while I was still paralyzed by Maija's spell. He drained Mudren dry and left him for dead, but Havoc turned me into *this*—" he bared his teeth again. "And until Dania and her friends so kindly obliterated him, I was forced to obey his commands. Which reminds me, Dania, I never did thank you."

"Believe me, the pleasure was all mine," Dania said. "I would have killed you, too, if I could have."

"And if I can ever return the favor, I will. Anyway, I think Dania knows the rest of the story, or most of it. Havoc led us to the Tablet—"

"You found it?" Dania interrupted. "We were never sure."

"Oh, yes. We found the Tablet right where Havoc had left it a hundred years ago. Maija spirited it away, breaking her word to Havoc. And Dania and her friends barged in right after that, when Havoc was about to tear Maija's throat out."

"If only we'd come a few moments later," Dania said.

"I said that's enough, Dania," Janik said.

Dania got to her feet for the first time. "Well, I'm not going to stop until you get it through your head that this isn't just some lark that Maija is pulling on us. Don't you see? If

Maija has the Tablet of Shummarak and she's here, that means she's trying to release whatever fiend lord is imprisoned here. She might as well be plotting to destroy the world!"

"And of course we're going to stop her," Janik said, "but that doesn't mean we're just going to cut her down."

"What if that's what it takes? We're not just going to talk her out of it, either. What do you have in mind?"

"We are talking about my wife, damn it!" Janik's face was a hand's width from Dania's. "I will take up arms against the Sovereign Host before I kill her—or let you do it!"

"She is not your wife any more, Janik, any more than she is the friend I once loved. Evil has consumed her! There isn't any Maija left."

"You talk as if evil were a monster, like the chuul we fought on the shore. Evil doesn't eat people, Dania. What are you saying? That she's undead? That she's been turned into a vampire, like Krael?"

"I don't know, Janik! She's not a vampire, she's definitely still alive, but—" She stopped abruptly. "Wait," she said to herself.

"But what? If she's not undead, then what do you think happened to her? What kind of evil could consume her and leave nothing behind?"

"The undead aren't the only great evil in the world, Janik. Look around you! We've been fighting fiends in the flesh since we entered the desert three weeks ago. This whole place was erected by a force of evil so great—" She broke off suddenly.

"What, then? You think she's been turned into a rakshasa?"

"Hosts of Shavarath, how could I be so blind?" Dania whispered. "Janik, I think you might be right!"

"What do you mean?"

"We're here because the Keeper of the Flame sensed something—an evil spirit escaping into the world about the time that we were here. Janik, what if that spirit possessed Maija?"

CHAPTER 17

"Possessed?" Krael said. "That would explain a great many things."

"So you're saying that the evil spirit we accidentally released while we were here is Maija?" Janik said, incredulous.

"It's in her," Dania said. "It has taken up residence in her body and controls her actions."

"And that's the evil that has devoured her?"

"That's just it, Janik! If I'm right, then Maija is still in there—like a passenger in a carriage the fiend is driving, helpless to stop it. And that means we might be able to save her—if we can drive the fiend out of her!"

Janik could not speak. He had clung to shreds of hope for so long without having any idea what to hope for. Now, when hope seemed justified, he wasn't sure how to deal with it.

"Dania?" Auftane said, looking up from Mathas. "What makes you think she's possessed?"

"Look," Dania said, "all along we've been baffled by what happened, unable to explain such a sudden and dramatic shift in her behavior. It was like it came out of nowhere, and we felt like she must have been keeping up an incredible charade for over a decade. But if I'm right, that's not what happened at all—it really was a sudden change. She wasn't lying to us all those years. When the spirit entered her, that's when she turned against us."

"So that makes it desirable to believe your theory," Auftane said, "but what evidence supports it?"

"Evidence? There's the stink of evil on her, which is stronger than the mere taint of a corrupt heart. It overpowered me back in that room. Even Krael's evil odor isn't strong enough to do that."

"I'll have to work on that," Krael said.

Dania ignored him. "Then, there's the connection with this place. It was here that she changed, as if the evil of the spirit imprisoned here had seized her. And, once she found that tablet in Karrnath, she brought it back here, as if she were obeying the orders of the rajah. And finally—" She paused a moment, searching for a conclusive argument. "Krael—you said possession would explain things. What things?"

Krael grimaced. "Well, as I said to you in Karrnath, I never thought much of Maija. I always thought of you and Janik as my real enemies, Mathas to a lesser extent, and Maija as sort of the annoying accomplice—Janik's good little wife. Believe me, I was as surprised as you were when she brought me the Ramethene Sword. And when she gave me to Havoc, I was stunned. I never trusted her, but I would have expected her to go back to Janik rather than betray me to a hundred-year-old vampire."

Janik scowled and opened his mouth to speak, but Krael cut him off.

"And then, just before we found the Tablet of Shummarak, she killed a man—a priest of the Blood of Vol, really just an innocent bystander. She used a spell on him to split him open. Blood oozed from his eyes first, then his skin erupted. I asked her where a cleric of the Sovereign Host learns magic like that."

"Exactly," Dania said. "A cleric of the Sovereign Host doesn't use spells like that. But ancient demons of Khyber do."

"I'm convinced," Janik said, and Auftane nodded as well. "So what do we do?"

"If we can drive the fiend out of her, then we can confront it on a different footing, perhaps destroy it. No matter what, Maija should be restored to her right mind."

"I liked the plan of killing her better," Krael said.

"Careful, Krael," Dania said. "There are three people in this very small room who have been hoping to kill you for fifteen years. Don't provoke us."

"Without weapons, I'm fairly certain that Sever would rip all your arms off before you managed to hurt me," Krael shot back. Sever accentuated Krael's point by slamming one fist into his open hand.

"Krael, help me here," Janik said, dropping to his knees in front of the vampire.

"What?" Krael said, one eyebrow arched in surprise.

"You stole all my books that have anything to do with Mel-Aqat, damn it. I assume you had a reason for doing that besides spite. What is the spirit possessing Maija?"

"Dhavibashta?"

"Don't be stupid," Janik said, and Krael grinned.

"What are you talking about?" Dania said.

Janik got to his feet. "Dhavibashta is the name of the rajah imprisoned here, according to the *Serpentes Fragments*. But it's clear to me that whatever spirit has possessed Maija is trying to release the rajah, so it's obviously not the rajah."

"I'm glad to see you can function without your books," Krael said.

"I still want them back."

Mathas sat up, his desire to participate in the conversation finally overpowering his weakness. "Is it possible," he said, "that the imprisoned rajah could extend its will beyond its prison to control Maija, while most of its essence remained trapped here?"

"That would mean the rajah could be using Maija to try to free itself," Dania said. "And I confess I don't know enough about this kind of thing to say for sure. Kophran might have been able to answer that, but—"

"But we wouldn't want to be locked in this tiny room with a pompous ass," Auftane said.

Janik ran his fingers through his hair. "I want to consider the more likely possibilities first."

"And what are those?" Dania asked.

"That's what I'm trying to figure out," Janik snapped. "If my theory is correct, the city of Mel-Aqat was built long after the rakshasa rajah was imprisoned. The ziggurat was built to mark the site of the rajah's prison, and the city was built around it."

"Who built the city?" Auftane asked.

"Based on the scale of the ruins, most of the city was inhabited by giants."

"Giants?" Auftane exclaimed. "Not the areas we've been in so far!"

"Right. The subterranean chambers, which include the chamber where we found the Ramethene Sword, were neither built nor used by giants. It suggests two possibilities. The pattern often seen elsewhere in Xen'drik is that of giant-sized main structures, plus attached quarters built on a human-sized scale that were used by the elf slaves of the giants. The chambers we've seen don't fit that pattern. They don't look like slave quarters—they're far too well built and extravagant. And they're not decorated with the typical elven motifs of skulls and scorpions. Instead, we find stylized tiger faces."

"Hmm," Krael said with mock seriousness. "Now who would have carved tiger faces in these ancient stone walls?"

"Right," Janik said, ignoring Krael's sarcasm. "I have long argued that Mel-Aqat was built by a fringe cult of giants that worshiped the rakshasa rajahs. I think now that this cult was led by a smaller cadre of rakshasas—a force of zakyas responsible for direct control of the giants, and smaller echelons of the more powerful fiends above them."

"So you think that one of these rakshasas might be the spirit possessing Maija?" Dania said.

"That's where my theory was heading," Janik said.

"The Fleshrender," Krael said.

"What?"

"The Fleshrender," Krael said. "That's the spirit in Maija."

Janik's brow furrowed. "The Fleshrender is a name for the Ramethene Sword," he said.

"I thought so too, until just now. But what's the one text that uses that name?" Krael asked.

"One of the *Serpentes Fragments*." Janik searched his memory for a moment, then quoted:

The Sunderer smote to the dragon's heart,
and its blood formed a river upon the land;
The Fleshrender drew forth the serpent's life
and its blood gave life to the gathered hordes.

"It's a clear textual parallel, the Sunderer in the first couplet and the Fleshrender in the second, both referring to the sword." Janik was thinking out loud.

"And what's the next couplet?" Krael said.

"Something about the blade and the hand that wields it. I don't remember exactly."

" 'For the blade drinks the blood, and the hand that wields it feasts on the life.' The two couplets are parallel, but not synonymous. The blade is the Sunderer, drinking the dragon's blood. But the hand that wields the blade is the Fleshrender, feasting on the dragon's life. See?"

Janik opened his mouth and closed it again, raising his eyebrows in surprise.

"I think you might be right, as much as I hate to admit it. But what makes you think this Fleshrender is the spirit possessing Maija?"

"Two things," Krael said, "neither one more than a gut feeling. First, there's the kind of magic Maija used in Karrnath. I suppose any fiend might use such spells, but they seem particularly well suited to one called the Fleshrender. Second, consider the connection to the Ramethene Sword. Like it or not, Janik, I think you released that fiend when you pulled the Ramethene Sword from its place."

"I don't like it, but I can't argue that right now. So—we have a name for our enemy—though not a very pleasant name. How do we get the Fleshrender out of Maija's body?"

"First, we get out of here," Krael said.

"We?" Dania said. "I don't plan on letting you out of here alive, let alone helping you escape."

Krael looked distinctly uncomfortable and Janik felt a strange twinge in his chest. A large part of him agreed with Dania. Krael had caused him so much misery and difficulty over the last few months, to say nothing of the previous fifteen years, that helping him and accepting his help in return seemed unthinkable. At the same time, he couldn't avoid seeing himself in Krael's situation: helpless and at the mercy of his worst enemies. Krael had been cooperative, and, well, useful—probably because he knew he needed the help of his enemies if he was to escape.

More than that, though, Janik somehow felt that Krael wasn't fundamentally different from himself. He had not seduced Maija away from him—Janik had grown so used to blaming Krael for what happened that he had a hard time separating his anger at Krael from his despair over Maija. And he was here for the same reason that Janik was: to claim revenge against the fiend that had destroyed his life. They had some common goals, both in the short term and in long-range pursuits.

"You need me," Krael said. "You'll never find your way out of here without my help, and you'll never find Maija."

"She might very well find us if we escape from here," Janik said.

"And she'll overpower you again, probably kill you this time," Krael said. "With me and Sever along, you've got a fighting chance."

"I don't think so," Dania said. "Now that I know what we're facing, I think our victory depends entirely on my ability to force this Fleshrender out of Maija's body. Two extra swords aren't likely to make the difference—assuming we can recover our weapons."

"Both of us are very effective without weapons."

"Krael, stop begging," Janik said. "It's embarrassing."

Krael visibly bit back another sarcastic retort and looked away, toward the door.

"Seems to me it's an open question how any of us will escape, whether we decide to help each other or not," Janik said. "But it's certain that sitting in here arguing with each other isn't going to get anyone out of this room."

Dania looked at the floor. "Sorry, Janik."

"Auftane, how's your patient?"

"I'm fine, Janik," Mathas said. "Tired, but fine."

"Glad to hear it, old friend," Janik said with a warm smile. He fought down the lump in his throat and turned back to Auftane. "Would you have a look at the door and see if there's any way you can open it?"

"Sever's tried that, too," Krael said.

"Not to judge too hastily based on Sever's appearance, but I suspect that Auftane is capable of more subtlety," Janik said.

"Agreed, Martell," the warforged sneered. "All I can say is that the door's too strong for me."

"And that probably means it's too strong for any of us to break down, but my hope is that Auftane can find another way to open it."

The dwarf was peering into a tiny hole near the right edge of the door, about halfway up its iron surface. "I suspect this is the other side of the keyhole," he said, "but it's too small to get at the mechanism."

"I believe the door is barred as well," Sever added. "Your lockpicks won't lift the bar, Khunnam."

"He's right, Janik," Auftane said, shrugging his shoulders.

Janik ran his fingers through his hair and stared at the door in silence for a moment. Finally, he sighed and shook his head. "Auftane, why don't you take a look at Krael's manacles. I want an assessment first, before you open them. Mathas, can you help him?"

"I'll try."

Auftane and Mathas huddled together behind Krael, examining the strange blue metal bonds as Sever watched over their shoulders. Janik stepped over to Dania, who had her head cocked as if she were listening to something outside the room.

"What is it?" he asked.

"Nothing," she said. "What are you thinking?"

Janik took her arm and drew her a few steps away from the others—as far as the tiny cell would allow. "What if Krael is our only way out of here?" he whispered to her.

Dania pursed her lips and crossed her arms. "There has to be another way," she said.

"We'd all like there to be another way, but no law of the universe says a means of escape must exist, let alone a second choice. What if he's the only way?"

"Do you think there's the slimmest chance we can trust him?" Dania said. "The instant he gets those manacles off, what's to stop him from turning to mist, slipping under the door, and leaving us here to rot?"

"I can't think of anything," Janik said, frowning.

"Janik?" Auftane called, standing up behind Krael.

"Yes?"

Staying behind Krael and out of his line of sight, Auftane pointed at the manacles and bobbed his head, an exaggerated expression of confidence on his face. Janik nodded his understanding and turned to Dania.

He lowered his voice further. "Assuming we can extract a convincing oath from Krael that he'll help us if we help him, are you willing to go along with that?"

"Are you asking me whether I can accept the lesser evil of helping him get free for the sake of the greater good of defeating Maija?"

"I guess so, yes."

Dania sighed. "I have to bring him to reckoning for the evil he's done, Janik. I have to. But if that happens after we've freed Maija from this Fleshrender's grip, I can live with that."

"Thank you," Janik said, clasping Dania's shoulder before turning to the vampire. "Krael?"

"Have you reached a verdict?" Krael said. "Decided my fate?"

"Your fate's up to you, Krael," Janik said, "though Dania assures me that she has a particular vision of it in mind. But in the short term, let's discuss what we can do for each other."

"A good idea," Krael said, eyeing Dania.

"Auftane here is confident that he can release you from these manacles. He's no doubt motivated by the opportunity to study them in more detail."

"I'm pleased to hear that."

"So we can set you free, and we ask for our freedom in exchange. We get you out of the manacles, you go under the door and open it from the other side. At that point, we're even."

"That sounds fair," Krael said.

"However," Janik continued, "once we're all out that door, I don't think we're done with each other, as much as we all might like to be. We have a goal in common, to extract our revenge from the Fleshrender. I'm not at all confident that we'll go about that in the same way."

"Whatever do you mean?" Krael asked.

"I mean that while Dania might be able to force the spirit out of Maija's body, I suspect you're more likely to force the spirit out by killing Maija. That's not an acceptable approach."

"Hmm," Krael said, a faint smile on his thin lips. "Perhaps it would be best to split up once we get out this door, and see who gets to Maija first."

"And let you tear her apart if you reach her first?" Janik said. "No."

"Besides," Dania added, "the two of you can't hope to face her alone. It seems that the six of us working together would have the best chances of reaching her, fighting through all the zakyas, and—" she caught herself.

"Killing her?" Krael said.

"And accomplishing our goal," Dania said, turning away from the leering vampire.

Janik crouched in front of Krael again, looking him right in the eyes. "I want to trust you, Krael, and I'd rather work with you than against you on this. Can you give me any assurance that you're not going to stab us in the back if we help you?"

"Long term? No," Krael replied. "Short term, though, it's just not in my interest. Leave you in here and try to face Maija and the Fleshrender alone, without even Sever beside me? That would be suicide—and believe me, I have little doubt that the Fleshrender would find some way to make sure I stay dead. You can always count on me to look out for myself, Janik. You know that."

Janik stared into Krael's red eyes a moment longer.

"Besides," Krael added, "if I had wanted to betray you, I would have taken this opportunity to dominate your mind, forcing you to release me without anything in exchange."

Even as he spoke, Janik felt the vampire's presence probing at the edges of his mind, but Krael made no assault, no effort to take control.

Janik tore his gaze off Krael and stood. "It looks like we're in this together."

"For now," Krael said.

Janik glanced at Dania, but she was distracted again. "Auftane, work your magic."

Auftane kneeled behind the vampire and spent several moments in intense concentration. As far as Janik could see, no actual magic was needed—the dwarf had produced a set of lockpicks and was working them in a small keyhole set into one of the manacles. He chanted quietly as he worked, and Janik wondered if he was just improving his own concentration, manipulating the flow of magic in the manacles, or just singing to himself.

"There!" Auftane announced, and Krael stretched his arms up triumphantly.

"Auftane Khunnam," the vampire said, getting to his feet, "I am indebted to you. Those were painful and damned inconvenient."

"I look forward to giving them further study," the artificer said.

"And now for my part of the bargain," Krael said. Even as he finished his sentence, his body dissolved into a cloud of billowing vapors. For a moment, the mist was still recognizable as Krael, but then it lost all form and drifted to the door. It churned slightly as it seeped through the tiny crack under the door—and in a moment, it was gone.

The room fell silent.

Janik faced the door, his eyes unfocused but his ears straining for any hint of what was happening behind it. He listened for the sound of a bar being lifted or the lock opening. Beside him, he was aware of Dania rocking on the balls of her feet and flexing her fingers.

No sound penetrated the iron door. Janik heard Mathas grunt softly as he got to his feet, and Auftane made some clanking sounds, fidgeting with the manacles he'd taken off Krael. Dania let out a long, slow breath. Janik closed his eyes, every sound around him becoming an entity in a field of darkness. He could hear each of the others breathing—Dania slow and disciplined beside him, Mathas heavy and a little labored, Auftane uneven. No sound came from the war-forged, or from the door before him.

A knot of worry formed in Janik's chest, clenching his heart. Had Krael betrayed them again, leaving them here while he made his escape? Or just as bad, perhaps he had encountered zakya guards outside the cell that had over-powered him, the iron door blocking any sound of the struggle.

He opened his eyes and glanced at Dania beside him. She caught the movement of his head out of the corner of her eye and turned to meet his gaze. She shook her head slowly, then closed her eyes again.

She's right, Janik thought. And she was right all along—we shouldn't have trusted Krael.

"Well," he whispered at last, "really, we're no worse off than we were."

"Except that our one hope is gone," Dania said.

Janik was about to reply when a terrible clatter shattered the quiet of the room—a metallic clanging against the door. That was followed by the distinct sound of a bar being lifted off the door, then a key turning in the lock.

The door swung open, accompanied by a metallic scraping, and Krael stood in the doorway, a triumphant smile on his face.

"It damn well took you long enough," Janik said.

Krael gestured to the floor at his feet. Scattered around him were all the weapons the zakyas had taken from them—

Janik's short sword and Dania's long one, Auftane's mace, and Sever's silver-black adamantine blade, as well as the pouch of wands that Auftane carried. His own massive flail was already tucked into his belt.

"I had to kill a guard, retrieve the key, and liberate our weapons," Krael said. "I think I accomplished all that rather quickly, truth be told."

Krael stepped back as Janik retrieved his sword. He slid his slender blade into its sheath, then stooped to get Dania's and Auftane's weapons.

"That's quite a sword you have, Dania," Krael said. "Even the hilt bites."

"Holiness hurts," Dania said.

"I'll keep that in mind," Krael said, rubbing his hands together. Janik thought he caught a glimpse of terrible burns on the vampire's right hand, but they were healing even as he looked.

Janik handed weapons to his friends and led them into the outer chamber, leaving the warforged to pick up his own sword. A zakya lay dead near an open door on the opposite wall. The creature looked shriveled—even its thick fur could not hide the way its flesh clung to its bones. Janik suspected it had been perfectly healthy before Krael got to it, and his stomach churned with revulsion. He tried to look away, but his gaze was drawn to its staring eyes, bulging in their sockets.

Auftane's voice shook Janik out of his morbid observation. "Where did you find our weapons?" he asked Krael.

"Heaped on a table in the next room. The guard was stationed there but he came running when I opened the door. It's entirely possible that there was a second guard who ran the opposite direction to raise an alarm."

"Great," Janik said. "Then we need to move. Where do we go, Krael?"

"This way," Dania answered, starting out the door. Janik shot her a quizzical glance, but she did not see it. She was moving slowly, her head cocked slightly to one side, her eyes not quite focused. Auftane and Mathas waited for Janik's lead, but Krael shrugged.

"That's what I was going to say," the vampire said. "We'll find Maija on the lowest level."

"Dania," Janik said, hurrying after her and grabbing her shoulder. "What's going on?"

"You don't hear it?" Dania said, facing Janik but not really looking at him. "It's calling me."

What in Khyber? Janik thought. He gripped both of her shoulders and brought his face close to hers, trying to force her eyes to focus on him. "What's calling you, Dania? Is that a voice you should be listening to?"

"I . . . think so," Dania said vaguely. "It's confusing." Her eyes suddenly focused on Janik. "I hear them both, Janik, the binder and the bound. Come on, we need to move!" She turned and continued walking. With a quick glance back at the others, Janik followed, drawing his sword as he walked.

Wait a moment, he thought, and looked back over his shoulder at Krael.

Sure enough, the vampire had the same distant expression that Dania wore. Did he hear the same voices? Seeing Janik look back, though, Krael caught himself and flashed a toothy grin at him. Janik shook his head and hurried to keep up with Dania.

Dania was nearly across the next room, which was more of a wide hallway than a chamber. A few quick steps brought

Janik right up behind her as she reached the door at the far end and threw it open.

Despite her distraction, Dania's reflexes were still razor sharp. She brought her shield up in a flash to block an arrow, and another glanced off an armor plate at her shoulder. Janik held his lantern up to light the room beyond, and nearly dropped it in surprise.

He could not see the archers. All he saw was the giant.

CHAPTER 18

The huge creature—a hunched, misshapen thing—stood a few paces from the door. Its skin was mottled gray, with splotches of pink like the scars of recent burns and patches of thick hair growing in haphazard places. Its eyes were widely spaced and uneven, and its drooling mouth had only a few teeth. The great hump on its back nearly scraped the ceiling of the large room. If it could have stood erect, Janik figured it would have stood more than three times his own height. One massive hand was clenched around what had been a stone statue—legs were still visible where the giant gripped it, but the rest was chipped and worn into a featureless club.

A gallery circled the upper level of the room, and Janik guessed the archers were perched up there, taking cover behind the columns that lined its edge. Yes, he saw them, peering around the columns as they pulled back their bow-strings for another volley.

Ignoring the archers and the arrows that clattered around her, Dania charged forward to engage the giant. Inspired by her, Janik found it hard to be afraid, despite the size of the brute, and he advanced behind her. The giant swung its stone club in a wide arc as they approached. Dania jumped back and the club swept the air in front of her chest, while Janik hit the floor and rolled forward under the giant's reach.

Janik came out of his roll facing the giant's knee. The monster tried to hit him with its club, but Janik easily dodged the awkward swing. The giant kicked at him, missing him with its foot but managing to brush his head with its rock-hard kneecap. Janik spun away from the blow, ducking between the giant's legs and slashing at its hamstring with the tip of his blade. He cut, but not very deep, and the creature wheeled to face him again, kicking clumsily at him as it turned.

That gave Dania the opportunity to close in past its wildly swinging club, and Sever charged up beside her. Their blades swung as one, biting deep into the giant's legs. A blast of lightning from Mathas's fingers engulfed the giant's upper body, and Janik took advantage of its distraction to come in close and drive his sword up into its belly.

The giant howled as a gout of blood splashed down on Janik. The stone club clattered on the floor, and for an instant Janik thought he had dealt a mortal wound.

Then the giant's arms closed around him, pulling him off the floor and squeezing him against the bloody wound in its gut. Janik's arms were pinned to his sides, his sword hanging uselessly from his hand, and he struggled to breathe with the giant's arms clenched around his ribs. He dropped his sword and started kicking, hoping to connect with a tender spot and startle the giant into letting him go. He heard Dania shouting, trying to capture the giant's attention, and felt tremors rumbling the thing's body as she and Sever continued hacking at it. The giant wheeled around to kick at them, but its grip did not weaken.

Janik's lungs started to burn and he changed his tactics. Instead of kicking blindly, he tried to bring his legs up between his body and the giant's, hoping to work himself free of its grasp. It almost worked. Feeling its grip slipping, the giant wrapped one meaty hand around Janik's neck and shoulders. Janik's head swam as the beast swung him like a club at Dania. His legs crashed into her chest, and she sprawled backward onto the floor.

Over the top of the giant's fist, Janik saw Sever slash with lightning speed, taking advantage of the creature's reach to cut its wrist. The adamantine sword bit deep and the behemoth released Janik with a howl of pain, sending him flying through the air. He slammed to the floor just behind Dania, dizzy and gasping for breath.

He lay helpless, the room spinning around him. Sever had the giant's attention, his blade whirling, lines of blood trailing every time it connected with the giant's flesh. Dania forced herself to her feet, and Mathas sent another arc of lightning to engulf the giant. Auftane stood right behind the warforged, touching various parts of Sever's strange plated body and causing them to glow with a series of spells. His spells had a visible effect—Sever did not weaken or tire, and kept the giant almost entirely on the defensive. It had not managed to retrieve its stone club from the ground, a minor victory in itself.

Wait, Janik thought. Where's Krael?

Even as the thought passed through his mind, a movement on the upper gallery caught his eye. Krael pushed the limp body of one of the zakya archers over the railing, then hopped up to perch on the railing himself. Krael was by no means a small man, and his plate armor dramatically increased his bulk. Janik was impressed by the grace of his movement and the apparent ease with which he balanced on the narrow railing.

Janik rolled slowly into a crouch, and saw Dania charge up beside Sever, her sword crackling with silver fire. Krael was watching the giant carefully, his huge flail in hand. As Janik stood, Krael jumped, flying through the air and landing on the giant's hump shoulder. He swung his flail as he leaped, smashing hard into the side of the giant's head.

Janik shook his head and quickly regretted it, putting a hand on the wall to steady himself as the room started spinning again. Dania's sword struck true, erupting in flame, and the giant choked out a final roar as it fell to its knees.

A month ago, if Janik had tried to imagine fighting alongside Krael and his warforged assassin, he would have thought himself touched by Xoriat's madness. But here they were, not only fighting a common foe, but working well together.

Krael balanced on the giant's grotesque hump. He brought his flail around for another mighty blow that broke the creature's neck with an audible snap.

Janik leaned against the wall and let himself sink down to the floor. This day had brought too many surprises already.

❧ ❧ ❧ ❧ ❧ ❧ ❧

Janik felt much better after Auftane worked his magic with his wands. Or at least his body did—his mind was still reeling at the bizarre company he found himself in, and he sat against the wall as Auftane checked each of the others. With the battle over, Krael and Sever shifted into a more distant attitude, whispering together apart from the others. But Janik couldn't shake the powerful impression he'd had of the six of them working as a team.

Dania reverted to her previous search for the mysterious

voice. Janik frowned as she cocked her head, looking around at the upper galleries as if trying to find the source of the whispers that only she could hear. She bounced impatiently on the balls of her feet, heedless of the bruises she'd suffered in the fight and eager to chase the mysterious voices. Janik rubbed his forehead, thinking of her words just before they found the giant. Could she really be hearing the voices of Dhavibashta and whatever spirit held the rajah beneath the earth? Could she possibly distinguish one voice from the other?

And what about Krael? Janik thought he saw that distant look in Krael's eyes again, though the vampire was clearly trying to hide it more than Dania was. That worried Janik, suggesting that Krael was listening to a voice he didn't want Janik to know about. But Krael had no reason to collude with the rajah, did he? Not with the grudge he clearly bore against the rajah's lieutenant, the Fleshrender inhabiting Maija's body.

Sea of Fire, he thought. *I never know what's going on.*

Auftane had tended to everyone, using his wands on the living and his own peculiar magic on Sever. Janik got to his feet. Only one other exit remained on this level—a huge door, large enough for the giant to duck through, opposite the enormous door they'd come through. But two smaller doors were visible up in the gallery.

"Which way?" Janik said.

"Up," Dania said, pointing toward the gallery.

At the same instant, Krael pointed to the large door and said, "Down."

Janik gaped at the two of them. Dania's eyes were wide, while Krael wore his insipid grin again. This was exactly what he had feared.

"What's going on?" he said.

Krael shrugged. "We'll find Maija in the heart of the temple," he said. He pointed to the great door again. "That door will take us there."

"Dania?" Janik said. "Did you have some other destination in mind?" Damn, he thought, did I just side with Krael against Dania? Could things turn any more upside down?

"The pinnacle," Dania said vaguely, her eyes still on the gallery.

Janik sighed. Dania wasn't making it easy for him to take her seriously. Krael seemed perfectly reasonable, squarely meeting Janik's gaze and pointing the group toward the destination they had agreed on. By contrast, Dania was completely distracted and hesitant to offer any explanation. He put his hands on her shoulders and tried to capture her eyes.

"Dania," he said quietly. "Talk to me. What's at the pinnacle? Why do you want to go there?"

Her eyes finally met his, but she seemed to be speaking out of a dream. "It's so beautiful, Janik," she said. "Like the couatl we saw in the air, and so kind and wise. It wants to help us defeat the Fleshrender. It can help us, Janik, if we go to the pinnacle of the temple."

"Janik," Krael whispered, as if Dania wouldn't hear, "I'm not sure Dania is entirely in command of her faculties."

"Shut up, Krael," Janik spat, but he wasn't nearly as sure as he sounded.

"Perhaps I can help resolve our impasse," Mathas said.

"I'm listening," Janik said. He still held Dania's shoulders, but she was no longer looking at him. She reminded him of a small child, easily distracted, looking anywhere but at him.

"I could send my eyes along the route that Dania suggests," Mathas said, "just as I scouted the ruins yesterday.

We could attempt to determine the veracity of her assertions without putting ourselves at significant risk."

Janik gave Mathas an approving smile, but he caught Krael's scowl out of the corner of his eye. Interesting, he thought. That suggests that Krael knows something about what Mathas might see, and doesn't want him to see it.

Or else he's just impatient, Janik thought. Anxious to bring this thing to an end, and put off by Dania's ridiculous ramblings about the couatl.

"Perhaps we should declare our partnership concluded," Krael said. "We have helped each other escape from that little cell, and I have shown you the way to the heart of Maija's temple. If you'd rather not go that way, it's your affair. But I know what I came here for—I will have my revenge."

"I can't let you kill Maija, Krael," Janik said.

"If you intend to stop me, then you'd better come down with me," Krael said, his voice low. "And if you think your dreamstruck paladin can do anything to get the Fleshrender out of your dear wife's body while Maija is still alive, you had better drag her along as well. Frankly, though, I'm losing confidence—and patience."

So that's it, Janik thought. Perhaps I was imagining that look on Krael's face, or reading too much into it. He's not hearing the voice of the rajah—he just wants to go and get this over with.

He turned back to Dania. "Dania, please look at me." Her eyes were fixed on the ceiling of the chamber now, and she seemed not to hear him at all. Janik took her shoulders again and shook her gently, then a little harder. "Dania!"

Her eyes did not move, and she spoke so quietly he could barely hear. "The pinnacle first," she whispered, "and then the rajah's prison."

"Sea of Fire!" Janik shouted, pushing Dania roughly away from him. She stumbled, but Mathas caught her, shooting Janik a reproachful glare. For a moment, Janik considered suggesting that Dania lead Mathas and Auftane to the pinnacle while he went down with Sever and Krael. But it would be too dangerous, he thought. He was confident that the six of them could handle anything, even Maija, but split into groups, they'd be vulnerable, especially against another giant. Besides, without Dania, what hope did they have of forcing the spirit out of Maija?

He put his hands to his temples and squeezed his eyes shut. All he could see was Maija sneering at him, Maija casting the spell that had knocked him out, Maija stretching her mocking grin into a thin, cruel smile. Her words raked across his heart: "I lied."

No, damn it! he thought. That wasn't Maija, that was the Fleshrender. Maija is still there somewhere—trapped in her body, powerless to stop what the fiend made her do and say. And if Maija is still there, then there's hope.

He opened his eyes and looked at Dania, who still gazed dumbly up at the ceiling. And that hope lies in Dania, he thought, as crazy as she seems right now. I have to trust her.

With that thought, new memories sprang into his mind. He remembered when Maija first introduced him to Dania, and so many joyful, exciting, harrowing adventures they had shared since then. He remembered the conversation he'd had with Dania—was it just the night before? He realized he had no idea how long they had been in the cell. And then he remembered the couatl they had watched as it danced across the sky.

"Krael," Janik said, "our bargain is concluded and our alliance ended. Go where you want, but we will follow Dania.

We won't harm you as you leave this room, but if I see you again—"

"Oh, you will see me again," Krael said.

"If I see you again, I'll do my level best to kill you. Thank you for your help. Now get out of my sight."

Without another word, Krael stalked over to the massive door and threw it open, Sever following close behind. And then they were gone.

"Oh, thank the Sovereigns," Mathas said quietly.

Janik placed a gentle hand on Dania's shoulder. "I hope you know what you're doing."

Dania's eyes met his again briefly, and she smiled a faint, beatific smile. "Up," she said quietly.

* * * ◉ * * *

Mathas used his spell of levitation to launch himself up to the gallery, then he tied a rope to the balustrade so the others could climb. Once her feet were on the gallery floor, Dania set off toward one of the small doors, leaving Janik to help Auftane over the railing and pull up the rope before hurrying to catch up with her. She led them along narrow hallways, not even hesitating when the passages branched. Here and there, they made their way up short flights of stairs, marking their gradual progress toward the top of the ziggurat, assuming that Dania was correct.

As they walked side by side down a long wide hall, Janik held Mathas back briefly and spoke to him quietly.

"What do you make of this, Mathas?" he asked.

"There is definitely a presence in this place," Mathas said thoughtfully. "I cannot distinguish it—to me, it's almost like being in a dark room and feeling someone else with you, but not being able to tell whether it's a friend or a drooling monster." He paused. "I must say, I wish that comparison were not so vivid."

"So why does Dania hear it so much more clearly?" Janik said. "She claimed she could hear two voices, the binder and the bound. How does she know she's following the right one?"

"Dania is far more sensitive to the realm of spirits than you or I, Janik. I believe she knows what she is doing."

Auftane hurried along and caught up with them, pointing ahead to the end of the hall. "Excuse me," he said, "but she seems to have found something."

Dania had reached a door and thrown it open, revealing a staircase spiraling upward. She quickly reached the top of the stairs and pushed open a trap door in the ceiling, releasing a flood of argent light into the hallway. As Janik watched, she climbed through the trap door, a small dark shape silhouetted against the warm radiance, and disappeared. Cursing himself, Janik ran to catch up to her.

He stormed up the stairs and through the trap door, then stopped dead. Behind and below him, he heard Mathas gasp and Auftane swear quietly as they reached the top of the stairs.

They were at the pinnacle of the ziggurat, it was clear. Long, low windows set into the massive stone blocks offered them a spectacular view of the city around them and the desert beyond. Somehow, even the barren golden desert seemed vibrant and alive in what must have been midday sunshine—as if some spirit of the ancient jungle still remained, teeming with the life of its thousands of inhabitants.

The chamber was hard to see clearly in the intense brightness. Their eyes were accustomed to the dim light of Janik's lantern in the dark passages, and the daylight alone would have made them blink and squint. Janik tried briefly to convince himself that the daylight was the source of the radiance that had spilled into the hallway below—but that did not explain its strange silver hue.

No—the stone chamber was on fire—blazing with silver flame, or perhaps *the* Silver Flame, for all Janik knew. Lines of argent fire covered the entire floor in an intricate pattern, like snakes twisted in endless coils. Where the lines crossed each other, they sometimes flared as high as Janik's knees. Dania was kneeling in the midst of them, numerous tongues of flame caressing her, but she was clearly not in any pain.

Dania was on her knees, her body erect from her knees to her shoulders. Her head was thrown back, her helm lay on the floor beside her, and her arms were spread wide to her sides. Her eyes were open and seemed fixed on some point out the window ahead. Her face wore an expression of utter rapture.

The flames pulsed along the lines on the floor. The rhythm of its movement reminded Janik of the couatl's flying dance, and he began to feel a connection. As he looked at the elaborate stonework in the chamber, he noticed serpent imagery everywhere—snakes ringed the windows, their heads meeting above the center, and the columns were shaped into majestic winged serpents.

What is this place? Janik thought. Why would a cult of giants and rakshasas dedicated to the imprisoned rajah build this shrine to the couatl that bound it?

As he resolved to pursue further research about serpent cults among the giants, the floor erupted into a storm of leaping flames. What had been tiny rivulets of fire exploded into blazing ribbons reaching almost as high as the ceiling, roaring like a hungry tiger. Janik drew his sword instinctively, and he felt Mathas and Auftane startled out of their own reveries.

Dania did not move.

The flames closed around her, forming a ring and then a column to engulf her. Janik started to rush forward, reaching out to grab her and heave her free of the fire before she was consumed, but the instant he touched her, the fire stopped. The column winked out, the lines on the floor went dark, and the daylight seemed dim by comparison.

Dania's arms dropped to her sides and she slowly rose to her feet.

"Dania?" Janik said quietly, gently lifting her by the elbow. "Are you hurt?"

She stood, her head hanging limply and her hair covering her face. Slowly, she brought a hand up to her throat. She lifted her head to look at Janik, brushing her hair out of her face. His gaze fell first on a gleam of silver at her throat, a torc shaped like a twisting serpent coiled around her neck. He was quite sure it had not been there before the fire engulfed her.

Then her eyes met Janik's, and he took a step back in surprise.

They had been a dusky blue, like the sky before a storm, but not any more. They were like pools of quicksilver, firmly focused on him and, he felt, seeing perhaps more than he would have liked.

She smiled, and her eyes glistened as she took his hands in hers. "I'm fine, Janik," she said. She held his gaze for a moment longer, then her eyes settled on Mathas and Auftane, lingering for a moment on the dwarf before turning back to Janik. She raised a hand to touch his cheek and smiled at him again. "Do not let your heart be troubled, Janik. I have chosen this path, and I am not afraid."

Janik had no idea what she meant, but there was a certainty in her gaze and her voice, and a warm comfort in her touch that eased the worry from his brow and softened the knot of anxiety in his heart.

"We need to move," Dania said. "Krael and Sever have already entered the heart of the temple."

Dania picked up her helmet and settled it on her head as Mathas and Janik shared a helpless glance. Auftane was distracted, staring out the window as he waited for Dania to lead the way.

She gripped her sword, and with a quick glance back to make sure the others were following, started down the stairs. She retraced their steps almost all the way back to the chamber where they had fought the giant, but led them instead to a steeply descending staircase. Another maze of passages greeted them on the lower level, but Dania led them with as much confidence as she had shown earlier—except this time, she kept glancing back to make sure her friends were following.

"We haven't seen a single guard since we killed the giant," Janik observed as they hurried after Dania, hustling to keep up with her purposeful strides.

"True," Mathas said. "I'm not sure how to interpret that."

"I know," Janik said. Part of him was relieved—he wanted to reach Maija as quickly as possible, especially if there was any chance that Krael might kill her before they arrived. But he also worried. "I wonder if Maija—if the Fleshrender—called all the zakyas back to this 'heart of the temple' to defend her."

"Not to mention more of those giants," Auftane piped up from behind them.

"I had hoped no one would mention the giants," Janik said with a grim smile. "That could be the end of it."

"There is another possibility," Mathas said. "Perhaps the Fleshrender is overconfident. It's possible that it never considered that we might escape. Maybe we've already slain what few guards could be spared."

"I prefer that possibility," Janik said, "and for that reason, I doubt it."

Dania stopped and looked over her shoulder at him, smiling. "Sometimes, Janik, the worst possibility is not the one that proves true."

"Maybe so, but I find it's generally better to prepare for the worst. Unless you've got information you haven't shared, I'll brace myself."

"See for yourself," Dania said, rounding a corner. They stopped before a towering stone door that yawned into an enormous vaulted chamber. An elaborate tracery of lines and symbols writhed over the floor, inlaid with a dull silver but echoing the lines of flame in the pinnacle chamber. A massive stone block stood at the center of the room, carved with snarling tiger faces—a motif also repeated in the carvings on the walls. A large stone tablet leaned against this block, which Janik presumed to be an altar. Runic symbols were carved into the surface of the tablet.

The ceiling gave off a dim red light that illuminated every corner, but darkness seemed to hang in the air despite that light, as if the shadows had substance. A palpable presence was in the chamber, brooding and malicious.

No giants waited and no zakyas threatened. Maija stood a few paces in front of the stone altar, her fingers twisted in the gestures of a spell. Krael faced her, snarling, his flail swinging slowly in his hand. The warforged lay motionless on the floor, cut in half at the waist. An enormous sword, looking like it was made of pure midnight, hovered in the air near Krael, dancing around him and occasionally lashing out to cut him.

Janik realized that Krael looked very weak. The magical sword bit and sliced him faster than his undead body could regenerate, and Maija's spells had taken a toll as well. Janik wasn't sure how much longer Krael would last, and he noticed in himself a strange urge to rush forward and help his old enemy—help him defeat Maija.

"Dania," Janik said quietly, "it's time. Whatever power you have to fight this thing, I sure hope it works."

Though Janik had spoken in a mere whisper, Krael heard it, for he turned his head to glance at the doorway. In that instant, Maija completed her spell, engulfing the vampire in a blinding burst of sinister, red-black flame.

When the blaze of hellfire subsided, Krael was gone.

DEATH

CHAPTER 19

J anik, my love," Maija said with a sneer, "how kind of you to come and offer yourself in sacrifice."

The floor rumbled as though the fiend imprisoned in the ziggurat were stirring, restive in his bonds. Janik's eyes grew wide as he looked around for any sign that Dhavibashta might be breaking free.

"Janik," Dania whispered, "there is still time. I need you all to keep her busy, and we need to weaken her if I'm going to force it out. Go!"

Janik needed no further encouragement. Drawing his sword as he ran, he closed the distance to Maija but came up short as the midnight sword slashed through the air in front of him, missing his throat by less than a hand's breadth.

"Hang on, Janik!" Mathas called from near the door. "I'll see if I can eliminate that sword!" Janik heard him chanting, but watched Maija's mouth curl into a wicked smile.

"I don't think so, dear Mathas," Maija said, thrusting her hand forward as if to punch, launching an invisible force that sent Mathas crashing against the wall behind him. With the wind knocked out of him, Mathas couldn't continue his spell. Janik brought his short sword up to block the slashing arc of Maija's magical blade. The clash of the ebony force and Janik's steel sent black sparks crackling into the air, stinging Janik's eyes.

Dania advanced just behind Janik, moving with caution, her sword flaring with holy power in her hand. Auftane came up next to her, holding his mace in both hands but looking a little unsure what to do.

"Don't hold back, Auftane!" Dania shouted, sensing his hesitation. "At least not until I can get the spirit out of her!"

"Cast me out of this vessel, Dania?" Maija said, an expression of genuine surprise crossing her face for an instant. "That seems unlikely."

With a quick gesture, she directed her sword away from Janik to slash at Dania, catching her off guard and making a long, shallow gash in her upper arm.

"And extremely inconvenient," Maija added.

Janik, no longer threatened by the sword, tumbled forward past Maija, coming out of his roll right behind her. He aimed a fierce jab at her lower back—a potentially crippling blow, if placed just right. At the last instant, Maija turned slightly and his eyes met hers.

So many nights he had gazed into those warm pools of brown. Her eyes had always been windows to him, letting him see everything that was in her heart, anything that troubled her—and all the love she held for him. Was it some trick of the rakshasa that he thought he saw that love still? Or was Maija showing herself to him despite the Fleshrender's control?

His attack lost its strength and glanced off an invisible force surrounding her body. He stood helpless, transfixed by her eyes.

"Janik," she murmured softly, "heart of my heart . . ."

"Janik, no!" Dania screamed. The first thing he noticed were Dania's inhuman, quicksilver eyes, but then he saw the flash of fire in Maija's hand. He leaped backward, throwing himself onto the floor as another blast of flame roared over him, searing him with its heat though it failed to engulf him. He landed hard but kept rolling until he could get his feet under him again. Maija's fiendish cackle echoed louder than the blast of fire.

Auftane made a wide circle around Maija and hurried over to Janik. "Let me help you," he said, one of his curing wands in his hand. Janik saw Mathas, leaning weakly against the far wall, launch a bolt of lightning from his fingers toward Maija.

Janik gaped in horror as the lightning forked to pass harmlessly around Maija. With a flick of her wrist, she deflected part of the spell back at Mathas. The lightning crackled up and down his body. He fell to the floor and lay still.

"Help Mathas, damn it," Janik barked at the dwarf. He had better be alive, Maija, he thought, or . . . or what?

Or I'll never forgive myself for bringing him here, he thought. He shifted his grip on his sword and advanced warily toward Maija again.

"So you're playing the cleric, are you, dwarf?" Maija growled, and she thrust her palm in Auftane's direction, sending him sprawling on his face. The wand clattered across the floor. "Tinkering with the power of the gods?" She emphasized her last word by slamming her fist into her open hand. Auftane convulsed once with the force of an unseen blow, then lay still.

In that instant, Janik managed to land one solid blow on

Maija, his sword jabbing into her shoulder. Her cry of pain sounded like the roar of a zakya, but she ignored him, turning her attention to Dania instead.

"Now you, Dania," she snarled. "I always knew you lusted after my Janik."

"It wasn't lust," Dania said, still on the defensive against the wildly swinging sword. "Not love, either."

Janik cocked an eyebrow as he managed to nick Maija's other shoulder with his blade. Maija gestured dismissively at him, knocking him back.

"The truth is, Maija," Dania said, "I wanted to be you."

Maija stepped backward at that, making Janik wonder whether some remnant of Maija's own will expressed her surprise that way, or whether Dania's response had taken the Fleshrender aback. In any case, it was the distraction that Dania needed. With one mighty blow, she smashed her sword into Maija's dancing magical blade, shattering it into tiny shards of darkness that melted into the floor. Then she extended her arm straight out in front of her, the tip of her sword leveled at Maija's throat.

"Out," Dania said.

Janik wasn't sure what he had expected, but that wasn't it. Some elaborate ritual, perhaps, or a lengthy prayer invoking the power of the Silver Flame. But not this, just a simple command—spoken with such authority that if Janik could have stepped out of his own skin, he would have. Dania's voice echoed in the chamber, resonating with power.

Maija stood transfixed, her eyes locked with Dania's. Slowly, Dania's sword arm lowered, but both of them were otherwise motionless. Janik stood helpless, watching as silent conflict raged between the two women.

Silence settled on the room. In the stillness, Janik felt

some resonance of the battle he was witnessing, and he realized what had failed to sink in before: Dania was no less possessed than Maija. At least four wills were involved in this battle, with Dania and the spirit inhabiting her body pitted against the Fleshrender and the far greater evil that rumbled in the earth beneath the place. Janik wondered whether Maija's will played any part at all, or if she was just the battleground, the piece of land these titanic forces were fighting over.

Janik had spent months arguing with Dania, but he had to admit that she had been right. This was different than the Last War. He had served Breland, even described his work for the crown as the true conflict, from which the massed armies and bloody battlefields were a mere distraction. But all his intrigues and exploits were no more than a shadow.

The real war was being fought right in front of him, and it was a war Janik didn't know how to fight. He shifted his sword in his hand, suddenly aware of its irrelevance.

The floor of the cavern began to shake—the merest tremor at first, not enough to break the silence. But it grew, until first the stone tablet rattled against the altar, then Dania's armor softly clanked, then the room rumbled. Trickles of dust started falling from the ceiling. Janik's body tensed for action, but he had no idea what to do.

The rumbling stopped, and Maija cried out and convulsed.

A shadow seemed to seep from her body, a smear of darkness without form or feature. It slowly separated from Maija and then sloughed her off as if stepping out of a robe. Maija slumped to the floor, discarded.

Dania didn't move. Her hands hung at her sides, her sword dangling from one and her shield from the other. She didn't lift either as the dark spirit slid forward, engulfed her—

And melded into her.

"No!" Janik cried.

As the darkness sank into Dania's skin, Janik saw a spasm of pain cross her face, and she dropped to her knees, her mouth stretched in a silent howl. She drew a long, tortured breath, then began wrestling her face and body under control.

But whose control? Janik had no idea whether the Fleshrender, the argent spirit that inhabited Dania, or Dania herself was the will that moved Dania's body. Whichever it was, it moved her body with agonizing slowness—lifting one knee off the floor and planting the foot, dragging her arms forward to rest on the raised knee, shifting the weight forward and dragging the other foot until the body stood erect. Dania's face was calm except for a muscle twitching wildly beside one eye.

Janik stood tensed in a defensive stance, his sword gripped firmly between him and Dania. He watched carefully for a sign of who was in control and what her intentions were.

Slowly, Dania's head lowered and turned to the right. Then her right arm rose, the sword hanging limply from her hand.

"Janik," she said, her voice a hoarse whisper.

She extended her arm, holding the sword out toward Janik and lifting its point toward him. He stepped back.

"Take . . . take my sword," she said.

"What?"

"Take it!" Her voice was regaining strength.

Janik sheathed his sword in one smooth motion. Hesitantly, he stepped forward and lifted the sword from Dania's fingers. His hands tingled where they touched it, but the sensation was not unpleasant—certainly not the biting pain Krael had endured.

"Now, Janik," she said. "Do it now."

Janik's eyes widened. "Do what?" he asked, knowing and yet dreading the answer.

"Kill me," Dania said.

"No!"

"Kill me!" she repeated. "And the Fleshrender dies with me!"

Her eyes met his, and he realized with a start that they were again their normal dusky blue. They pleaded with him in a way her voice could not manage, even as one eye twitched, reflecting the struggle that raged inside her.

Her words at the pinnacle of the temple came back to him. "Do not let your heart be troubled, Janik. I have chosen this path, and I am not afraid." He had not understood at the time, but now he grasped her meaning. She had known that this was how she would defeat the Fleshrender.

And she had been counting on Janik to do it, to kill her. His fingers shifted on the unfamiliar grip of her sword.

"Janik," she said, gaining a little more control over her voice. "Back in Karrnath, I swore an oath by everything holy that my sword would bring an end to this. Please—" her voice was a desperate gasp—"fulfill my oath!" A spasm of pain passed across her face, a sign of the struggle for control that raged within her.

Janik lifted the sword and stepped back a little, testing the heft of the weapon, thinking about swinging it. For a moment, he almost convinced himself he could do it.

Then he saw her eyes again. The sword slipped from his fingers and clattered to the stone floor, sparking motes of silver light.

"I can't, Dania." His gaze fell on Maija, lying on the floor like a discarded robe. "I can't do it."

"Janik!" Dania cried, but he turned away.

As he turned, he saw a small cloud of shadow detach itself from the ambient gloom of the chamber. It quickly congealed into a human form, then Krael stood before him. The vampire ducked past Janik to pick up Dania's sword.

Silver light flared as Krael's hand touched the hilt, and the smell of burning flesh reached Janik's nose.

The vampire's voice was choked with pain. "I told you I'd return the favor if I could, Dania," he said, grimacing in agony as the sword continued to sear his hand.

Dania did not move to defend herself. Janik felt paralyzed. He thought a flicker of a smile crossed Dania's face, and she began to nod—or else bowed her head in acceptance.

Then Krael swung the sword with all his strength, cutting deep into Dania's shoulder. Krael screamed along with Dania's cry, smoke and silver fire surrounding his hand.

Janik's heart was suddenly a lump of stone in his chest, and he couldn't seem to draw a breath.

"No." His lips formed the words, but he had no breath to give them.

Krael dropped the sword and stepped back. Dania was drenched in blood but her body was slow to fall to the ground. A soft white light surrounded her, a contrast to the shadow that emerged as she fell.

Janik's heart pounded again, a brief terror seizing him as he saw the Fleshrender take shape before him. The spirit was clearly visible, like a zakya with ebon fur. It was a black flame raging, shadow streaming from its insubstantial form like a radiant darkness. Even as the life ebbed out of Dania, Janik could see the life pouring out of the fiend, for it bore the same mortal wound in its shoulder. As Dania slumped to her knees and then, lifeless, onto the floor, the fiend staggered away from her, falling to the floor a few steps away.

As Janik continued to stare, the fiend's body dispersed into wisps of darkness and was gone.

RECONCILIATION

CHAPTER 20

Janik fell to his knees and stared blankly around the room. Mathas was near the door, slumped against the wall, his head lolling to one side. Auftane lay on his face halfway between Janik and Mathas. Maija's crumpled form was close, and Dania lay in a spreading pool of blood. The serpent torc was still coiled around her neck, and the eyes seemed to stare up at him.

He looked over his shoulder at Krael.

"What was that you said about returning the favor?" he said. His own voice surprised him—it was flat, emotionless. He felt a sea of rage and pain churning inside him, but managed somehow to float on its surface, not letting himself feel it. He merely observed it, noted it, and tried to keep from collapsing on the floor.

"She helped kill Havoc," Krael said, "and freed me from his control. And I freed her." Krael's voice was shaking as he cradled his wounded hand to his chest.

"Then you accomplished a great deal with that one blow," Janik said. "You repaid your debt to her, fulfilled Dania's oath—which I presume you prompted, one way or another—and you got your revenge against the Fleshrender for making you a vampire."

"It's been quite a day."

"It certainly has."

"What about you, Janik? Is it time for your revenge?"

"What?" Janik said.

"Aren't you going to kill me?" the vampire said, his voice growing stronger. "I assume you still loathe me, after all our history, and I did just kill your dearest friend."

"So you did," Janik said, his gaze falling on Dania again. "I find I've lost my taste for revenge. Just go, Krael."

Krael walked slowly to the door. He peered intently at Auftane as he walked past, and kneeled briefly beside Mathas.

"Leave him alone, Krael!" Janik called. "Leave before I change my mind."

Krael stood and stepped into the doorway, then turned back. "They're still alive, you know. They need some attention."

"I'll take care of it."

"Janik . . . I'm sorry it had to end like this. Dania was a worthy adversary, a woman of spirit and purpose and conviction. I'm . . . I'm sorry she had to die."

Here comes the pain, Janik thought, and he bowed his head so that Krael wouldn't see the sudden rush of tears.

When he looked up, Krael was gone.

❀ ❀ ❀ ❀ ❀ ❀ ❀

It took all his strength to get to his feet. He knelt beside Maija first, fearing the worst despite Krael's words, and gently rolled her onto her back.

She looked like she was sleeping—she even made the quiet whimper she used to make when Janik would extricate himself from her arms early in the morning, trying not to wake her. He felt her pulse—strong, slow, and even—and then hesitantly brushed the back of his hand down her cheek. He wanted to stay there, to watch her until she woke up, to be the first thing she saw. But Auftane groaned and twitched, so Janik hurried over to check on the dwarf.

Auftane was a mess. His forehead and nose were scraped from his encounter with the floor, and a trickle of drying blood ran from his mouth into his beard. His once-shining breastplate was caved in on one side, and Janik set to work on getting it off so the dwarf could breathe. As he did so, Auftane's eyes fluttered open briefly and one corner of his mouth twisted into a half smile.

"Janik," he whispered. "Did we win?"

Janik returned Auftane's smile, but found that he didn't know how to answer. "Are you going to make it, Auftane?" he asked instead.

"Dolurrh can't have me yet," the dwarf said. "Too much to get done."

"Glad to hear it." Janik took off his coat, rolled it into a bundle, and tucked it under Auftane's head. "Rest a bit. I need to check on Mathas."

The old elf lay so still and looked so frail that Janik could hardly believe he was still alive.

"Oh, Mathas," Janik muttered as he started tending to his friend, "I'm sorry for this. Please, pull through for me, and I swear I'll never drag you along to Xen'drik with me again."

Mathas's eyes did not open, but his mouth moved. His words were a hoarse murmur Janik couldn't understand.

"What did you say, Mathas?"

"Then I'll have to go without you," the elf repeated, only slightly louder.

Janik laughed long and loud as a fresh wave of tears spilled from his eyes.

Auftane worked himself upright, sitting on the floor and looking for the wand he had lost when he fell. Janik spotted it and handed it to the dwarf, who coaxed enough power from it to heal even the scrapes on his face. Looking worlds better, Auftane stood and walked over to crouch beside Mathas.

Mathas's eyes flickered open at last as the first wave of magic from the wand poured into him.

"That's better," he said, and he smiled as the dwarf continued to tend to him. "Janik, what happened? Where's Dania? And what happened to Maija?"

Janik didn't answer, but turned around to face the two bodies on the floor—Dania lifeless, Maija still lost in sleep. I wonder what she's dreaming, he thought as he watched Maija's face twitch, her brow crinkling slightly. Let her sleep, he reminded himself.

He heard Mathas draw in a sharp breath behind him, and looked over his shoulder. The elf's eyes were wide, a look of horror on his face.

"Are they both. . . ?" Mathas said, his voice trailing off.

"I think Maija will be all right," Janik said quietly. "She doesn't seem badly wounded—I think she's just asleep."

"And the fiend has left her?"

"Yes. Dania cast it out."

"What happened to Dania?" Auftane said, following Mathas's gaze.

Janik walked over and dropped to his knees beside Dania's body. He had been dreading it, but he had to do it—to look at her face once more. He had to say goodbye.

Slowly and gently, he rolled her onto her back. The front of her armor was tacky with drying blood. Her helmet was twisted around to cover part of her face, so he took it off, then brushed her red hair from her face. He was only dimly aware of Auftane and Mathas coming to stand behind him. Mathas's whispered prayers to the Sovereign Host were a comforting drone in the back of Janik's mind.

Her eyes were still open, staring blankly past him. He reached out and closed them. Auftane handed him Dania's sword and he took it, feeling the holy power within it but loathing it at the same time. He turned it over in his hands and noticed for the first time an inscription in the blade, carved in small, flowing script: *By my life, my honor, and whatever is holy.*

"Your oath is fulfilled, Dania," he said quietly. "Rest easy." He laid the sword on top of her body, folding her hands over its hilt on her chest.

"Janik, what happened?" Mathas asked quietly, putting his hand on Janik's shoulder.

Kneeling beside Dania, he told them. "Do you remember, Mathas, on the boat on our way here, when Dania punched me? She was talking about sacrifice, making sacrifices in order to fight the evil in the world?"

"I remember," Mathas said.

"I think she knew, even then, that something like this was going to happen. Do you remember the last thing she said that night? 'You will understand, before this is over.' She knew."

He sighed, rubbing his temples with his fingertips.

"In the pinnacle, when Dania was surrounded by the fire, she allowed a couatl, like the one we saw flying—maybe the same one, I don't know, or maybe the ancient one that binds Dhavibashta here—anyway, I think she let a couatl possess her, just like Maija was possessed." His eyes fell on the torc around her neck. "Except that she was still mostly in control. But the couatl gave her power, and she used that power to force the Fleshrender out of Maija's body."

His eyes were glued to the silver torc, but he no longer saw it. The scene replayed itself in his memory, every detail etched there like a scar. The shadow emerging from Maija and entering Dania. . . .

"The Fleshrender left Maija just like that"—he gestured vaguely toward Maija's body—"and entered Dania's body instead. I don't know, maybe Dania forced the fiend into her body, but I think she just used herself as bait. Once it possessed her, she was able—or, I guess, the couatl in her was able to bind it to her just like the couatl binds Dhavibashta in the earth beneath our feet. Just as our own spirits are bound to our bodies. The Fleshrender's life was bound to Dania's life."

Janik fell silent for several moments.

"I couldn't do it, Mathas," he said at last. "I couldn't fulfill her oath for her, I couldn't help her. I couldn't kill her."

"Of course you couldn't," Mathas said. "Of course you couldn't."

Janik took a steadying breath and went on. "Krael reappeared," he said, "and picked up Dania's sword. He did it. Krael killed her and destroyed the Fleshrender."

Janik fell again into silence, and his friends were lost in their own reflections on what had happened. Suddenly, Maija gasped loudly and sat upright, a look of terror on her face as she stared wildly around the room.

Janik was beside her in an instant. "I'm here, my love," he murmured. He put one hand on her shoulder and fumbled with the other, trying to grasp her hand. But she pulled her hands up to her chest, turned her shoulder away from him, and winced as though his touch hurt her.

"Don't touch me!"

"Maija, it's me. Janik."

She began to curl in on herself, turning away from him. "I'm so dirty—don't touch me," she whimpered.

Janik reached out again and gently stroked her brown hair. It was tightly braided and coiled close to her head, though she used to wear it long and free. She flinched at his touch but did not pull away.

"Dirty?" he said. "Oh, Mai, no." Tears sprang to his eyes, joy and relief and sorrow all mingling together.

"I did so many terrible things!" She looked at him for the first time, and he saw the tears streaming down her face.

"You didn't do anything," he said, his voice soft but firm. "The fiend did them, not you. You don't need to feel any guilt or shame about what happened. You didn't do anything wrong. The fiend was using you, that's all."

"That's all?" Her voice grew louder. "Do you have any idea what it felt like to be the tool in her hand? Like—like the shovel used to lift manure?"

"Shh, I didn't mean that." Janik kept his voice low and continued gently stroking her hair. "It must have been terrible for you."

"Oh, Janik," she sobbed. "I felt so helpless. I couldn't do anything to stop—" She choked on her words and turned away from Janik again.

"It's not your fault," Janik said. He lay his hand between her shoulder blades and felt her take a deep breath, trying to steady herself.

"But I saw it all, I remember it all as if I had done it. My hands and my voice cast those vile spells, said those terrible things to you. I let Havoc kill Mudren Fain and turn Krael into a vampire. My hands killed . . . I killed so many people. So many innocent people."

Janik drew her into his arms. She pushed away at first, but soon melted and curled up against him, sobbing into his shoulder.

"That's it," he murmured, stroking her hair. "Mourn for them, for all those people." His eyes fell again on Dania's body. "But their deaths are not meaningless, not in vain."

"How can you say that?"

Tears sprang to Janik's eyes again. "Because Dania gave them meaning."

Maija pulled her head away from his chest and looked up at him, then followed his gaze to Dania's body.

"Oh, Dania, no!" she cried. She broke out of Janik's arms and crawled over beside her fallen friend, wailing her grief.

Janik followed her on his knees. "She gave her life to destroy the Fleshrender, Maija. And somehow I think she took the death of everyone the Fleshrender killed and—and made it part of her own death, her sacrifice. She . . . she sanctified them, Maija."

Maija's crying did not abate, but she nodded as she wept, understanding what Janik could barely put into words. He wrapped his arms around her again and they mourned and celebrated Dania together.

● ● ● ◉ ◉ ● ● ●

Janik stood and helped Maija to her feet. She began fumbling with her hair, picking at the braids to let it flow freely over her shoulders again. It was wavy and wild after being tightly bound for so long, but Maija reveled in it, shaking her head to make it fall in a tangle down her shoulders and over her face. Then she looked up at Janik, the first hint of a smile barely visible on her face under the cascade of hair. Janik laughed, and Mathas came to join them.

"I am very glad to see you again, Maija," Mathas said, smiling broadly.

Maija threw her arms around Mathas, clutching the old elf to her chest. "Oh, Mathas. I'm so sorry for everything."

Mathas returned her embrace and clasped her arms as she pulled away. "Dear friend, you have nothing to be sorry about. You were a victim, a prisoner. You carry no responsibility for the evil that spirit did through you."

Tears sprang again to Maija's eyes and she pulled Mathas to her again.

"Thank you, Mathas," she murmured. When she finally released him, her cheeks were streaked with tears, and she wiped awkwardly at them. "Now where is the dwarf?" she said. "I'd like to meet him and thank him as well."

Mathas gestured vaguely. "He's—" He looked around the chamber. "I don't know where he is. I'm afraid my attention has been elsewhere."

"I'm sure he'll turn up," Janik said with a small laugh. "And what was so demanding of your attention?"

"Well, I've been studying the floor in here—I know, it sounds fascinating. As near as I can tell, the bonds that hold the rakshasa rajah below this place remain intact. But I believe I understand the erection of the towers around the city."

"Oh, yes," Maija said. "She hoped to use them to break the couatl's grip on the rajah."

"Well, I'm pleased with myself for deducing it before you told me," Mathas said. "We should probably take steps to topple them again."

"Yes, we should," Maija said.

"And one other thing concerns me," Mathas said. "Janik, I assume that Krael has not been decisively destroyed. Should we be worrying about completing that task?"

"No," Janik said. Mathas arched an eyebrow. "I let Krael go."

"I beg your pardon," Mathas said carefully, "but was that wise?"

"I believe so." Janik sighed. "I realized something important here, something I'm not sure I can explain. I realized that Dania was wrong. Back on the ship, as we crossed the Phoenix Basin, she said that vampires were the scourge of the earth, that Krael had to be purged from the world. But she was wrong, and I think she realized that before she died."

He took another deep breath before continuing. "When Dania was struggling with the spirit, forcing it out of you, Maija, I was watching, feeling helpless. And that was really the first time I became aware that there's more going on in the world than the struggles among nations. Dania had been trying to tell me that, but I think it's bigger than even she realized. It's almost as though the ancient war between the dragons and the fiends was still going on—a war between, well, between good and evil, for lack of better words.

"I didn't believe in good and evil. I mean, I clung to my way of doing things, trying to keep to the moral high ground—thanks mostly to you two and Dania steering me that way, keeping me from stooping to Krael's level.

"But everything that's happened here has pointed to a much larger struggle. The conflict between the couatl and the rajah it binds isn't just a legacy of some ancient war between nations. It's fundamentally a conflict between life and destruction, between an affirmation of beauty and goodness and life and the denial of all that."

"But Janik," Mathas interjected, "I think I'm echoing Dania when I remind you that Krael is a vampire."

"I haven't forgotten that, Mathas. But he's still human as

well. And like any of us, he can choose sides between good and evil. And today he made a heroic choice. He chose differently than I did, but I still think he chose for the good. He destroyed the Fleshrender when I couldn't. And in that moment, I didn't want to fight any more."

Janik fell silent. Maija was staring at the ground, her brow furrowed, and Janik put his arm around her shoulder. He looked at Mathas, whose expression suggested that he was a little perturbed.

"What is it, Mathas?"

"I am not accustomed to learning wisdom from those who are so much younger than I," the old elf said. "And particularly from you, Janik Martell." His face broke into a broad smile, and he clapped Janik on the shoulder.

"Where in Khyber has Auftane gone?" Janik said, partly to hold off another rush of tears. He squeezed Maija closer as he cast his eyes around the room. "Auftane!" he called, his voice echoing in the chamber.

A moment later, he called again. "Auftane!" The smile began to melt off his face.

"Do you hear anything, Mathas?" Janik said. "Sounds of combat or cries for help?"

Mathas concentrated for a moment, then shook his head. "Nothing. And Auftane is not particularly quiet."

"We need to look for him. But let's attend to Dania first."

"Shall we build her a pyre outside?" Mathas said. "I believe that is the way of the Silver Flame."

"If she is to be burned," Janik said, "there is some part of me that would rather see a grand pyre built for her at the cathedral in Flamekeep. She deserves it."

"She deserves all the honor the world can bestow, Janik,"

Maija said, "there is no doubt of that. But I can't see her desiring it. I think she would prefer a battlefield honor, if you know what I mean."

Janik nodded. "You're right." He walked over and stood beside Dania's body in silence for a moment. "Wait," he said. "What happened to the torc?"

"The silver torc?" Mathas said. "It was still around her neck when Maija woke up, was it not?"

"Yes, I remember looking at it," Janik said. "But it's gone now."

Mathas arched an eyebrow. "Auftane?"

"He's got some questions to answer," Janik growled, then he knelt to lift Dania into his arms. With Maija leading the way and Mathas behind him, he carried her out of the ziggurat of Mel-Aqat, into the searing desert sunlight. They encountered a small gang of zakyas, but the fiends fled at the sight of Maija, as if they recognized that the power of their commander had been broken.

Janik shouted Auftane's name at intervals as they walked, but no reply came. When they passed outside the walls of the ruined city, Janik set Dania's body down and began gathering dry shrubs and stunted trees from the Golden Desert. While Maija prepared her friend's body for the pyre, Mathas sat on a stony ledge and chanted the words of a spell. Attuning his mind to the web of magic suffusing the world, he searched for ripples from Dania's silver torc. When Janik brought a bundle of brush back a short time later, Mathas opened his eyes, shook his head, and stepped down from his perch.

"Any sign?" Janik called.

"No," Mathas replied. "It is possible that the torc dissolved back into nothingness, in much the same way as it first appeared around Dania's neck. The other possibility, though, is that Auftane carried it outside the range of my spell, possibly using teleportation magic to leave the area quickly."

"Damn it," Janik said. "And damn Auftane, if what I'm beginning to suspect is true."

"What do you think happened?" Maija said. "Do you think he took it to Krael?"

"There would be a certain disturbing symmetry to that," Mathas said.

"I don't know," Janik said. "Somehow I don't think Krael is involved. But I don't have any better ideas. Without knowing more about the torc, it's hard to know who might want it and why."

"I'm disappointed," Mathas said. "I really trusted him."

"As did I," said Janik. He shrugged, then looked down to where Maija knelt beside Dania's body. "But in the grand scheme of things, it just doesn't seem that important."

Maija had removed Dania's armor, dressed her in clean clothes, and washed the blood from her face and hair. Janik could almost convince himself that she was sleeping.

She has found her peace, he thought.

He finished assembling her pyre and carefully laid her on it. He knelt beside the pyre and worked carefully to kindle a flame. As he did, he thought of the fire engulfing Dania at the top of the ziggurat. Finally, the wood flared to life and he stood back, putting an arm around Maija.

Maija wept in his arms as the pyre did its work, but Janik found that his tears had run dry. He watched the dancing flames, leaping red and gold and blue—and here and there a tongue of silver, as if to remind them that her death was something sacred. Slowly, the flames consumed her flesh.

And as he held Maija, Janik remembered what the Keeper of the Flame—no, what the Silver Flame itself had said to him in Thrane five months before: "What you have lost lies still in those ruins, still within your grasp." He offered a silent prayer of thanks to all the Sovereign Host, to the Silver Flame, to the couatl of Mel-Aqat, to every power of holiness that had played any part in bringing Maija back to him.

EPILOGUE

With an almost audible pop, the dwarf appeared in a comfortably appointed chamber.

"Home, sweet home." He sighed, walking to stand in front of a tall mirror, shedding his pack and bags and pouches as he went. Fidgeting with the silver serpent in his hands, he looked at his reflection—covered with the dust and dirt of two months spent traveling through the Wasting Plain and the Golden Desert. Blood was still crusted in his beard, which was, at least, still neatly trimmed. He set the torc on his dresser, put his hands to his cheeks, and breathed a deep sigh, exhausted and deeply relieved that he was able to use magic to expedite his return to Fairhaven.

He took off his clothes, first draping his long coat over the back of a nearby armchair, then his vest, and his frilled shirt. He left his high boots on the floor, placed carefully together. Stripped down to his breeches, he turned again to the mirror.

He liked this body. Dwarves were solid, strong. He liked the feel of the muscles, the firmness of the skin, vaguely reminiscent of stone. And Auftane had a fine sense of style.

But it was time to bid Auftane farewell. He sighed and watched in the mirror as the reflection changed.

The squat, solid form of the dwarf grew taller and much thinner. The dark brown skin faded gradually to tan, then pasty white with freckles. He enjoyed the freckles and paid close attention to their pattern on his skin. The neat beard and waxed moustache disappeared, and he rubbed a slender hand over his smooth chin. His shoulder-length black hair became short, tousled, and sandy brown.

He always saved the eyes for last. Finding just the right shade of amber took him several attempts, then he stepped away from the mirror, taking in his full reflection.

"Welcome home, Haunderk," he said to himself. "You need a bath before you can report to ir'Darren."

He made his way to the door of his suite and rang the bell that would summon a servant to fill his bathtub. His eyes fell once more on the silver torc, shining on the dresser.

"And won't Kelas be pleased with you."